THE INCOMPLETES

BY

LINDA SMOLKIN

E-book ISBN: 978-0-9986171-8-3
Paperback ISBN: 978-0-9986171-9-0

Cover design: Sasha Smolkin (Site: linktr.ee/smolkinart)
Cover Photos/Images: João Vítor Duarte, kiwihug, Marjan Blan, Steve Johnson, Benjamin Lion, Thomas Lenne, Yulia Ogneva, and Tatiana Mezhenina.
Book layout: Ebook Launch

This is a work of fiction. Names, characters, businesses, places, organizations, events, and incidents portrayed in this story are either a product of the author's imagination or used fictitiously, and they are not to be construed as real. Any resemblance to actual persons, living or dead, events or locales is entirely coincidental.

Dedicated to Sherron Mayes

Your legacy lives on in every word of this story.

We take a final breath before escaping

There's no way out, no forgetting

In reverse, I see you

In reverse, I remember you

In reverse, you cast your shadow upon me

   —The Incompletes

Chapter One

Richmond, Virginia
2010

Curb appeal sells a house, but the bones make you want to buy one—at least that's what they say on all those TV shows. Yet, whenever I mention the thought of buying my first place, everyone wants to give me all kinds of advice—which neighborhoods are best; what to look for when checking out a house; the deal-breakers and the must-haves. For me, it comes down to one thing: emotion. A feeling that comes over me when finding the right home, and I've had that feeling a few times already.

For the past two months, Susan's used to showing me a bunch as she paints on a smile, knowing we've already looked at a dozen without success—townhouses, Cape Cods, ramblers, you name it. There's nothing we haven't seen in my price range.

Lately, I've been cautious after putting in a few offers already and losing out to other buyers. But I'm not going into a bidding war, overpaying on a house when my expenses are already tight.

My phone pings with Susan's text, and I slip my feet into a pair of Converse, say goodbye to Dad, who wishes me luck, and lock up behind me.

"Good to see you again, Emma," she says as I settle onto the leather seat of her fancy four-door sedan.

As usual, my real-estate agent is dressed to perfection, this time in a red pantsuit with matching lipstick and nail polish. Her blonde hair is pulled back in a bun, showing off diamond stud earrings.

"Good seeing you, too! What's on the list for today?"

Susan turns down the radio and hands me a printout. "There's a new one on the market," she says while backing out. "Built in 1993 with an updated kitchen, two full baths, and two sizable bedrooms. No garage though."

"Bummer about the garage, but everything else sounds good." I hang my sunglasses on my shirt and thumb through the details. The rooms in the photos look nice and match the description, but I've learned my lesson. It's best to see the property in person before passing judgment because a camera with its wide-angle lens can do wonders these days. I flip the sheet to the other side and read more. "Ooh, nice, there's a basement. Do you know if it's finished?"

Susan comes to a red light and puts on her turn signal. "Not sure. The details are slim to none. Let's hope for the best."

"Odd they'd have photos of everything else, don't you think?"

"Depends. Sometimes they don't include them when the condition isn't that great. Whatever the case," she adds, "I bet you could spruce it up in no time. Maybe your folks can give you a little handout if it's a bigger project?"

Susan loves to act like my parents have cash lying around, which is the farthest thing from the truth. It's not the first time she's brought it up while talking down to me. Maybe because I'm living at home. Or because I'm always in worn jeans and concert tees. Who knows? I haven't always lived with my parents, but it has helped me save for a down payment these past few years, especially on my teacher's salary.

"Don't worry," she continues. "The owner replaced the roof and HVAC a few years ago. That's a plus since those can get expensive. And that'll let you show some TLC to the basement if needed."

Twenty minutes later, Susan pulls into a neighborhood with beautiful homes, long driveways, and lush trees. It's an easy commute to my job, but the street makes me double-check the price because they're mostly two-story Colonials that look way out of my range.

After another block, the spacious Colonials get exchanged for modest ramblers with colorful doors and shutters. Pretty yards with flowerbeds and manicured shrubs make an appearance. Long driveways and walkways lead to covered porches with benches. Susan takes a final turn and parks in one of the driveways at the end.

"Cool, a cul-de-sac! I've always dreamed of living on one."

She smiles, and this time it seems more hopeful— and might catch me a break in my real-estate endeavors. We walk up the path and while Susan fidgets with the lock box to retrieve the key, I look around.

Out of all the houses, it's the only one where the yard needs some work. The grass needs cutting, the flowers look thirsty, and ivy has taken over the brick walls under the windows. But I love it so far. It's warm and cozy, at least from the outside. I imagine sitting on the porch while grading papers and drinking my Diet Dr. Pepper. The neighbors greeting me while kids whizz by on their bikes and skateboards. Dad offering to tame the yard. And Mom coming over eventually to give decorating advice.

Susan unlocks the door and closes it behind us. A small foyer leads to a living room on the left and a dining room at the back with a sliding glass door. I make my way through the two rooms and open the door to step outside on the small deck. The yard, which sits on a small hill and backs to a creek, has pine trees scattered throughout. A concrete patio juts out below with built-in seating on one side with neglected flowerbeds, like the front.

Susan's heels tap in a steady motion on the wooden deck as she joins me outside. "Isn't this great?" she says, looking toward the back.

"No neighbors behind me? I'm sold! Where do I sign?"

Susan laughs, but it doesn't last long because she's preparing herself. She knows how this works—excitement can take over, blinding you to the risk of another potential buyer who can make an offer and whisk your hopes away. "Let's take a look at the rest," she says. "See if the appeal holds up?"

"Should we check out the basement first?"

"How about we leave that to the end?" she asks.

"Good idea, in case I need to brace myself."

We head back in, close the sliding glass door behind us, and take a quick look at the kitchen with its stainless-steel appliances and white granite countertops before heading down the hall. The bathrooms have been updated with a fresh coat of paint, chrome fixtures, and new tubs. The bedrooms are spotless and painted in an off-white. I envision setting one up as an office that converts into a guest room with a colorful futon.

We make our way back to the kitchen, and Susan pulls out a business card from her purse, places it on the counter, and signs the welcome sheet. "So, what do you think?"

"It's awesome." I look out back once more. "Let's check out the basement?"

She snaps her fingers. "Almost forgot about that! Got so excited about this yard."

Susan opens a door from the kitchen and flips on the light. We head downstairs, and she sighs as we enter the dusty space. "No wonder they didn't have pictures. Sellers never listen. Basements are usually in need of a facelift. This takes the cake."

As we look around, I wonder whether it's the same house, one that only moments ago made a great impression, as if we were on a first date. Wood paneling on the walls makes the basement dark and closed-in. Orange carpeting, torn and stained, has seen better days and perhaps a few parties. On the left, several hardcover and paperback books stand at attention within the dusty shelves.

Toward the back, a built-in bar with a backlit mirror showcases another grimy shelf with empty carafes and cocktail glasses. Susan walks ahead of me to check out the utility room, and as I turn the corner to follow her, I spot a drum set.

"Oh wow!" I wander toward the abandoned kit and run my hand along the outer edge. "Ooh, it's a Gretsch."

"A what?" Susan asks.

"Oh, sorry. Gretsch is the name of the drum company. They've been around forever," I add and wonder why the set's still here, ready and waiting for someone to sit on its throne and play. "I'm a drummer. Well, actually, used to be."

"Really? Let me guess, you were one of those child prodigies."

"Far from it! I didn't start until eighth grade. Had a couple of bands in high school and college."

"That's so cool! I'd love to see you play."

"Honestly, I haven't picked up the sticks in years."

"Too busy?" she asks.

"Long story. Maybe over a beer sometime."

After Susan hands me a tissue from her purse, I make my way around the kit to wipe off most of the dust, or at least what will come off with one try. I step back a few feet and admire the full set. It's a five-piece with two crash cymbals, a ride, and a hi-hat, similar to mine that's packed up and stored away at my parents' house. It has been forever since I've been this close to one. For the first time in a long time, it makes me want to play.

"The space is decent, right?" Susan asks. "A little paint could do the trick."

"And maybe the dingy carpet can come up," I add while staring at the drum set a moment longer before we make our way upstairs.

We take one more peek through the rooms, imagining how the furniture would look before checking the size of the closets. Susan locks up and as we drive off, a few kids on the block grab my attention.

The sunny day has brought them out to play, with parents pushing strollers and neighbors walking their dogs. I don't have kids, or a dog, cat, let alone a hamster. But I like the family vibe and I'm tired of living with my parents. It's not that we don't get along. I'm grateful they let me move back in after grad school. It's simply time to be independent, have a place of my own, and enjoy some privacy—a way to move on and out without feeling guilty that I'm not spending enough time with Mom after what she's been through.

"Do you want me to drive through the neighborhood again?" Susan asks. "Or would you like to look at the other two properties?"

"No need. Let's make an offer." It's the first time I've said these words in weeks, but the house speaks to me.

Susan makes her way onto the main street that leads to I-95. "I was hoping you'd say that. It's a lovely starter home."

"I'm willing to try. Again."

"Maybe it's time," she says. "Who knows…could be fate, with the drums and all."

"Can we write them into the contract?" I ask. "That the sale is contingent on me keeping the set?"

"That's a first," she teases. "Usually, buyers want a home inspection."

"That, too. But I have a feeling it's gonna be in great shape."

CHAPTER TWO

The following month, we take our seats at a large wooden table and wait for the lawyer. The AC blasts above my head, making me wish I'd brought a sweater. A woman comes in and apologizes for the delay, saying they're almost done with another closing.

Susan walks to the side table and pours us both some coffee and grabs a cookie as I review the listing once more. Today, I've traded in my usual jeans-and-a-tee look for black slacks and a not-too-wrinkled button-down. Susan still out-dresses me in her striped pants, silk blouse, and gray blazer.

All seems in order, but I'm still nervous about things falling through at the last minute—even though the home inspection went well, and the owner agreed to everything, including the drum set. As we wait to get started, the Realtor, who's acting as the seller's rep, pulls out a note and hands it to me.

Dear Emma,

I'm sorry we didn't get to meet in person. I hope you'll be happy in the house my husband and I called home for many years. I loved your note about this being your first place and what you liked about the property. We also enjoyed the backyard and the view from the dining room. It's especially beautiful in the fall. Your comment about wanting to keep the drum set warmed my heart. I'm so glad it will be put to good use.

Congratulations and all the best!
Josephine Hensley

After reading the note to myself, I read it aloud for everyone at the table. We have a good laugh when Susan says the neighbors might feel otherwise about the drumming—or, rather, the noise that accompanies my once favorite pastime. While sharing stories about hobbies we had as kids, the lawyer flies into the room, looking disheveled and holding a pile of paperwork, pens, and one of those notarizing gadgets.

He joins us at the table, passes the contract around, and asks us to review and sign wherever he's put a colorful sticky. A moment later, he asks for my driver's license and sets it beside him. My hand throbs after signing and flipping through what feels like a hundred pages. Before long, the lawyer gives me a huge file with a large binder clip and the seller's rep wishes us well after handing me the keys.

As I hold the keys and walk outside with Susan, it hits me. I own my first place and feel more independent than ever.

Susan takes off her blazer and throws it over her shoulder. "You did it! You got your dream house and that beautiful backyard."

"I know! I love not having neighbors. Means I can sunbathe topless…or my friends can."

"Don't forget your sunscreen. Or the neighbors to the side!"

I chuckle at the thought. "Oh yeah, that! Thanks for the reminder."

"You know me, I'm all about the details." She fans her face with a brochure. "Can you spare a minute? I have something for you."

"Sure." I stop by my car to throw the paperwork on the back seat.

When we arrive at her sedan, she plops down her briefcase and jacket on the passenger side and leans into the back seat. Dipping her head out of the car, she straightens up, holding something behind her back. "Surprise!" She sweeps a shiny pink bag in front of me.

My eyes widen as I take the gift from her and look inside. Digging my hand in, tissue paper flies out as I uncover a bottle of champagne, a fancy glass container for oil and vinegar, and a cute soap dispenser.

"I figured you wouldn't mind a little bubbly to celebrate the occasion."

"What a sweet gesture, thank you! Can't wait to pop it open tonight in my new kitchen."

We hug goodbye and before Susan drives off, she rolls down the window. "Congrats, again. And I do hope those drums get some good use!"

***

I head over to my middle school and eighth-grade class. A teacher waves at me through the hall and with ten minutes to spare before the second period starts, I run into the bathroom and change into jeans and a tee.

The day's history assignment and lesson plans have already been mapped out. Yet now that I'm in front of my students, it's hard to concentrate after the closing. *I'm a homeowner. A bona fide homeowner.*

Thoughts about where to put the furniture make me drift off until I'm interrupted by one of the kids asking a question. I answer absent-mindedly and then wonder about the drums. What was I thinking by asking to keep them? Will they collect more dust and sit unused in the corner? I haven't touched a pair of sticks in years. Maybe it was fate—that discovering the drums made the house feel like home. Or maybe I'm supposed to play, to find my passion again and work through the sadness.

On the way home from work, I drive through my new neighborhood, checking out the other homes before heading to mine. It has officially sunk in. I'm going home. To my place. Not to my parents' or a rental. To my very own.

I pull into the driveway, fumble in my pockets to find the house key, and look up the path. The Realtor's sign is still up, causing me to do a double take, to make sure it doesn't still say For Sale or Under Contract. Instead, it's stamped Sold! *To me. Emma Meade.* And not for a penny over the asking price, making me proud of the negotiation skills Dad taught me.

Thirty minutes after settling in, there's a knock on the door. My friend Jenna gives me a long hug and hands me a card. She kicks off her flip-flops and spins around, taking in the living room. Tonight, we're popping the champagne that Susan gave me.

Jenna and I have been friends since high school, going through all the usual boyfriends, breakups, and petty drama. We never moved that far away from home except for college, and always came back between breaks. My brother Cory had the biggest crush on her and when she graduated from high school, he mourned for her until, of course, he got a crush on a new girl and Jenna became a thing of the past.

"So excited for you!" She follows me to the kitchen. "I can't wait for the full tour."

I pull out the champagne from the gift bag Susan gave me and plastic cups grabbed from the teachers' lounge. Jenna walks to the sliding door for a look outside and jumps when the cork makes a loud noise, ricocheting off the microwave and onto the floor.

"It's still sinking in," I say and fill up our cups.

"You're all grown up now."

"Hope not," I joke before we guzzle down the bubbly.

With the champagne seeping through our veins, I show her around. We go through the main level of the house, stopping in each room. Jenna peeks into the closets and mentions the good storage space and updated faucets and floor tiles when we reach the bathrooms.

"You were right," she says. "It's totally move-in ready."

"Wait until you see the basement," I add, and we walk back to the kitchen, open the door to the lower level, and head down the stairs.

"Wow," Jenna says as she takes it all in. "Am I dreaming, or have we been cast in a *Cheers* episode?"

She walks around and stops short in front of the kit. "Emma," she whispers, "why didn't you tell me about the drums? Did they come with the house?"

I nod, wanting to say it slipped my mind, but she'd call my bluff right away, so instead, I stay quiet.

"Odd they didn't take it with the rest of their stuff. Well," she pauses, "I'm assuming there was nothing else left behind."

"I asked for them in the contract."

"That's great, Emma." She walks closer to the set and runs her fingers across the sticks that lie crisscrossed on the snare. She pauses before adding, "Maybe it's time?"

We stare at the set for a moment longer and then look at each other. Her question makes me anxious. I can feel the pressure building up, not being able to speak, and Jenna notices. Going behind the kit, she stops short once more, remembering my sadness that started three years ago. Looking at me for approval, I nod back as confirmation, and she sits down and picks up the sticks. Jenna tightens her grip on them, way too tightly, as if she's a kid and someone's trying to take her toy away.

Jenna hasn't played the drums a day in her life and it shows. She pretends to be my favorite drummer—Neil Peart from Rush—and not only butchers his last name but the drum solo, throwing the sticks around the kit in a haphazard way. It should give me a headache, but instead, brightens my day.

"Hit the snare again," I say as she continues making noise.

"I'm that good? By the way," she adds with a grin, "which one's the snare?"

I point to the middle drum in front of her. She hits the piece over and over, and each time, it makes an odd rattling sound.

"Hand me one of the sticks." I lean over the set. As

Jenna stands up to watch, I tap the snare a few times and then take it off the stand. The piece is heavier than I remember, and when it's in both hands, I shake it and hear something inside.

Jenna leans in to listen. "Sounds like some bugs died in there."

I place the snare back on the stand, and we search the bookshelves and drawers for a drum key to remove the head. When our search comes up empty, I go back to the kit and turn the snare upside down. Even though the bottom has a clear head, it's hard to make out what's inside. It looks like a piece of white cardboard, or the inventory tag got stuck. Without a drum key to open the snare, there's no way of telling.

"What could it be?" Jenna asks.

While lifting the lever to turn off the snares, I notice a loose screw. "Not sure, but it could use a new head and," I place the snare back on its stand, "the throw-off needs tightening or a repair, something the store can help me figure out."

Jenna nods as if she understands my lingo, and as we head upstairs to finish off the remaining champagne, I think about the drums. Getting the snare fixed means being one step closer to sitting on the throne again. And another reminder of the last time I played.

CHAPTER THREE

There's never a dull moment at Mo's Music. With its great customer service, knowledgeable reps, and in-stock availability, people flock from all over Richmond and central Virginia to buy their gear or get repairs.

It's a Saturday morning and the parking lot overflows with cars and people carrying guitars, keyboards, and amps from the store. Along the way, kids jump up and down with excitement, and it brings back memories.

Growing up, I'd bang on pots and pans with wooden spoons and Dad always said it was music to his ears. He thought I'd be a natural drummer—and after several months of me begging, he managed to convince Mom. And then I got the biggest surprise of all on my thirteenth birthday.

My parents said we were going out for ice cream to celebrate. The four of us, including my brother Cory, piled into our Chevy station wagon. Once we'd finished our ice cream, instead of walking back to the car, we continued down the sidewalk. Out of the blue, my mom asked, "Emma, what's your favorite color?"

"Blue. Why?"

A moment later, their little decoy made sense when we stood in front of Mo's and my dad said, "Let's pick you out a drum set!"

The ice cream shop was two blocks from Mo's, and it didn't dawn on me that we'd be heading to the music store afterward. After looking at a few floor displays, I pointed at a Tama starter kit—a blue sparkle one with five pieces. My mom was surprised that the cymbals on display weren't included in the price. So, they bought me a more affordable cymbal starter pack, which I used until saving up enough money from my high school summer job waiting tables.

Back home, my brother Cory helped me set up the kit in my parents' basement, moving the pieces a few inches here and there and adjusting the rug underneath. From that moment and every day after, I'd bang away and even throw in some fancy stick work and rim shots when Dad came down to watch. My parents put up with the noise until well after I graduated, allowing my confidence and creativity to grow. And whenever the neighbors mentioned how much they enjoyed my brother's playing, my dad would grin and say, "That's my girl. Isn't she awesome?"

That childhood memory has always stuck with me, mainly because it's bittersweet—a time when the four of us were happy and all together. My blue Tama set is now packed away in boxes in the corner of my parents' basement. Maybe one day I'll set it up and play. Until then, I'll focus on fixing the Gretsch, which brings me to Mo's today.

I pop the trunk and pull out the snare, tapping the top as I walk toward the store. A few teenagers with green hair rush out, holding the door open for me. Nice tattoo, one says, and points to the hummingbird on my inner arm.

"Thanks. Cool hair," I say in response and head inside. Nirvana blasts through the speakers while guitarists show off their riffs, clerks change strings on guitars, and teenagers with headphones move to the beats in the DJ section.

Holding my snare feels awkward, and I switch sides, placing it against my right hip before walking toward the drum section in the back. A guy with long black hair and wearing a purple Mo's T-shirt chats with a couple and a teenager. I listen in, wanting to give advice but bite my tongue.

No, you don't need a huge kit with all the bells and whistles. No, you don't need those extra two cymbals (get a combo first and save money), and no, you definitely don't need an expensive cowbell.

The mom offers to buy the set the clerk recommends if they throw in a cowbell and some drumsticks for their son. As the clerk walks off to find the manager, the man, who must be the dad, turns around and smiles. "Is that for your kid?" he asks.

It's not the first time hearing this, and I want to say so many things back—but being impolite isn't my nature, so the thoughts stay in my head.

Do I look old enough to have a kid?
You don't think a woman can play drums?
Haven't you ever heard of Sheila E.?

"Nope, it's mine," I say politely.

Without a word or a smile, his family of four turns around and stares at me like I'm a freak of nature. It makes me want to get behind one of Mo's floor models, hit the bass pedal with force, do a fill around the toms, and crash the cymbals as if my life depends on it. Anything to take my frustration out on anyone who's ever judged me.

Because even though it doesn't matter to anyone other than myself, I used to be damn good. I used to be great.

Mo's clerk comes back and finalizes their deal. I wish them luck and half-joke about getting ear protection for the drummer and everyone in their family, including pets if they have any.

"Hey there, how can I help you?" the clerk says to me.

Before putting the snare on the counter, I shake it so he can hear the noise.

"Hmm, that's odd." He gives the snare a once-over. "But also, cool. I haven't seen a classic Gretsch in a while." He picks up the piece and looks all around the side before turning it upside down. "Would you like me to open it up?"

"Please. There's something wrong with one of the screws—and something's floating around in there. I couldn't find a key at home."

"Totally get it," he says with a grin. "They seem to disappear into that black hole where all our socks go."

In between laughs, I ask him to replace the head while he's at it. He pauses, and I'm waiting for a condescending remark about a woman playing the drums.

"Do you want to stick with coated?" he asks, referring to the type of head, relieving me of my preconceived notion of his opinion about me.

"Definitely coated. And if you have the Remo ones, I'll go with those."

He bends over and goes through the shelves, running his hand across the thin boxes. Looking back at me, he pushes his long hair to the side. "Sorry, we're all out. But we've got Evans."

I nod in agreement, and he pulls out the box, similar in size to a small but thinner pizza container, and sets it on the counter next to the snare. He goes through the drawer in front of the computer and pulls out a drum key to loosen the head. I'm about to offer some help to make it go faster, but once he starts there's no stopping. Within seconds, he loosens all eight lugs with both hands like he holds the world-record for spinning plates. He pulls the lugs up and takes off the head.

The clerk looks into the snare, making me lean over and do the same. "If this is where the treasure's stashed, let me know." He pulls out a piece of paper folded numerous times into a square the size of a fortune cookie. On one of the edges, there's white tape.

"And this whole time I thought there was a bee in there with a friend or two."

"Who knows, they might be inside, squashed to hell after partying it up." After handing me the paper, he pulls out a tool from the top drawer and tightens the screw. "Should be good to go. Would you like me to put on the new head and tune it?"

I turn around and notice there's no line behind me. "Sure, if you don't mind. I'm out of practice."

It's sometimes hard to admit that, although I used to kill playing at gigs, tuning never came easy. I'd often turn the key this way and that way, while knocking on the head with my knuckle, hoping the sound was perfect, while making it "just good enough" to get me through a playlist until the next time.

The clerk pulls the new head out of the box, and I open the piece of paper that was trapped inside, hesitating at first, not knowing what awaits me. No squashed insects. No maps for finding a hidden treasure. Only a list of names—eight after my counting—in all caps all crossed through, except the last one. I'm deep in thought while staring at the clerk as he tunes my kit.

Who leaves a note in a drum set?

Who are the people listed?

Why are they all crossed out, except for one?

Folding the note up, I stuff it into my pocket for now. I ask the clerk to add drumsticks to my purchase, hand him my credit card, and sense someone watching me.

A guy about my age looks over. Floppy cinnamon hair, eyes the color of black coffee, scraggly facial hair some might call a beard, and a spackling of freckles. He smiles before looking away.

A minute later, he's standing next to me. And when he's closer, his eyes become more intense. I'm lost in them for a moment too long until the clerk thanks me for the purchase and makes a joke to call him when the treasure's been located. I joke back, telling him not to worry, and that he won't be forgotten when I'm dripping in jewels or building out the ultimate music studio.

I glance once more at the stranger, grab my snare, and head to my car. After putting the snare inside the trunk, I walk to the driver's side when the cute, cinnamon-haired guy comes toward me.

"Hey, you forgot these." He hands me the drumsticks and receipt.

"Oh, thanks! If my head wasn't screwed on, I'd forget that, too."

"Which one? Yours or on the snare?"

His smile makes me lose focus. It takes me a minute to get his joke but then I laugh a little too hard.

"Was that a snort?"

"Me, snort? Never!"

He reaches out to shake my hand. "I'm Zev, by the way."

"Emma. Nice meeting you."

"Are you in a band?" he asks, something I haven't heard in a long time.

"Not at the moment. Used to be in a few."

"What happened?"

"You know…life, college, that sort of thing. What about you?"

"Same here," he says. "We went our separate ways after graduating. But I've wanted to start one up. Any interest?"

"Honestly…" I pause, choosing my words wisely, not wanting to overshare. "Not sure. I haven't played since our band broke up a few years ago."

"That's too bad. But you were getting the head swapped out, so maybe you're ready to start up again?"

I shrug. "Thinking about it but taking baby steps."

"What kind of music are you into?" He leans on the car next to mine.

"Rock. Some pop. Reggae's cool now and again. But mostly rock."

He nods and shoves his hands into his pockets. "Wanna exchange some songs we both know? It might save us time learning new ones. We'd just need to see if we mesh."

"Are you in sales? I never said I'd join your band."

He smiles and pushes the hair away from his eyes. "Not a band. Let's jam, for starters. And no, I'm a barista. Something my mom loves reminding me of."

"Why's that?" I ask.

"Supposedly, I'm a disappointment because I didn't go to law school or become a doctor or engineer."

"I'd say ignore the haters. But it's hard when they're our parents. Besides, she probably just wants the best for you."

"She wants what *she* thinks is best, not what will make me happy. Anyway, enough about that. Wanna swap numbers in case we decide to jam? No pressure."

"Sure," I say as we exchange phones.

He hands mine back and before putting it into my pocket, I chuckle after looking at what he typed.

"Your last name is Guitarist?"

"Didn't want you confusing me with the Fender guy."

"Or the gazillion other Zevs I know?"

"Hey, do you sing?" he asks. "I'm not that great but can be backup if needed."

I shake my head in response. It's hard enough drumming, let alone drumming and singing at the same time. We chat for another minute and as he walks off, I watch him. His posture could be better, making me wonder if it's from all the standing at his coffee counter.

Zev must feel my eyes on him and, a second later, turns around and puts his phone into his back pocket. "Have a great weekend, Emma!"

I wave as he spins back around and heads off. "Thanks, Zev Guitarist."

CHAPTER FOUR

When I get home from Mo's, it's early enough in the day to make some noise. Three years have passed since I've played, but nobody forgets the sound from an acoustic set, especially when you're not wearing ear protection, or you live next door to a drummer.

One of these days, I'll soundproof the basement. And maybe do what my mom did all those years ago—write a nice note and bring cookies to each neighboring house, making a promise not to play too early or late.

Before the day gets away from me or apprehension takes over, now's the time to try out the once-dusty set. But I can't stop thinking about the note with the names, the one that peeks out from my pocket. I change into joggers and put the note on the kitchen counter along with the drum key thrown in as a freebie from my now-favorite salesclerk.

I eye the thick pile of documents that sits on the dining room table. The former owner didn't show up for the closing, but I remember the sweet note she wrote. Would she be able to give some clarity on the eight names? I take off the large clip holding the papers together, dig through and find two separate documents:

the sales contract and a few others to make sure the names match. Josephine Hensley is written on all of them, with only a post office box in Richmond.

I spread out the rest of the papers on the table and look for an address or phone number, anything, to find out more about the seller. Susan, my agent, said the house only had one owner, but what if Josephine had kids and the note is one of theirs? The only way to know is to ask or do some research.

I open a browser on my laptop and put Josephine Hensley into the search bar. More than one result pops up, so I do another search on my property and come across Josephine and Dean Hensley. On the second page of results, there's an article with the headline: *Couple's 60th Anniversary Celebration at Spring Valley Manor.*

In the article, the journalist shares how the couple met in France in 1946. Dean, who was in the military—and a drummer—set off for Europe during the war. He was twenty-five and from Ohio. She was eighteen, a young French woman growing up outside of Paris.

Josephine and Dean met at the store where she worked and struck up a conversation one day about books after he admired her from afar. They married the following year and came back to the States. Dean stayed in the military until he retired twenty years later, began his second career as a music teacher, and moved to Richmond in the nineties.

The rest of the story reveals how Dean passed away just weeks before the anniversary celebration, but Josephine decided to go through with the party to honor him and their beautiful marriage. There's only one photo of Josephine in the article. She's stunning, an older version of Audrey Hepburn from *Breakfast at Tiffany's*, wearing a black dress and pearls, with her silver hair pulled back.

The story highlights Dean's career and his love for drumming, with a few photos of him thrown in. Dean in his uniform, standing tall and proud. One with him and his bandmates. Another with students holding their instruments.

The final photo shows Dean standing in front of a drum kit. Is it the same one that was left behind in my house? If so, it's a treasured keepsake, so why wouldn't Josephine take the set or give it to someone she knows?

I close the article and do one more search on Dean Hensley and add the word "funeral" to the end. A legacy page comes up that shares how Dean, who grew up in Cincinnati, died in his sleep at age eighty-six. After figuring out the difference between their two ages from the article, that makes Josephine about eighty years old now.

The page says that Dean left behind a wife, one daughter, a brother, and three nieces and nephews. He played several instruments but loved the drums and spent extra time after school teaching those who needed a more creative approach. I scroll to the bottom of the page and read some of the comments.

Mr. Hensley was my favorite teacher! I had him for band practice forty years ago and still remember his lessons to this day, wrote someone named Andy.

Dean was a great guy. He bought instruments for students who couldn't afford them, posted one of the parents.

He could light up a room with his smile, and his drumming, Deena, the school's counselor, shared.

I open up a new browser to try a different search, one focused on the names from the note. While wondering where to start, I glance at the snare and sticks on my counter. Knowing more about Dean gives me a connection to him and his drums. But is it enough to get me behind the set?

Since Cory died, it has been too difficult. My brother loved watching me play and it made me miss him all the more, so I avoided the drums, hoping that one day my courage would return and my old Tama set would be ready and waiting. Out of sight and mind, as they say; it's what I needed most at the time. But now, having a set in my own place forces me to look at them to try and overcome my fear and guilt. Maybe that day is today, a day to face my grief head-on.

I close my laptop and head downstairs. The basement looks bigger and brighter since the facelift. The wood paneling has been painted an off-white, the carpet pulled up and replaced with throw rugs, and windows covered with mini blinds. A beanbag, along with a hand-me-down loveseat and coffee table, gets me ready—and hopeful—for some entertaining, especially considering the bar has been dusted off and polished.

The drums look bare, almost sad, with its missing centerpiece—the heartbeat of every set. After placing the snare back in its spot, I sit on the throne for the first time in three years. The seat is comfy but loose, and I bend over to tighten the spindle, so the chair won't spin.

The sticks feel heavy and unfamiliar, not like before where blisters on my fingers and palms would turn to calluses and offer some protection. Now, my hands are soft after years of not playing and will suffer the brunt of gripping.

I remember what my drum teacher Mr. Taylor told me the first time we had a lesson together: "If you don't hold the sticks right, everything goes wrong." Suddenly, he's next to me, in spirit, coaching me, telling me what's good and bad, what I need to work on. I then pretend Cory's at one of my shows, cheering me on, whistling or giving a fist pump in the air after his favorite songs.

I place the sticks on the snare and decide what to play. There were a few originals from my first band in high school, mostly now forgotten. Besides, they were pop songs and all I want now is to play loud and hard, to wail on the drums without a care in the world. I'm alone, so I can be sloppy and mess up, play however the mood strikes me, as long as the sadness doesn't take over or my neighbors don't complain.

Before choosing a song, I put on my headphones and get ready for the warm-up exercises. Mr. Taylor insisted all his students go through rudiments before any real playing. "Like any good musician, athlete, or performer, if you don't warm up, you're headed for failure," he'd always say when we'd whine for the first twenty minutes of band practice. We hated waiting to get to the fun parts, but looking back, that's what we needed before doing the fills, the tricky cymbal work, and the drum rolls. Getting to the cool stuff meant we had to build a foundation first and practice over and over.

I start the metronome and grip the sticks. First single strokes, right left, right left, one after another at various tempos, starting slowly. I work my way into double strokes until the tempo gets fast enough and a messy drum roll plays out, followed by crashes on the cymbal. It's loud, even with my headphones on.

I get up and peek out the window to see if anyone's looking, wondering about the noise. Then I remember:

the Gretsch was Dean's. And Dean's legacy lives on. At least that's what I tell myself when heading back to the set.

Blink-182, a band my brother loved, is the first that comes up in a long-forgotten playlist aptly named Band Beats. I choose Cory's favorite, not knowing if it's even possible to get through the song after all these years. But I want to play it; I need that adrenaline to rush through my body.

With a fast track and tricky parts, it would challenge any drummer, even a great one. I press play and fix the headphones more securely. I destroy the song—in a bad way, missing half the beats and crashing the cymbals two seconds too late each time. It makes me think of Cory and how he'd encouraged me to continue playing until I got it right. "Sprinters don't have the fastest time when they start," he'd say. "They work hard at it. Give it time, Em." To this day, he's the only one who'd call me Em.

I switch songs, choosing a few easier ones, and come back to blink-182. After playing at the right tempo and crashing the cymbals without a delay, I want to share my improvement with Cory. To tell him I killed the song after all these years. To see him smile and believe in me. Instead, I play another favorite of his and cry and scream over the music until a loud banging reaches through my headphones and makes me jump up from the throne.

Chapter Five

Wondering if a neighbor is about to complain, I tiptoe upstairs and toward the front door. I already know what to say, that I'm following the city rules by not making loud noise in the evening, and that the former owner wants me to pay homage to her late husband by playing. That last part is a lie but it's Plan B to pull on their heartstrings with a sweet story and a smile.

I peer through the peephole and see a delivery guy holding a plant with a lavender ribbon tied in a bow. After opening the door, I take the plant and place the container on the side table, wondering who sent me the gift.

He hands me his clipboard and awaits my signature. "I know it's none of my business. But are you doing okay?"

His question doesn't make sense until he points to the tattoo on my wrist, then lifts his arm to show me his, the same design as mine but bigger: a gradient heart with ellipses on both sides. The ink represents the end of someone's life and the agony brought to those who love and remember them. It's also for those who need a reminder to continue with their recovery.

"Thanks for asking," I squeak out. "Hanging in there. It's for my brother…unfortunately, he didn't make it."

"Oh man, I'm so sorry," he says. "That was me ten years ago until my family had an intervention. Make that two, because the first one pissed me off so much that I cut them off and lived in my car for three months. The shit I put them through with my addiction still eats at me." He hesitates, maybe realizing he's over-sharing with a stranger. "I'm really sorry about your brother."

"Me, too. One day at a time, as they say."

"That's for damn sure," he adds, and for a split second, our eyes lock in a comfortable way—a silent connection that will stay with me long after he leaves. With a reach of the clipboard, he breaks the silence and wishes me well before walking off. He turns and waves goodbye, as if we've become good friends holding a thread of hope for others who've gone through trauma.

I pick up the plant and close the door. The note includes a nice message from my Realtor's boss, who owns the agency. She adds a sentence at the end about referrals being the lifeline of her business. I put the note in my pocket and as I decide where to put the housewarming gift, my phone pings with a text.

Hey Emma! Are you giving your drums a beating?

I didn't expect to hear from Zev Guitarist the same day but my heart races when his name appears on my screen.

They didn't have a chance. Just kidding. I sucked!

Doubt that! Any more thoughts on jamming? I'll go easy on you :).

Not sure if I'll have time. You know, a job, life, etc.

Lame excuse! Who doesn't?

LOL, okay—I need another month to practice before meeting up.

Cool, but don't worry—let's just see where it goes.

I give his text a thumbs-up and put the plant on my dining room table before picking up the note with the eight names on it, still wondering why all but one's crossed out.

There's something unusual with each name. Their first names appear more commonplace: John, Thomas, Anthony, and Monica. But their last names have bizarre spellings. They have more than one consonant next to each other like BL and NT, as if they're a different language. The last one listed has both undecipherable first and last names. Next to the name, there's a line of numbers with letters and decimal points.

I go down the list and enter the name on the first line into a search engine, then the others one by one. Nothing comes up on any of them. My brain hurts as my fingers go to work. I tap continuously into the search bar, trying to discover who they are without any luck. I give up and search for Josephine once more, and not much comes up either, except for an article about how she loves to cook and often took home the yearly prize for a French cuisine cook-off at a restaurant in Shockoe Bottom.

After reading through the article, I scroll through the search results and find out more about Dean and his time in the military playing in the orchestra. A separate article talks about how he got started. His mom, a piano teacher, also worked part-time in a music store and would bring Dean with her when he was too young to be left alone. Even though she tried to get him to play piano and the clarinet, he gravitated to the drums, always throwing a tantrum—his mother said—when she made him sit at the piano. First, he'd sit on the bench with his arms crossed. Other times, he'd stomp off, crying, until he stood behind the drum set the store had on display and began playing.

When he turned seven, his mom stopped fighting him on the instrument and let him choose. Once Dean got behind the kit, he could pick up the beats of almost every song, all by ear, getting even the trickiest rhythms down.

As time went on, the storeowner, captivated by the boy's talent, allowed Dean to come after school so he could continue to play, because they couldn't afford a set and didn't have the space at home. The drum instructor also gave Dean free lessons twice a month and that helped him improve. But even without the lessons, Dean had a passion for drumming that continued throughout his school years before he joined the military band.

After finishing the article, I'm about to give up my search on the names when I eye the numbers listed on the note's final entry. I type them into the search bar without the accompanying name, just as they're written, with their two decimal points and spaces in between. Right away, there's a match.

A map shows up in the results, followed by an online encyclopedia. What I thought at first might be a serial number for a product turns out to be coordinates for Sobibor Museum in Poland.

There's still a lot I don't know about the Holocaust, but you can't teach history and WWII without knowing about Sobibor. It was an extermination camp, one of many and with one purpose: to kill as many Jews as possible.

If my search is correct, what does Sobibor have to do with the note? Does it contain the names of those who perished during the war? Possibly a connection to Josephine, Dean, or someone they knew? Or something completely different, which makes me shudder to think of the possibilities—considering only one isn't crossed off the list. Why eight names and not ten or fifteen? And why would Dean leave the note in the snare? Or did Josephine put it there, purposely for a drummer to find? Curiosity eats away at me.

I look at the plant on the table and an idea comes to me. Maybe my real-estate agent can help. I dial Susan's number, and she picks up on the first ring.

"Hi, Emma! How's it going?"

I'm about to answer before she continues. "Wait a sec, let me roll up the window so I can hear you better. The life of a real-estate agent, practically living in my car. But no complaints…glad I'm busy!" The outside bustle recedes, and she continues. "Okay, sorry about that! So, how's the house?"

"Fabulous. Loving the backyard. I spruced up the front and gave the basement a few minor improvements. Looks much better."

"Oh, good! Hope it didn't set you back too much. Bet it looks great!"

"It does." I hesitate. "Susan, I have a bit of an odd request. Is there any chance you or the other agent could reach out to the seller, Josephine Hensley, and see if she'd meet with me?"

"You're right. That is a bit out of the ordinary. May I ask what it's about? Because I'm sure her agent will want to know."

"I found something in the house that might belong to her."

"Could you send it to me? I can mail it to her. Not sure where she lives, but I can find out."

I pace within my living room and continue with a lie. "It's too fragile and it might get lost with the way the mail can be these days."

"Oh, not a problem. Why don't you drop it off at my office and we'll get it over to her agent."

Susan seems uncomfortable giving me the address, so I'm about to lie again because she can't know the reason. Maybe Josephine doesn't even know about the note. "Susan, this will sound cryptic, but it's a very personal item. I'd hate to send it to her without any explanation. I'd really love to give it to her in person."

"Okay, no worries. I'm about to head into a showing with a client. Let me reach out to the seller's agent and explain. See what she says."

"Of course. I definitely don't want to mail it. So, if you could make sure to relay that, please."

"Will do. Oh, before I forget, did you get the plant?"

"I did! It's sitting beautifully on my dining room table."

"So, it has a nice view of your yard?"

Her comment makes me smile and look out back to take in the view. We chat a little longer and she gives me advice on which plants would do well in different parts of my yard depending on the amount of shade and sun. I hang up, hoping to hear back soon about the seller. Before putting my phone down, a text from Dad comes through.

See you tomorrow. Noon, right?
Your mom's not in the best of spirits.
We'll need to cheer her up.

CHAPTER SIX

Dad answers the door and steps outside for a long hug. I start pulling away, but it takes him longer to let go. "I've missed having you around," he says, and I grin while hoping our embrace doesn't squash the card and chocolates tucked under my arm.

He holds the door, letting me slide past. "Why didn't you use your key?"

I shrug while kicking off my shoes. "Didn't feel right now that I no longer live here. How's Mom?"

He leans in and whispers, "You know, Mother's Day is always a hard one. She's in the den."

"And you?" Anytime I ask about Mom, it's as if I'm on autopilot, desperately trying not to forget about Dad. He's the strong one for Mom, always putting his emotions on the back burner. Not a day goes by when I don't think or worry about them both.

"Grateful every day for you, sweetheart."

He often says this, his go-to line to make an impossible situation a little more positive. But I'm onto him, always have been, with the way his voice creeps up—and how he looks away—with his response.

We walk into the den, where my mom is sitting in her favorite chair while reading a book. Her legs rest on the ottoman and the sun streams onto her, adding a golden highlight to the cover of a pink and blue book she's holding. Mom doesn't look up, and our gray tabby, Random, who sits on the edge of the ottoman, keeps her company. They're two creatures of habit, spending alone time together in their own little worlds.

"Happy Mother's Day!" I say, hoping my chipper greeting will make this moment a little easier. Aside from Cory's birthday and the anniversary of his death, this is the hardest day of the year. Three's a charm, they say, but in this case, three's a tragic reminder.

She looks up with a smile before closing her book and setting it on the side table. My mom, who grew up in Northern California and went to George Washington University in DC, hoping one day she'd get into politics, still has the hippy look she adopted in her youth. She moves her salt-and-pepper braid to her back, slips her feet into Birkenstocks, and pulls her faded denim shirt down.

I walk toward the chair and hand her the Mother's Day gifts. Random looks up and sniffs the air. Realizing there's nothing exciting awaiting him, he puts his head back down, closes his eyes, and starts to purr.

Mom takes the truffles and sets them on the side table. She opens the card, reads the message, and comes in for a hug. Like my dad, she holds on to these moments. "I'm so glad you're here. But I definitely don't need any more chocolate." She pulls away, patting her belly.

I'm about to tell her to live a little, that a few chocolate truffles aren't going to kill her. Often I hesitate, having to think twice before saying certain words and phrases for fear of upsetting her.

A moment later, my father chimes in. "Deb, there's always room for more chocolate!"

"That's right," I add. "Better eat them up before Dad steals them! In fact, you might want to hide them."

We laugh in unison, something we often do together to ease the pain, to try to make this day a celebratory one. In the past on Mother's Day, my parents always invited the neighbors over for a cookout. We'd barely notice the holiday or pretend it was like any other day. This year, Mom isn't feeling it. And Dad just got over a bad case of poison ivy while working in my yard. He puts on a happy face one minute and scratches his arms and legs the next. I don't miss having the neighbors over either and still feel tired from the recent move. So, today, it's just the three of us.

Out of the blue, and while Dad's flipping burgers in the backyard, Mom blurts out, "Can't believe it's been three years. I still have Cory's last message—listened to his voice this morning. And I still have his phone number in my contacts. Can't bear the thought of deleting either one." She turns away and walks toward the sofa to sit down.

Her comment catches me by surprise because she rarely talks about Cory. Whenever my brother's name is brought up, she changes the subject quickly, so I don't often mention him in front of her.

I pause to collect my thoughts, fearful that the wrong words will come out. This is how my life has been with Mom for the past three years. *Walking on Eggshells, the Grievers' Edition*. I have no idea what she's going through. And I don't pretend to. But sometimes I worry I'm becoming the mom, giving advice, not knowing what to say or what's right. "You don't have to get rid of anything," I wind up saying. "Especially if it helps to hold onto the memories."

"But maybe I should, to move on and start healing. Not to forget about him and what happened, but to stop blaming myself."

This is the first time she's shared so much with me. She's been seeing a therapist for the past two months, so maybe that's helping her open up. For years, Dad tried to get her to see one and she kept putting it off, saying she could work through the pain and loss by herself, not with a stranger in an office with fancy degrees and motivational quotes framed and hanging on the wall.

I also blame myself for Cory's death but never mention it, because Mom doesn't need to deal with my grief when she's dealing with her own. So, today, instead of telling her that the feeling's mutual, I sit beside her on the sofa and listen. I move closer, wanting to hug her, but she's suddenly closed off, unlike a few moments ago.

"Mom, you know Cory's death had nothing to do with you."

"I should've been stricter about the driving. He wasn't like other kids his age. He was so nervous and wanted to wait. And what did I tell him? Practice will make him better. Such bullshit!"

I pull away as her voice rises. At the same time, Random jumps straight into the air and his tail gets bushy. Unsure what's happening, he moves quickly back to the ottoman, keeping his eyes wide open before settling down.

"I shouldn't have pushed him to get behind the wheel if he wasn't ready. I should've seen it as a sign, that he was nervous and needed to build up his confidence," she continues in a calmer voice. "At the very least, I should've asked your dad to spend more time with him on the road, especially at night."

"Mom, I know you're hurting but it's not your fault. If you want to blame someone, blame the doctor. She's the one who should take responsibility." I'm trying to ease her guilt and shift some of the blame away from me that I'm still dealing with. We all miss him so much.

She fidgets with the bottom of her shirt and looks away. "I don't know. What's the point in blaming her?"

"Blame who?" my dad asks when he comes through the sliding glass door with a plate of burgers. "A little help here?" he demands in a playful manner when we don't answer, as the door gets stuck when he tries to close it. "Don't want those blood-suckers to attack us," he adds while cussing out the mosquitos.

"Talking about the pesky neighbors again?" I say and close the door behind him.

He laughs, which makes me hopeful that his cheerfulness and our lighthearted banter will help Mom's mood. But she's off in her own little world again, back in her favorite chair and into the book she set down a moment ago.

A few minutes later, Dad calls for us from the kitchen and we finish setting up the table, bringing over the potato salad, condiments, and utensils. While having lunch, we catch up on what's going on at my job, but mostly about my new house and the minor projects I have in store. Mom hasn't seen the basement yet. When she got the tour, I told her the basement was a complete mess and off-limits for now. Truth is, I haven't brought up the drum set yet.

Whenever I'd play growing up, she'd often put in earplugs or leave the house for her daily walk. But the noise factor isn't the reason. Being behind the kit was my happy place, once: something that brought me joy like nothing else. I'm sure she'd find the story interesting about how the drums came with the house. But my last gig brings back painful memories—when Cory's life spiraled out of control.

CHAPTER SEVEN

The recent visit on Mother's Day has put me in a slump. All week, remembering Cory hits me hard. I'm crying in the morning, in the shower, between class breaks, on the way home from work, before bed.

It hasn't been like this for a long time because I usually shut down my emotions before the weeping begins. Or I distract myself with funny pet videos or *Friends* reruns. Something, anything to help. This time, nothing does the trick. Not the French fries and donuts. The chats with my friend Jenna. Or even banging the toms and crashing the cymbals hard and fast.

After trying everything, I find myself searching online for the nearest support group. I've never thought of joining one but after watching a movie where the husband dies and the woman goes to one, it seems like a good place to start. Turns out, our local community center has several, and I choose a group for those who've lost loved ones, held on the first Thursday evening of each month.

I make my way over for their next session. The parking lot is packed, making me drive around several times until a woman walks down the sidewalk with keys dangling from her hand. I step on the gas and follow her slowly until she gets to her car, situates herself, and pulls out of the spot.

People pour in and out as I enter the lobby, where there's a sign with a list of the day's events: mystery book club, music therapy, and yoga. And finally, the support group meet-up on the last line.

A man at the front desk greets me, sending me on my way down the hall, up to the second floor, and to the third door on the left. Both doors to the room are open and there's not an empty seat. Having second thoughts, I stand by the entrance and do a quick count of nine people while an older man with salt-and-pepper hair grabs a chair for me from the corner. They all turn around and look at the newbie. A few of them smile and get up to make room for the extra chair the man has set within the circle.

"Please, come in," he says. "I'm Gerald. Thanks for joining us today."

He extends his arm, and we shake hands. His hair's messy and matches the haphazardness of his beard. I sit down and take a look around the room while trying not to stare. Even though there's a mix of ages, most of them appear much older than me.

Gerald looks at his watch and says we'll get started in a few minutes. Two middle-aged women next to each other start chatting about the best coffee shops in the city. One swears by a cute little cafe near VCU and the other says it's mediocre at best. A man, with thinning red hair, rolls his eyes and flaps his hand like a beak as if they can't stop talking. He makes me giggle, and I look down quickly, pretending to laugh at something on my phone.

"Okay, everyone," Gerald says. "Let's get started. We have a couple of new faces this month, so let's go around the circle and introduce ourselves. Just your name if that's all you want. If you'd like to add more, that's totally fine.

But let's try to keep it short so we have enough time to chat. I'll go first. I'm Gerald and I'll be leading the group talk, which I've been doing for about six years. I volunteer here once a month, but I also have a full-time practice in Henrico."

Gerald looks to the right and points as we start going around the circle. Most people just say their first name, a few say their name and age, and one of the women states why she's here—her husband recently passed away and she's finding the daily routine challenging.

Eventually, it's my turn. "I'm Emma. And I'm twenty-seven." When they stare at me, wanting more, I hesitate and look to the person next to me, the last person in the circle. He introduces himself before Gerald continues.

"Who would like to go first?"

There are a few moments of silence, and everyone looks around. Margaret, who a minute ago was sharing coffee-shop chatter with another, chimes in. "I'll go," she says.

Margaret weaves a story about how the anniversary of her husband's death was last week and she found herself crying for hours because, of all things, she decided to watch romantic comedies where people fall in love.

She has done this every year since his death, and she still cries her eyes out. Margaret can't explain why she keeps watching them, knowing she's a mess afterward. "My friends want me to meet someone," she continues. "Some of them want to set me up or think I should try online dating. But I can't. It feels weird, like I'm cheating. I miss Dave so much."

She pulls a crumpled tissue out of her pocket and wipes her eyes. We wait for her to continue but she looks up at Gerald.

"Margaret, thank you for sharing. Moving on to the next phase of your life isn't easy. And there's no need to rush into dating if you're not ready. Take the time you need. And if your friends can't understand, then it's completely fine to set boundaries."

She nods and wipes her eyes again. "I know they mean well. But I really just want to tell them to fuck off."

The circle laughs, and I'm not sure why. Perhaps Margaret doesn't usually use profanity. Or they want to be a fly on the wall when she cusses them out.

"That's kind of harsh. I mean, they're just trying to support you," another woman says.

Margaret stares through her as if she wants to tell her to fuck off, too.

Gerald notices the tension rising. "Thanks, Sabrina. They are probably trying to support her but that doesn't give them a pass. Sometimes friends don't understand because they haven't dealt with grief. Or they don't understand that everyone's different. They can support her in other ways, and she has every right to say so.

"Margaret," he turns to her, "a good approach would be to say, 'I know you mean well, but I'd appreciate if you stopped bringing up dating. I'll let you know when I'm ready to go out with someone.' If they love and respect you, they'll keep their opinions and advice to themselves."

She nods in agreement, and Gerald looks around the room and catches my eye. "Who'd like to go next?"

It's hard to get a feel for the room and how they'll react when they hear my story. I'm reminded why I'm here, because I need someone to talk to, someone who's not my mom, dad, or close friends. Someone who can relate. I raise my hand and put it down quickly after having second thoughts.

Gerald nods and gives me a warm smile. "Yes, please, Emma, go ahead."

I shift about in my chair to get comfortable and realize nobody knows me or my story. How much do I share? And is it possible without crying? In an attempt to not hog the entire night's conversation, I decide to start at the beginning and make it quick.

"My brother died three years ago. It's long and complicated but basically, he was in a car accident, which caused severe back pain. He got addicted to pain meds and overdosed. Sometimes I think it was suicide, but I'm not sure. Nobody knows for sure." I pause and look around. All eyes are on me.

"I'm so sorry. He must've been so young," Margaret says.

I look down and nod, while playing with the edge of my shirt. "The effed-up part is…" My words trail off and my voice cracks. Suddenly I'm searching for a tissue but not prepared like Margaret, who seems to have one in every pocket. She walks over and hands me her travel pack. The room sits quietly, waiting for me to continue.

"The accident wasn't even his fault. He was hit by some asshole who didn't stop at a red light, but my mom blames herself. She thinks she should've insisted he practice more before driving alone. And I blame myself because he was on his way home from one of my gigs when the accident happened. I was a drummer in a band. He was so supportive, came to all my shows."

"Emma," Gerald says. "I am so sorry. Losing a loved one is so difficult, especially a sibling. I'm sure you've heard this before. You are not to blame for this. It's not your fault."

"I say the same thing to my mom, year after year. Why can't I believe it for myself? I'm working through it—but it's still hard. I guess I'm making progress…did some drumming recently for the first time since Cory died."

"That's good. Great, actually," Gerald adds. "I hope you'll continue drumming, and please keep coming here to talk. It can help to be around others familiar with what you've gone through. Many have lost spouses but there are a few who have lost friends and siblings. You must've been close?"

I nod and, at that point, I'm ready to pass the baton and let the next person go. Maybe I'll share more next time, if there's a next time. Sitting around the circle hearing sad stories and crying isn't the best for me—and I think about the drumming again, how that was progress. Maybe jamming with Zev would also help and somehow honor Cory in the process.

A few more from the support group raise their hands and talk, mentioning how they start feeling a little better and then have a huge setback. Gerald comforts us by saying that it's natural to have good and bad days. After a few more turns, Gerald looks at his watch, rubs his hands together, and stands up.

"This was a great session, everyone. Remember, we're here the first Thursday of the month and if you need some extra sessions in between, just reach out. Other centers throughout the area can accommodate. Or come see me privately. Whatever you do, know we're here for you. There's always someone to talk to if that's what you want."

Gerald looks at me when he says this last part and it makes me thankful, knowing I'm not alone. I help him put away the chairs, thank him again for the support, and wander toward the lobby.

A woman walking a few steps ahead catches my attention. She's got a dirty-blonde bob and wears black cargo pants and off-white Doc Martens. As we walk toward the parking lot, she turns around and smiles my way. She's got a certain style and energy that makes me want to strike up a conversation.

"I was gonna ask if you're a musician, but that's a pretty stupid question, considering you're carrying a guitar."

She pops the trunk and places her case into the trunk. "Actually, don't tell anyone," she whispers, "but it's one of my rifles. I'm a killer for hire."

I laugh, which helps my somber mood. "Like that movie with Antonio Banderas and Selma Hayek…can't remember the name."

"*Desperado*," she recalls effortlessly.

"That's right. Wasn't he also a guitarist?"

"Yep," she says, "killing two birds with one stone."

"Or bullet. So…what are you doing here with a guitar?"

She throws her bag on the back seat and turns around to face me. "I teach music therapy. What about you? What brings you here?"

I'm suddenly reminded of the sign in the lobby and ignore her question. "That's awesome. I've heard it really helps."

"Seems to. This is my second year helping out. Are you into music?"

"Yep, love it," I say but don't tell her anything about my drumming or how live music used to be a huge part of my life.

"Cool. If you don't have plans tomorrow night, I'm playing at Deacon's. Just me and my guitar. And the five strangers I've paid to fill the space," she jokes. "You should come."

"Sounds like fun. You know, me and my big plans on a Friday night. So many choices."

She walks toward the driver's side and opens the door. "My set starts at seven. Feel free to bring some friends! Sometimes the crowd can be kind of blah. But it's a Friday, so there's hope. I'm Katie, by the way."

"I'm Emma. I'll definitely try to make it."

Before she drives off, I wave goodbye, thinking about tomorrow night and doing something fun for a change.

Chapter Eight

Deacon's is pretty empty when I arrive. It reminds me of the first time we played here in 1999—that's the part I left out when chatting with Katie in the parking lot. My high school band had several gigs here, and my parents had to sign a waiver because I was only sixteen, even though it was an all-ages show.

On that first night, Dad insisted on driving me. He wanted to make sure the place was acceptable for his teenage daughter. Cory, who was three years younger, whined about not being able to go. As we continued to play other gigs, Dad lightened up and allowed him to come as long as his homework and chores were done.

Often when Dad dropped me off for shows, he'd stop the car after backing out, roll down the window, and hold his hand out, clutching a drum bag or the sticks I'd forgotten to take from the front seat. He'd jokingly say, "What would you do without me?" before driving off. It's a bittersweet memory of my supportive family and how these few years have passed since I've drummed.

The first time we played was an earlier show, like tonight but on a weekday, so there was hardly anyone in the audience. At the time, I wasn't self-conscious about my mistakes or nervous. I'd been playing long enough, with enough confidence to get behind the kit with ease. Since then, a lot has changed at Deacon's. Different ownership, different menu, a more spruced-up stage. But some things remained the same, like the name, the affordable happy hour, and the graffiti on the walls that some would call art.

As classic rock blasts through the speakers, a few guys at the bar throw back their beers. Behind them, a large poster hangs on the wall with tonight's lineup. A server in cutoff jeans and a Deacon's tee smiles my way as she carries drinks toward a table near the front.

A moment later, Katie walks onto the stage with her acoustic guitar and rests it on a stand. She tunes another guitar before plugging the cord into the amp. After adding a few picks to her stand, she studies a notebook, flipping through the pages.

Practice helps settle the nerves before and during a performance, but even experienced performers can fumble. If you weren't a musician, you might think she's mumbling to herself, but I remember this well: Katie's going through the motions, mentally rehearsing the lyrics she's about to sing.

Soon after, she spots me at the bar and waves. A minute later, she walks over. She looks different, a little more rock-n-roll than the day before. Her hair is pulled to one side, revealing a turquoise streak at the nape of her neck. Last night, she wore a long-sleeved shirt under her tee; today she's in a black tank, showing off several tattoos on her arms. Her eyeliner is thick and catlike, her lips painted the color of raspberries.

"Hey! You made it, so you know what that means?"

I shrug and give a questioning look.

"I gotta be on my best behavior," she teases.

"That's no fun!"

"You're right. Never mind. You like tequila?" She motions to the bartender.

"For sure! But it doesn't like me, especially when I'm driving. Let me get yours, and we'll toast to a kick-ass performance."

The bartender brings over a club soda and a shot of tequila, both with a wedge of lime on the edge of the glass, and we clink our drinks together. Katie downs her shot and, after reaching for her lime, closes her eyes before sucking out the juice. I can't tell whether she likes tequila or drinks alcohol to calm her nerves before taking the stage.

"How often do you play here?"

"A couple of times a month, and a few other places here and there. Wish I could quit my job and do it full-time but, you know, it doesn't pay the bills, which includes a hefty student loan."

Katie opens up and tells me she's a lawyer, a couple of years out of school, making less than she imagined, with a sixty-thousand-dollar student loan left to pay off.

"Not sure what I was thinking going to law school," she says and waves to the bouncer at the door. "It sounded better in theory. Reading contracts all day bores the hell out of me. Don't mean to complain. Just thought it would be different."

"I get it. It's so hard to make it in the music business. You did the right thing by going to law school."

Katie shrugs and checks her watch. After realizing she's up in five minutes, she thanks me for the drink and heads to the stage. As we wait, more people arrive, and the crowd begins to grow. I put my jacket on the stool, order nachos from the bar, and head down the hall to the bathroom. There's a short line and while waiting, I read the signs on the bulletin board. There's a small one, printed on bright-pink paper with bold text:

> *Singer/guitarist with 10 years' experience*
> *Looking to join a band*
> *Prefers rock but indie and pop are fine*
> *Ask for Katie at the bar*

My heart races at the thought and the possibility. Could this be the same Katie? I push it out of my mind and make my way back to the bar.

Katie picks up one of her guitars, puts the strap around her shoulder, and greets the crowd. "Thanks for coming out. This won't be like seeing the Foo Fighters, but I promise it won't be as bad as a root canal. We'll make it a pretty great night."

The bar fills up and the crowd is deep in conversation, chatting up a storm and ignoring her jokey comments. But as soon as she starts to sing, the place goes silent, and all their attention focuses on Katie standing center stage. In a matter of seconds, we've been hypnotized by a beautiful voice, raspy with a wide range, as she hits the high and low notes with ease.

Katie covers several songs by Heart, Lady Gaga, and P!nk, and throws in a couple of originals while showing off her guitar playing and stage presence that seem to come naturally. As she talks to the crowd between songs, I think about the ad again and consider asking whether she'd want to jam with Zev and me. Then again, would she even be interested, given how good she is?

Katie finishes her set with a Fleetwood Mac song and a huge round of applause. People from the audience approach the stage to put money in the tip jar. She makes her way over to the bar, stopping along the way to chat with the crowd.

"Not sure what's better," I say when she approaches, "your voice or your playing. That was amazing. You're amazing!"

"I've seen better but thank you."

"You're being modest!" I take a breath and eke out some long-forgotten confidence. "By the way, is that your sign on the bulletin board? Are you looking for a band?"

She nods and gets the bartender's attention. After hearing Katie play, I'm surprised she needs to advertise. Musicians should be begging to work with her. When I ask why she's looking for one now, she tells me about her previous bands, stories that sound all too familiar. Some members moved away or started college. Others had too many responsibilities to find time to play. Some showed up late to rehearsals or didn't show at all. And so on.

I share my own band drama, leaving out the part about not drumming for a while and what happened to Cory. Traumatic experiences stay buried and not often shared—unless you're a delivery guy with a matching tattoo like mine.

"Why didn't you mention it before? So cool! I love that you're a drummer."

"You haven't heard me play."

"I'm sure you're awesome. Have you considered being in a band now?"

"Funny you should ask." I tell her about meeting Zev and how he wants to jam. My mind races as I wonder how this would work with two guitarists. "Do you know how to play bass?"

She shakes her head. "Never could pick it up. But I can play electric guitar. I love acoustic but, honestly, my fingers could use a break now and again." She raises her hand, palm up, and rubs her calluses, like the ones that were etched on my hands when playing the drums every day.

"I haven't said yes to Zev yet, but how would you feel about getting together?"

"Sounds good to me. The vibe has to be right, though." She hesitates. "I mean, the two of us would totally mesh. I'd just need to get a feel for Zev."

"Totally. I've only met him once, but he seems cool."

The bartender places another tequila in front of her. Katie picks up the shot glass before adding, "Guess we won't know unless we try."

We clink our drinks again before she heads to the stage for her second set. After a few songs, I pull out my phone, look up Zev's number, and send him a text.

Hey, it's your favorite drummer. Do you play bass?
Yep! Why?
Wait till you hear the guitarist I found.
Awesome! What's his name?
Her name 😌
Oops, sorry, her name?
Katie! I'm listening to her at Deacon's. And her voice, so good!
Cool, text me back with a time to meet up.

I finish watching Katie's set and wonder if I'm truly ready to be in another band. The reminder of Cory. The time commitment. The different personalities. But as Katie said, we won't know unless we try.

Chapter Nine

Zev shows up at my doorstep, followed by Katie five minutes later. We decide to jam at my house since the thought of lugging around my drum set would be a major hassle. Besides, they're both in apartments with neighbors at every angle who wouldn't be too happy with us. Before meeting, we emailed one another to share some songs and found fifteen we all liked to begin our practice.

Katie puts down her gear and introduces herself to Zev. In a few minutes, the two discover how much they have in common. They went to the same high school a few years apart, worked at the same shopping mall during summer breaks, and love all the same music. They're off to a great start, relieving some of my worry about Katie's comment about needing the right vibe.

While we hang out in my living room, Katie confesses she's had better luck with musicians in their forties and fifties because they're reliable and have more time on their hands. I wait for Zev's reaction because he's the youngest at twenty-five, but it doesn't faze him. He agrees and shares a few experiences of his own. We laugh, wondering why we'd want to join the same band.

"But we're different," I say. "We *are* responsible."

"Depends on how you define responsible," Zev says. "Just showing up won't cut it."

Katie chimes in. "At least Emma can't say she was late for practice because of the traffic."

"True, unless there's a backup from my bedroom to the lower level."

"That would be me," Katie adds, "tripping over everything in my apartment. I keep saying I'm gonna declutter and sell some gear but here we are, years later, still staring at the boxes."

As they follow me downstairs, I have a rush of nerves. They already know that it's been a few years since I've jammed with anyone. Katie says it's all about the energy—but they haven't heard me yet. I haven't even heard myself, other than escaping alone and with my headphones on.

Zev looks around, puts down his gear, and walks over to the bar at the back. "This is cool! We should hold our gigs right here. There's everything we need."

"Except for the liquor. People would need to get shitfaced, so I sound better."

Katie comes closer, instinctively putting her hand on my arm. "Don't worry, it's gonna be great."

Zev sets up his small amp next to my drum set and leans his guitar on the chair. Katie pulls out a paper with the list of agreed-upon songs and puts it on a table to the side. We go over them, trying to decide which one to play first.

"How about the Foo Fighters?" Katie asks after plugging her guitar into the amp and ripping into the beginning part.

While Zev watches her, I stretch and go through some arm exercises before sitting on the throne. My hands shake as I reach for the sticks. "Let's start with something easier, with a slower tempo. What about the White Stripes one?"

It's on the list and one we all know and like but won't show off Katie's amazing voice. We have plenty of time for that, and it'll have to do for now until we get warmed up and more comfortable playing together.

After running through the piece, we decide Zev will sing backup when needed. Some of the drum parts are messy when we go through the next song, and I ask to start again. Each time, Katie kills it—both on the guitar and vocals—and we go through a few easier songs before trying "Everlong." I screw up, unable to keep the tempo, which makes the whole song sound crappy. We try three times, and I still can't get it right.

"Damn it!" I throw one of the sticks and walk away from the set.

"Emma, don't worry, the song's tricky," Katie says. "Let's move on to another one; we'll try at our next rehearsal."

"No." I walk behind the kit and sit back down. "I don't want to wait. Let's try again."

Zev looks at Katie. They oblige me—or rather, my stubbornness—and we play the song a few more times until I improve. I wipe sweat from my brow and, at the same time, Zev rolls up the sleeves of his faded denim shirt.

We go through the song again and while playing, Zev's wrist catches my attention. Whenever someone has a tattoo, specifically a wrist one, it warrants a closer look to see whether we have something in common, and at the same time, hoping it's not the same sad story. Relief sets in when Zev's ink isn't like mine.

After playing for an hour, we give the neighbors a break from the noise. My arms ache and blisters have started to form on my palms. We talk about the songs that sound good, the ones almost there but need more practice, and those that will come off the list for now.

"You know…" Katie pauses to detach her guitar strap and places several picks into her bag. "Forget it, never mind."

"You know that's not cool, right?" Zev says. "If we're gonna be in a band—"

"Good try," I say. "Don't you mean jam?"

Zev shrugs. "I stand corrected. If we're gonna jam, we need to be honest. What's on your mind?"

While waiting for her to answer, part of me fears she's going to say we're not gelling.

"Actually," Katie continues in a playful manner. "I was gonna give us a compliment. I'm surprised how good we sound, considering this is our first practice."

"Me, too," I say, not allowing my insecurities to resurface.

Zev adds how he loved every minute and can't wait to jam again, putting the word jam in air quotes to tease me. I blush and look away.

We head to the kitchen and sit around the table, deciding on songs to add to our playlist that we'll practice separately before meeting again. Zev grabs his phone to check a text and his tattoo reappears. This time, I get a closer look. It's a Star of David outlined in dark gray and filled with yellow—the star that Jews during the Holocaust wore on their garments. I want to ask about the significance but don't want to be too nosy. After putting his phone down, he catches me looking.

"Cool ink," I say. "Well, cool isn't the right word… hope you know what I mean."

Zev looks down at his wrist as if he's forgotten the design. "Thanks. Got it a few years ago when my grandmother passed away. She was a Holocaust survivor."

I want to ask more but still don't dig. At my school, we've had survivors come talk to our students, and it's so sad to hear their stories. Most of them can't finish their speeches without crying. "I'm a history teacher and we study the Holocaust each year," I say. "Not to the extent that's needed. I'd love to fit more in, but standardized testing eats away the time. Makes me crazy."

Katie glances up from her phone. "At least you introduce the kids to it. Some schools probably never discuss the Holocaust."

Zev turns his attention to Katie. "Are you a teacher, too?"

"No, I'm a lawyer, pushing papers around, reading contracts until my eyes bleed. The most boring job ever."

Zev smiles and plays with his guitar pick, flipping it back and forth. "That's what my mom wanted for me. 'Become a doctor or lawyer, Zev,'" he says in a higher-pitched voice before continuing. "I'm a disappointment, at least compared to my architect brother who designs fancy office buildings and houses in DC for the rich and politically famous."

"Sorry, that must be hard," Katie answers, "but at least you don't have crazy student loans to pay off from law school."

"Oh, I have plenty. My mom said she'd only pay for college if I got a degree in engineering, or something she thought would get me a decent job. When that didn't work, she tried with the whole law school thing after I graduated. She's not eager to share I'm a barista. You should see her face if anyone asks what I do for a living." He pretends to be his mom, and we have a hard time holding back our laughter until he gets serious again. "She doesn't approve of any part of my life. She treats my boyfriend like a stranger and thinks it's a phase. I overheard her say that to my dad once—and that I'm a disappointment to the family."

"Wow, that's brutal," I say, with a hint of disappointment myself, but obviously for a different reason. My slight crush on him begins to fade away with each passing moment now that I know he's off-limits. Honestly, the last thing I need is a fling and a bad breakup, which could ruin a good thing, if the three of us keep playing.

Katie walks to the sliding door to look out back. "Sorry, Zev. You think she'd be supportive. It's not that difficult."

"I don't know, maybe it's different with Jewish families," he adds and walks over to join her. "There's so much pressure to get married and have kids. I've been avoiding family gatherings, so I don't have to listen. And don't get me started on how they act when my brother comes home with his fiancée."

When Zev changes the subject and asks about my tattoo, I decide to tell them, figuring we might be spending a lot of time together. At the same time, I want to make up a story, so they don't feel sorry for me, so I don't get the sad faces. When strangers ask about my tattoo, I usually don't share details and, instead, mention the artist's name. This time, though, my new friends put me at ease, with a connection not usually felt so quickly. My story unfolds, like the other night at the support group, without a ton of detail.

"And here I am talking about my mundane stuff. You've had some serious tragedy and trauma." Zev touches my hand. "Emma, I'm so sorry."

The way he looks at me with his dark eyes, similar to the way Cory used to look at me, makes me tear up. Other than that night at the support group, I haven't cried in a long time, and it always makes me uneasy. Wiping away the tears with my sleeve, I can't bring myself to say more.

Katie leaves the table and comes back with a tissue. She still hasn't spoken. Maybe she knows, from her music therapy sessions, that sometimes it's best to just listen.

A moment later, she sits down next to me. "Emma, I can't imagine what you've gone through."

"I'm fine, really," I lie.

"You shouldn't hold it in. But you have a good excuse to wail on those drums; it's like therapy," Zev says.

"Don't worry, it's been on my mind ever since buying the house." I pause, mesmerized by Katie's intricate Frida Kahlo tattoo.

She extends her arm and pats down the dirt in the plant, the one that the Realtor sent me, making me wonder if Susan has reached out to the previous owner yet. Maybe Susan's been busy, or the owner doesn't want to meet with me. I pick up my phone and check my texts. The icon shows one new message from my mom. I read it before putting the phone back down.

I'm ready to spread your brother's ashes.
Let us know when you're free.

CHAPTER TEN

Mom's waiting outside when I pull into the driveway. She glances over at Dad as he comes out and locks the front door. She's got a sweater draped around her shoulders and holds a rectangular rosewood urn: the one with Cory's ashes that has been sitting on their kitchen shelf this whole time.

They walk toward my car, and Dad has his hand on her arm. Both of them haven't looked the same since Cory's death. Dad, who's grayer at the temples and darker around the eyes, holds it all together, at least for Mom's sake. Sometimes his eyes appear bloodshot, or his nose turns red. It makes me think he's been crying on his own or holding back tears. Either way, I don't fall for the "my allergies are acting up" excuse he's sometimes used these past few years.

They open the car doors, and Dad slides into the front while Mom takes the back and places the urn and her purse beside her. We've already decided where to spread the ashes, an hour outside of Richmond near Charlottesville. Cory loved being away from the city and would often head out to Albemarle County for a weekend with his camping gear to breathe in the fresh air and look at the stars. He loved the quiet spaces and views, more so than Richmond. Often, he'd go alone to clear his head, as he'd say. He was never much of a beach guy, even though he'd tan easily, his dirty-blond curls turning platinum in the summertime, often making heads turn.

Once my parents buckle up, I put on some Rolling Stones, one of their favorite bands. As we head out of their neighborhood and onto the interstate, I roll the window down and turn up the music.

It was hard, really hard at first, for Mom to come to terms with his cremation. We had to convince her that's what he wanted. Even though Cory's death was sudden, Mom couldn't deny knowing about his wishes because she was there. We were all there.

It was less than a year before he died, and on his birthday. We were sitting around the table after he blew out his candles. Out of the blue, he blurted out that he wanted to be cremated if something happened.

We all thought it was morbid to talk about on his birthday. It's not like he had a premonition—at least I don't think he did—but looking back, maybe somewhere deep inside, he knew he wouldn't be around for long. When Mom said she didn't want to discuss death, especially on his birthday, they got into an argument. Cory wouldn't let up and told her that loved ones are selfish, doing things that don't respect the deceased person's wishes.

Later in the evening, as I was about to take off, Cory startled me when he opened my car door. "Jesus, you scared the crap out of me. A little warning would've been nice."

He slid into the passenger seat and closed the door behind him. "Mom's so freaked out about death."

"What do you expect? The thought of someone we love dying isn't something we want to think about."

"Em, death is part of life. We can't deny it."

"I'm not denying it."

"You are by not wanting to talk about it."

"Okay, fine… I'm all ears."

"We never know what's gonna happen. If I die," he said, "I want to be cremated."

"You made it clear, but don't you—"

"Let me finish. I'm afraid Mom won't respect that. So, I'm gonna make sure there's no question."

After fidgeting with the settings, he handed me his cell. "I want you to record me, and then I'm going to use your phone to record the same message, so you have a copy."

"Cory, are you sure you're okay?"

"Yeah, I'm fine, why?"

"All this talk about death. Wanting to record your wishes. I'm worried about you."

"There's nothing to worry about."

"Are you using again?" I whispered, as if other people were listening in.

"Oh my God, no! Can you stop with that?"

Cory was lying, of course. I could tell by the way his lip twitched. By the way he answered with such determination. By the way he stared me down. It was always a dead giveaway and something I'd noticed ever since we were kids. That's how I knew he'd lied about the drugs I found stashed while looking for a Band-Aid several months prior. He swore up and down, with this same determination, that they weren't his. At the time, my way of being supportive was to back off and not be the overbearing, older sister, something I've regretted ever since.

"Em, seriously, everything's fine. Can we get on with the recording," he added. "And stop with the interrogation already? It's like I'm on *Law and Order*."

"Okay, but, what if something happens to me first? Like being tickled to death. I've heard that's a thing," I said, trying to relieve some of the tension.

"Em, nothing's going to happen to you. You're gonna live to be like three hundred years old, like Aunt Jeanie."

I shrugged and then hit him on the arm. "You really want to do this?"

He nodded, cleared his throat, and sat sideways in the seat. I pressed record, and when he forgot to say his name and the date, we took one more video. He deleted the first one and watched the second with approval. We repeated the same video on mine.

After he got out of the car and shut the door, I leaned over and rolled down the window. "Hey, wait a sec."

He bent down and leaned on the edge of the door.

"I don't say it enough. I love you, Cory."

"Me, too."

That night was the last time we talked about the drugs. That's why, when people ask what happened, I always say I'm not sure whether his death was an overdose or suicide. He was already in a lot of pain and masking it. And he often lied about being okay.

When Cory died, no matter how hard it was, Dad had to gently remind Mom of my brother's request. We could've given in to her grief, her denial, especially in the days after his passing when she started to pick out coffins. She didn't recall the conversation at the dinner table. Or she chose not to remember.

Either way, that day at the funeral home, I bit my tongue in front of the director as he shared the various choices, from simple pine boxes to lavish options. It was a momentary, rough patch between us that had to be resolved quickly so the funeral home could finalize the details. I didn't want to show her the video but had no choice. A couple of days later, after frustrating discussions between us, Mom agreed as long as she decided when and where to spread his ashes. I never asked her again, not realizing it would take three years to get where we are today.

As we drive on the interstate toward Charlottesville, Dad asks me to pause the music so we can share stories about how Cory and I were so close, yet so different. He, the sports fanatic and athlete. Me, the book nerd and straight-A student. Cory would tease me about not knowing anything about baseball or football and I'd tease him about how the headlines and photo captions were all he'd ever read. My parents share more stories that make me laugh—and it makes the hour pass by.

We find a good spot and park the car within a neighborhood where the houses are large and set apart by several acres. Cows graze in one of the fields, and I stop to take pictures. A man on a tractor waves as we walk by.

"Do you think we look conspicuous?" Dad asks.

"Us? Carrying a box in the middle of the street with you two dressed like you're going to a Grateful Dead concert? No way," I answer, making Mom laugh, which makes my day and makes me wish she laughed more. Perhaps this trip to spread Cory's ashes is cathartic, helping her move on, whatever that entails.

We reach the end of the street that leads to a public park with a small playground, gazebo, and picnic benches. Mom stops for a breather and asks if it's actually legal to spread his ashes here. It doesn't matter, I tell her, because nobody's around and even if they were, I already have a story planned out in my head: We came here for the day to remember our Aunt Harriett—made up, of course—who grew up here fifty years ago. If they ask about the box, we'll pretend we're being nostalgic: we're filling it with dirt to help plant a tree in our backyard and to remind us of Harriett. It's a sweet, sappy tale that anyone would believe.

"Here," Mom says when we reach the gazebo on the edge of a grassy area. "Actually, not here. Over there." She points to the edge where another mountain peak juts out beyond the one where we're standing.

Dad takes Mom's hand, and we go down the slope to the edge, where cows graze and dogs bark in the distance. Mom holds the box, and we stand side by side.

"Do you want to say anything, Emma?" Dad asks.

At first, I don't say a word, even though there are many sweet childhood memories. Instead, tears build up and what comes out is much worse. "Yeah, I hate that doctor! Why prescribe all those painkillers to begin with? She should lose her license, that piece of shit."

Dad puts his hand on my arm. "Emma, not now. Let's remember the good times, the stories, not the sad stuff that happened. There's been plenty of that."

I walk away. "Not enough, if you ask me! How the hell can that quack sleep at night?"

"We have to keep going," he adds, "to find the joy in life. Cory would want that."

Something's going on with me, and I can't control it. My brain goes into overdrive, and I want to blame anyone and everyone, except my brother. "No, Dad! You're wrong. Cory would want to be alive, hanging out with his friends, going on dates—"

"Emma, stop! Stop it right now!" My mom throws her scarf toward me, and it lands on the ground between us. "Haven't we had enough pain to last a lifetime? I'm done with the blaming—even all that I've put on myself. We need to move forward. I need to move forward!" She picks up her scarf, sits down on the grass, and crosses her legs. Dad joins her, and I walk toward them and do the same.

Without a word, the three of us sit together until Dad breaks the silence. "I'll go first." He reaches for Mom's hand, and she wraps hers in his. "Remember when Cory got gum stuck in his hair and used that adhesive remover he found in the garage? It sure as hell got rid of the gum."

I can't help but laugh. "And the hair, too. He was so embarrassed that he knocked on my door in the middle of the night. At first, I thought he'd forgotten about an assignment due the next day and wanted my help, considering he was the world's biggest procrastinator."

"Whose idea was it to cut his hair?" Mom asks.

"Mine. It took forever to convince him that cutting the gummy part out would look way worse than cutting it all over. Didn't look that bad, did it?"

Dad laughs. "Yeah, when he wore a baseball cap. I'm pretty sure that was the last time he chewed gum. But he didn't learn his lesson with the hair, did he?"

Mom shakes her head. "Remember when he thought my hair tint was conditioner? Turned his beautiful blond curls bright orange. He cried for hours. But he looked so cute. I still have the picture." She pulls her phone out and starts to scroll. "Yep, here it is. Not the greatest quality, but it'll do." She holds the phone up.

Dad leans in for a closer look. He turns to me and smiles. It feels like we're sharing the same smile, a bittersweet one, the kind where you're happy you have the memory but sad you won't have new ones with the person who's no longer around. For my parents, they'd replace their smiles in a second, and any present-day moments of happiness, to have Cory with us today. We all would.

Mom stands up and wipes the back of her pants to get rid of the mulch. She picks up the urn and looks toward the mountain. We follow her as she takes off down the slope toward the edge. She glances around to make sure nobody's near and opens the box. "We love you, Cory." Her voice cracks, her hands shaking as she scatters his ashes.

"We love you, Cory. And miss you," Dad and I say, echoing the words.

My parents have, over the years, had their fair share of arguments but they're a team. In many cases, I've heard the loss of a child tears a family apart, causing couples to break up. Somehow, it has brought my parents even closer. Dad drapes his arm around my mom's shoulder as we walk up the hill. He motions for me to come closer, and with his free hand, grabs mine, and we hold hands while walking back to the car.

There's silence for most of the way home until Dad laughs and can't stop.

"Jim, what in the world's so funny?"

"I keep thinking about Emma's joke, us walking around like Deadheads."

"Dad's right, with joke being the operative word," I say. "Because you'll never catch me at one of their concerts. And you won't be hearing them in my car."

"You run a tight ship." Dad smirks. "The Stones are okay but not the Grateful Dead?"

The two of us get into a friendly debate about music when Dad says punk rock isn't really music, and I tell him one day I'll prove him wrong when he becomes a fan of the Ramones, Sex Pistols, and other bands that make Dad chuckle after hearing their names.

Once I swing into their neighborhood, my cell rings. It gets ignored, and after pulling into their driveway and saying goodbye, I reach for my phone and listen to the message:

"Hi, Emma, it's Susan from Twin Park Realty. Good news: Josephine Hensley, the former owner, would like to meet with you. Give me a ring, and I'll share the details."

Chapter Eleven

Josephine Hensley chooses the time and place: two o'clock at an ice cream shop a few towns over that's mostly lined with commercial buildings and retail plazas. I wonder if she lives nearby. Or is she being smart, not meeting me close to her place in case she wants to maintain some privacy considering she doesn't know much about me.

There's also no telling if she even knows about the note. Or what else has been left behind or hidden. What if she was—and still is—up to no good? I think about these possibilities and more on my way to Triple the Scoop, all while second-guessing my meeting with her.

The bell on the handle rings as I open the door and head into the shop. It seems like an odd place to meet rather than a coffee shop. Maybe Josephine has a sweet tooth and enjoys the flavors, all thirty-six of them, or so it says on a blackboard under their tagline *Live a Sweet Life Without Regret.*

Scanning the room, I don't see any customers fitting Josephine's appearance. And of course, she might look younger than her age. I've only got that online photo from a newspaper a few years ago to go on, the one that talks about her anniversary celebration, where she's wearing the beautiful black dress. I need to be careful not to mention that to her. My research tactics might freak her out.

It's busy inside, so I grab a table in the corner and throw my book on the chair, so nobody grabs the spot, and make my way in line behind a few people. A teenager with purple hair and a nose ring greets customers and takes orders. An older woman sits on a stool at the register, ready to take payment. This can't be Josephine, can it? The woman is around my parents' age. She's too young to be Josephine, so my thoughts disappear as I study the flavors in the showcase. Instead of tripling the scoop, I choose one—strawberry with chocolate sprinkles on top—pay the cashier and walk back to my table.

She's clearly not here and it's now five minutes past two. My nerves get the better of me. What if Josephine doesn't show up? What if she sends someone to size me up first? What if some burly guy accompanies her, telling me to mind my own business? To stop my imagination from going any wilder, I start skimming *Number the Stars*, a book my students read this time of year for an assignment and one I've already read three times.

Around ten minutes later, I feel a rush of energy as a woman walks toward my table. It has to be her. She's average height and slender, with her beautiful silver hair pulled back, the way she wore it in her anniversary photo.

"Excuse me, are you Emma Meade?" She has a French accent, which shouldn't surprise me. The article online stated she was from a town outside Paris.

"Hi, you must be Josephine." I stand up, and we shake hands. Her grip is firm. Her hands are manicured, which makes me think she wasn't the drummer in the family—or she hasn't drummed in a long time. She gazes at me for a moment with her dark eyes, then lets go of my hand, and glances at my half-eaten ice cream on the table. "I see you've already splurged. Can I get you anything else?"

"Oh, no thanks. And since I've asked you here, let me treat." I reach for my handbag.

"No, absolutely not," she insists as she meanders toward the line. She's dressed head-to-toe in black: a mock turtleneck, high-waisted trousers, and black heels. The only contrast is her gorgeous silver hair, which complements the silver buckle on her belt, and fire-engine-red lipstick that matches her nail polish. She looks shockingly young and stylish for a woman who's eighty. She pulls her wallet out of a bag and pays with cash, something I don't often see these days. As she walks back to the table, she starts on the ice cream in her cup.

"It's too delicious to wait," Josephine says and sits down. Placing her handbag onto the table, she digs into her ice cream again and as she takes a bite, closes her eyes.

Up close, she has smooth alabaster skin, with only a few wrinkles around the eyes and above her lip. I want to ask what her secret is—special moisturizers, juicing detoxes, maybe yoga? When she lifts her arm, charms from a gold bracelet dangle, moving back and forth. One's a cross and the others, a ballerina and a rose.

"Were you a dancer?" I ask to break the ice, pointing to her bracelet. I don't want to bombard her with my questions about the note right away.

"I was. Back in the day." She hesitates. "In France, we had ballet class every day after school. I wanted to perform but then the war broke out."

Josephine answers my questions about her dancing, how old she was when the war started, and where she's from in France. I already know some of the details but don't let on. After a few minutes of small talk, we discuss the house, and she shares stories about the wonderful years she had living there. I reach in my side pocket for the note, actually a copy of the original to make sure it's secure.

"It was a sweet request to keep the drums," she adds after taking another spoonful. "My Realtor suggested giving the set to a music shop or putting an ad in the paper, but I said to leave them just in case. I'm so glad it worked out. You know, I've never met a female drummer. Good for you!"

I love how encouraging she sounds, and this is my segue. It's now or never. "That's why I'm here, actually." I play with my napkin, delaying a moment to get the words out. "To be honest, it felt like fate, finding a house in my price range, let alone finding one with a drum set."

Josephine opens her purse and places a photo on the table. In it, a man sits behind the drums. I know who it is but play stupid.

"That's my husband, Dean. We met right after the war. He was a drummer and that set you have is the same one in this picture. It meant a lot to him. Playing was magical, something almost spiritual that drove him forward, made him forget about his wartime sorrows. After he retired from the military, he taught music at various schools. I always loved watching him play. We moved around a bit, and that kit followed us wherever we went."

She hands me the picture. It's a color photo of Dean, who appears to be around fifty or sixty. He's sporting a camel-colored turtleneck, has dark, wavy hair with long sideburns, and wears a big smile while holding up his drumsticks to pose for the camera. I imagine the two of us becoming fast friends and spending hours talking about drums and music. I reach across the table to hand the photo back.

"No, my dear, keep it and think of Dean while playing. I have more like this one at home." She pauses and looks up. "He was so passionate about playing that sometimes during our conversations he'd ask me to repeat what I said. It was cute because, in all honesty, he had drumming on the brain twenty-four hours a day."

"Sounds like a true musician." I reach into my pocket to pull out the note, becoming more nervous as each second passes.

She watches me unfold the piece of paper.

My hands tremble as I set it on the table and push it toward her. "Not sure if you've seen this. It's why I wanted to meet in person. I found this in the drum set."

Josephine picks up the note and studies it. She places the note back down on the table and eyes her empty dish. "They have the best flavors, don't you think?"

Maybe the note brings back hurtful memories. Maybe that's why she's avoiding my question. "Josephine, if you don't want to talk about it, no worries. I'll put it away and forget about the whole thing."

We gaze at each other until she glances toward the front. Is she planning to make a mad dash for the exit? Or is someone waiting for a signal from her?

"Emma," she turns back toward me, "what questions do you have?"

I can't tell whether she knows something about the names or is fishing for clues. It makes me nervous and wonder again about my decision to meet with her. "Do you know anything about the names and numbers on the list?"

"Before anything else," she pauses before adding, "let me say that nobody other than you, me, and my dearly departed husband know about the note. And we should keep it that way."

She still hasn't given me an answer, and my fears come to the forefront. I wasn't sure about the last person on the list. Her response makes me imagine the worst. "Of course I'll keep this between us," I say. "After a little digging, if I'm correct, those numbers are coordinates?" I point to the numbers listed with the last name, lean in closer, and continue in a whisper. "Can you tell me if that's right?"

She remains silent, playing with a charm on her bracelet.

"If it's any help," I add, "I'm a history teacher and know about Sobibor. Over the years, I've learned quite a bit about the Holocaust."

Her eyes widen. "You've done your homework."

"To be honest, I cut and pasted the numbers into a search bar. Sobibor came up right away in the results."

There's more silence between us. I want to come up with a silly joke to lighten the mood, but nothing seems appropriate.

"Sobibor is right," she says. "Unfortunately, it's a heartbreaking story. I'm not sure if you're ready to know the details."

Her response makes me tense. Is it a reminder of someone they tried to save who was sent to the extermination camp? Or where her family ended up? My heart pounds faster, and I reach across the table to touch her arm. "Please. I'd love to know what happened, Josephine. Who are the ones already crossed out?"

"So, you haven't figured those out yet?"

I shake my head.

"Emma, I have a question for you…" She continues in a whisper, "Do you believe that some people are so evil they deserve to die?"

Her question comes out of nowhere, and right away Cory's doctor comes to mind, the one who kept prescribing pain meds, knowing good and well how addictive they could be. "That depends on so many things," I reply.

"Such as?"

"Such as their character. What they've done. It's a tough one to answer."

Josephine pulls out a compact mirror from her handbag. Checking her face, she reapplies her red lipstick and then puts the compact back into her purse. "Emma, it's not that difficult, really. It's a yes or a no."

"Can I ask you a personal question—actually, two?" I say, trying to buy some time.

She nods and, at the same time, her phone rings. Ignoring the call, she focuses on me again.

I continue, leaning in. "Does the note belong to you? And what happened to the ones crossed off?"

"Good heavens, Emma, this is our first date. So many questions!"

She laughs, which makes me giggle nervously. Is she messing with me? Maybe the note means nothing. Maybe she's just a bored old lady with time to kill.

Then she continues with a more concrete response. "No, it wasn't mine. And I'm not ready to answer your second question."

My thoughts go into overdrive. If she's not ready to answer my other question, what in the world happened to these people and where are they now?

"At this point," she continues, "telling you doesn't feel like a confession because my husband's passed on, and honestly, I could die tomorrow, so it doesn't matter. Let's just say what's done is done. But, as I said, it's best to keep this between us."

So, did the list belong to Dean? I need to know more, but Josephine doesn't budge. She still hasn't told me much. But is she making a threat? Am I biting off more than I can chew? And then more questions fill my head. Was Dean a killer? A hired one or working alone? I'm surprised I didn't find a gun in his kit. Or maybe that's hidden somewhere else in my house, like behind a toilet, like in all those far-fetched thriller movies.

All I wanted was a house and a cool drum set, not some hidden drama. And now I'm freaking out inside, not sure what to do.

She seems to read my mind and pushes the note back toward me. "You can pretend we didn't meet. Put the note back in its place and never think about it again."

"Why didn't you take the note when you moved out?"

"Because, my dear, it doesn't belong to me."

What was so horrible that eight people made it onto some cryptic list? And now knowing the last one has something to do with Sobibor adds a sadder element. My mind races back to her initial question: Does an evil person deserve to die? I can't answer, because how can little old me play God?

Josephine gets up and hangs the strap of her purse over her shoulder. I stand up and follow her out. Once we get to the sidewalk, she turns to me after making sure nobody's nearby. "There's a small panel in the wall of the master bedroom closet," she says, "the one where you get access to the bathroom pipes if there's a leak. Once you open the panel, reach up with your hand on the wall. You'll find a piece of paper taped up there—unless your home inspector found it. But that's highly unlikely."

"A list of more names?" I ask with a forced smile.

"You're a drummer," she responds. "You'll figure it out."

"Not sure about that."

"Emma, the day you can answer my question with a resounding yes, without any doubt, that an evil person deserves to die, I will tell you about the last person on the list." She hands me a piece of paper with her phone number on it, and walks away with her head held high, turning the corner and disappearing from sight.

Chapter Twelve

Josephine is hard to read. Cool and collected, without a care in the world. I sprint to my car and plan to follow her, to see where she lives, or who she'll meet next and what she's really up to.

She hasn't confessed to anything and won't answer my question yet, which makes me wonder: Are the other people on the list dead? And if so, did Dean take care of them, or did the two of them go on their spree together? Maybe that's why she wants to know if I believe evil people deserve to die. Maybe, to her, killing evil people is a "pass" in a morality book on life.

Back at my place, I drop the keys on the table and rush into the master bedroom closet, with Josephine's instructions echoing in my head. The hangers and clothes get pushed to the side, uncovering the panel. I hadn't noticed it before, even when the inspector was going room to room, giving me lessons on home maintenance and cost efficiency.

I bend down and try to remove the panel's cover from the wall, but it won't budge. I grab a screwdriver from the basement and head back into the closet, hoping some prodding will do the trick. With a bit more force along the sides, the cover finally comes off. I set it aside and place my hand inside and against the wall, like Josephine instructed, and inch upward. Nothing unusual rubs against my palm; only the coolness of the wall holds my touch. I try again, up toward the right. Nothing.

After taking a deep breath, I reach up a little higher and to the left when something tickles the edge of my fingers. Something's there. How will it come off the wall without getting damaged or falling out of reach? And then it dawns on me, an item that might help see what's there: a selfie stick my dad gifted me years ago—as a joke—that's still packed away in my suitcase.

My dad had bought the gadget right before taking us on a family vacation to New York City after I graduated from high school. The whole time, we were embarrassed whenever he'd use the selfie stick and Cory would mumble *tourist* under his breath when Dad carried it around. Even Mom busted Dad's chops, especially when he dashed through the crowd after leaving it at a restaurant in Times Square. Back home and a week later, Dad confessed to hiding the selfie stick in my suitcase with a funny note and a photo from our trip taped to the top.

The stick hasn't seen the light of day since that trip. I reach up to the shelf, pull down my suitcase, and attach the gadget to my phone.

Holding steady, I move the phone up the wall and take several pictures as the flash illuminates the small opening in the closet. After looking at the photos, the tickling sensation makes sense. It's a piece of paper with torn-out edges, like the one found in the snare, folded to the size of a square napkin, and fixed to the wall with blue painter's tape.

I inch my hand up the wall like before and gently pull the tape from the sides. I'm scared it's going to rip, so I remove it slowly, as my hand and forearm start to throb. After peeling the note off, I close the panel, and my renamed "sleuthing stick" gets put back into my suitcase for another mission.

The tape is stuck on all sides and it takes several minutes and a pair of scissors to detach. After opening the note, I'm confused and disappointed because it's similar to the other note…until closer inspection. Someone has sketched pictures of drums along the border and highlighted one letter in each of the last names of the seven that are crossed off. Each highlighted letter is in bold, and not in any particular order within the name. It reminds me of those word puzzles my mom used to solve where you have to find a word within a bunch of mismatched letters. There's also a year written after each one of the seven names. When I follow the highlighted letters down in a vertical pattern, it spells NOSLLEB.

My mind races with the possibilities. What does NOSLLEB mean? Is it another person or code for something? I recall what Josephine said: *You're a drummer. You'll figure it out.* Her words of encouragement consume me. And then I remember how anagrams work and rearrange the letters in my head.

Grabbing a pen, I write out NOSLLEB on another sheet of paper, and underneath I write it backward: BELLSON. Because I'm a drummer, it comes to me right away that it's not just BELLSON—it's Louie Bellson, a jazz drummer and one of the best. We studied him in high school music class.

What does Bellson have to do with those on the list or with Dean? I want to call Josephine and ask her to tell me, or at least give me more clues. But what if she's messing with my head? If so, I need to figure out what's going on in hers.

On this second note, the last name on the list, the one that's not crossed off, doesn't have any letters highlighted and the name is still undecipherable with its mismatched letters. Josephine says she'll tell me more about the person—only if I answer her question.

For now, I focus on the clue for the other names and head to the dining room table. I open up my laptop and type all the names in the search bar, one by one, minus the highlighted letters from spelling out BELLSON. I choose the one that has the most unusual name of the bunch, hoping my search might go a little faster if fewer people show up in the results.

My hunch is that he's no longer alive, so I click on the second result, a legacy page, from 1999. It matches the year that's listed next to his name on the note, and I read further about this man. On the legacy page, his obituary states that he died in a car accident on the way home from work and is survived by a wife and two small children.

I keep the legacy page up and open a new browser, typing the same name in the search bar. Other articles show up—how he was acquitted of a crime back in 1991 and again in 1994 in Columbus, Ohio, both times of rape. Not enough evidence. Witnesses won't talk. Tampered evidence, the author states, and so on. I remember one of the articles about Josephine and Dean. Before moving to the Richmond area, they also lived in Columbus and Chicago.

I focus on another one on the list with an uncommon last name. This time, a different offense: beating up an elderly man on his way home from work who died from his injuries two days later. The man on the list was charged with homicide and a hate crime. The result, again: not enough evidence and no witnesses to come forward. Also from Columbus. Dead five years after acquittal, in 1997.

I work my way through two more on the list. A man who stole homes from elderly couples by forging deeds. A woman who embezzled money from a fund intended for mothers to go toward child support. Both with the same story: not enough evidence to convict or nobody wants to come forward. Both dead five years after being acquitted, like the others.

Shit. Was Dean an assassin, killing the scum of the earth who didn't pay for their crimes? People who were evil and who he thought deserved to die?

Did Dean work alone? Did someone hire him? Did he or Josephine want someone to find the note to "take care" of the last person on the list? Crazy thoughts cloud my head.

What have I gotten myself into? The way Josephine walked with such innate confidence and without a care in the world: Was she sending me a message? Was somebody, sooner or later, going to deal with the last one and I should keep my mouth shut?

After letting the information sink in about these crimes, it's hard not to think about Cory. I look at the tattoo on my wrist, the heart that's front and center—a daily, sometimes hourly, reminder of him, and the doctor who prescribed his painkillers, knowing the harm they'd do.

Who knows how many other patients have suffered or died from her carelessness? And what about all the loved ones, like my mom, drowning in grief and unable to cope? Cory's doctor still gets to practice. She's still alive and making a living. Does someone like her deserve to die for ruining so many lives?

I slam down the cover of my laptop. I pace from one end of my house to the other, wondering what to do with the note, and if I'm ready to hear about the last one on the list.

Chapter Thirteen

The few days after meeting with Josephine leave me shaky, distracted, and sad about Cory. To help calm my nerves, I attend another support group session at the community center. It's been a month since the last one and that helped some, putting things into perspective, especially with the others who shared their own tragic stories.

Gerald smiles my way, and I take a seat next to Margaret. She's chatting with the same woman from before, and I look around the room for the man who made the funny gesture last time and made me laugh. He's not here, which makes me hopeful that whatever's troubling him has begun to subside, allowing him to move forward and heal.

There's a new couple across from me, a woman with black, wavy hair pulled back on the sides, wearing a light-blue tunic and dangly turquoise earrings. A man sits beside her with salt-and-pepper hair and sunken eyes. He's holding a pamphlet and when he reaches for her hand, she's not responsive. The couple holds a heavy expression, similar to one my parents had for years: Of grief and worry. Of sleepless nights. Of parents who've lost a child.

After introducing ourselves like last time, when it's my turn, I say that it's been a rough week without going into more detail.

Margaret nods. "A rough year's more like it," she interrupts and plays with her tissue without continuing.

Gerald crosses his legs and focuses on her warmly. "Margaret, I'm sorry. Would you like to talk about it once we get to your turn?" He says these words in a way that shows he runs a tight, yet tender ship, a place where everyone has to wait their turn.

She shakes her head and whispers, "Maybe next time."

He turns and asks me to continue. When I tell him there's nothing more, Gerald asks if anyone else would like to share.

It's quiet as I glance at the couple. They've only shared their names during introductions, and I have no idea why they're here. He looks at the woman next to him and reaches for her hand. This time, she doesn't pull away or seem distant, as if she's warming up to the idea of being here. He opens up, and their tragic story unfolds about their eight-year-old son dying in a bus accident.

You'd think everyone around the table would gasp after listening. Instead, the room remains quiet because when hearing something so dreadful, any response can only seem superficial. So, it's okay to be silent. Sometimes, those who grieve just want to be heard.

Gerald steps in to offer support. "Thank you for sharing something so painful. I know how hard it can be to open up."

Minutes later, I'm so affected by their words that I stammer while offering my condolences, and then fight back tears when they hold up a picture of their son. This time, Margaret doesn't need to pass me a tissue. I've come prepared and dab my eyes. Their honesty somehow enables me to talk more about Cory and how I found him lifeless in his apartment. Margaret switches seats with one of the guys and moves next to me, reaching for my hand. Suddenly, she's the strong one and I'm a mess when it's my turn to speak again.

"My parents always loved having me and my brother over for Sunday dinners," I begin. "It was really important to my mom, because her father traveled a lot for work and wasn't around much. So, my mom planned these dinners so we could stay connected and talk about our week." I grin while reminiscing. "We had to be there by four thirty, sharp, so we could eat by five because my parents got up early for work and couldn't miss their morning walks. As a joke, Cory would always arrive at four twenty-eight and tell them he was being fashionably early.

"One Sunday, Cory didn't show up. No call or text to cancel or say he was running late. We tried calling a few times, but it went to voicemail. After waiting an hour, we decided to go ahead and eat, figuring he was out with his friends and got the days mixed up. In the back of my mind, something wasn't right, but I didn't say anything. And..." I pause as my voice cracks, "that's another thing that still eats at me."

All eyes are on me. I should stop here to keep my emotions in check, but everyone keeps staring, knowing there's more to the story. "Cory told me time and again that he didn't have a problem with addiction. If I'd done something, my parents might've been able to help. It's as if I was protecting them from worry. It's usually the other way around, you know, parents protecting their kids. But Mom was beating herself up about Cory's car accident when he was forced to give up baseball, something he loved. So, it was Cory's secret. And mine, too, and I feel so guilty."

When he realizes I'm too upset to continue, Gerald interjects. "Emma, we can all look back and want to change so much. What's important is how we're dealing with things now and if that trauma is making it difficult to lead our lives. That's why these meetings are so important, so we can share our deepest fears and stop beating ourselves up."

He hesitates and leans forward, putting his hands on his lap. "I don't mean any disrespect to your brother—and please know that your grief isn't being minimized when I say this—but, maybe, it was the drugs talking or he was scared of what your parents would do. And that's why he lied to you. The only way for you to truly heal is to realize that it wasn't your fault."

"Still…maybe we could've saved him from what happened," I interrupt. "When he wasn't answering our calls, I stopped by his place after dinner. His car was in the lot and any normal person would think nothing of it. But seeing the car made me nervous. I knocked a few times before letting myself in. That's when I found him, lying on the bathroom floor.

"I shook him, hoping he'd wake up, but he didn't respond. After calling 9-1-1, I waited for what felt like hours until the EMTs showed up. But he was already gone. The police also came, asking me all kinds of questions, like I was under interrogation."

My voice cracks when I talk about going over to my parents to tell them the news. They didn't believe me. My mom grinned at first, as if I were playing some sick joke on her. When his death finally sunk in, she shrieked, until her legs gave way. She slid to the floor, and my dad held her while she wept.

"Oh, sweetie," Margaret says. "You've been through so much."

"What was it? Oxy? Fentanyl?" a guy from the circle calls out.

"Sam," Gerald whispers. "We don't ask those questions here."

"Sorry, it's just…that's exactly what happened to my friend, and I really fucking miss him."

"No, it's okay," I respond. "At first, it was oxy; then, from what I can tell, he took whatever he could get when the pain wasn't manageable. They found heroin in his system."

My words trail off while thoughts overwhelm me about Cory, my parents, Josephine, and that list with those horrible criminals on it. I pick up my bag and head toward the door. "I have to go."

"Emma, wait," Gerald says as he stands up.

But I can't. I'm done for today—spent, exhausted.

I rush out as Gerald pokes his head out the door. "Are you okay?"

"I'll be fine," I call back and run into the bathroom at the end of the hallway.

The door swings open, and Katie's washing her hands. She grabs a paper towel from the counter and turns toward me. "Emma? What's wrong?"

"This damn support group. Not sure if it's helping to rehash what happened."

"I'm so sorry. Can't even imagine the pain. You know what you need?"

"What's that?"

"Tequila!" She belts out, making me laugh.

"I'm more of a vodka girl."

"Vodka. Chocolate. Pizza. Whatever works." She throws the paper towel toward the wall and makes the bin with one try after it ricochets off the tiles.

I bend down to splash water on my face. "Are you done with your music therapy?"

"In a few. Wanna hang out after and watch a funny movie? I hate seeing you like this."

I turn off the faucet and look in the mirror at my red nose and puffy eyes staring back at me. "Thanks for the offer. I'm gonna head home and get into my cozy PJs. See you in a couple of days for practice?"

"Definitely!"

We walk down the hall and toward her classroom. Before heading in, she adds, "Not sure if you and Zev will be up for it. But I wrote a song."

"That's awesome!" Her students turn around, and I continue in a whisper. "Can't wait to hear it."

She waves goodbye and heads to the front of her classroom, picking up her acoustic guitar that's leaning against the wall. The circle turns toward her, and I wonder what kind of trouble, sorrow, or loss they've had and if it's worse than the person sitting next to them.

Chapter Fourteen

My fifth-period students are acting up. Although, it's mostly Eric who's making the noise. Whenever given what his parents call busywork, he procrastinates or ignores the assignment completely. Today, he's tapping his pencil on the side of the chair's metal leg. He does this repeatedly while looking out the window, until several students call out his name and tell him to stop. He laughs as he keeps tapping, and I tell them all to settle down.

Funny how I'm the only one who doesn't find the tapping annoying. He's able to keep a solid beat while throwing in some accents. All he needs is a drum set, which he may already have at home. For now, though, I tell him to leave the drumming for later so we can focus on the lesson.

It's not the easiest time of the year, curriculum-wise. We've been studying World War II for the past couple of weeks. I sometimes worry about how the topics we study— and how the Holocaust survivors' testimonies— might affect my students. Before presenting, the survivors who come to my class ask me what they should talk about. I leave it up to them to share whatever's comfortable. Every time, the survivors focus on what it's like to be taken from their homes, not knowing whether they'd ever see their families again. At the end of each classroom visit, my students amaze me with their thoughtful questions.

Last week, Walter, a survivor who's seventy-five and lives in the DC suburbs, stood in front of the class. I'm still thinking about him and what he went through in France. Being detained in a concentration camp called Rivesaltes before being separated from his parents soon after. Having to hide during the war, only to find out years later that his parents didn't make it out alive. There are many similar stories about the tragedy of war and the brave souls who risked their lives to save others.

This week, we're discussing liberation and the Nuremberg Trials. For the assignment, each student had to write a report, and those who enjoy presenting can come up to the front. Presenting isn't part of the grade, but I do expect participation, even if it's just adding to the discussion.

Lindsey and Anna get up and stand by the chalkboard. Lindsey tapes construction paper to the board, featuring a map of Germany on one and a list of names on the other. After, she stands in the center of the room, holding a few index cards while Anna stands to her side.

"Nuremberg is in Germany," Lindsey begins. "Where the Nuremberg Trials took place. Having Walter here last week to talk about his childhood experience during the war made me cry."

Sudden chuckling from the corner of the room makes my hackles rise. After walking toward the laughter, I discover that Eric is playing on his phone under his desk. Lindsey pauses as I hold out my hand.

Eric looks up at me, dazed and confused. "What?"

"You know what. Hand it over."

Eric rolls his eyes and gives me his cell.

I turn back to the center of the room. "I'm sorry, Lindsey. Please continue."

She situates herself and flips to the next card. "For almost one year after the war, many Nazis went before the International Military Tribunal for war crimes." She points to one of the papers taped to the board. "Twenty-four people, to be exact." She names half of them and then moves back a few feet as Anna steps forward.

Anna reads the names of the final twelve war criminals before continuing. "They were tried for their participation in the Holocaust as well as crimes against humanity. It was held in Nuremberg because it was thought of as the birthplace of the Nazi Party. Out of the twenty-four brought to trial, twelve were given the death penalty, six were jailed, and the rest were either acquitted or the judges couldn't reach a decision. Like Lindsey said, after hearing Walter's story and reading more about Holocaust survivors, I'm glad these criminals were brought to trial. It makes you think about your own life and how good you have it. It makes me never want to complain about stupid stuff again."

Lindsey and Anna finish their presentation and take their seats. A couple of others, who enjoy presenting, go through theirs and then we open up a discussion. They're empathetic and reflective. In the end, the students agree with the tribunal's decisions but don't show any hatred toward the convicted. Several students think that the Nazis shouldn't have been hanged but, instead, kept alive so they could evolve to see the good in all people without prejudice.

One student says that Holocaust survivors should be the ones who choose the punishment of war criminals and whether they should get a death sentence or life in prison. Eric, who finally participates, says the class should choose how trials are conducted by writing our decisions anonymously on a piece of paper.

I gather the papers, mix them up, and read the results aloud. They turn out mixed, with twenty-two students saying survivors should choose the punishment and the other nine saying it should be judge or jury.

I'm not sure how the survivors would react if given the choice, and it reminds me of Zev and his grandmother. Zev only brought her up once, in response to my asking about his tattoo. He says he's proud of her and wants to remember what his grandmother went through during the war. I wonder if she ever talked about her experience to students like mine. I make a mental note to ask him more when the moment feels right.

The bell rings and the students gather their belongings and disperse from the classroom. Eric's taking longer to put his textbook and notes in his backpack, and he's the last one to leave. Before heading out, he glances over, as if he's about to say something and then changes his mind.

"Hey, you," I call out, and he stops before getting to the door.

He turns my way, straight-faced, not knowing what to expect until I hold up his phone. Eric walks toward me and takes the device from my hand.

"That was a great idea to share our thoughts anonymously. I'm glad you participated today." I don't mention how it'll help his score because there's one thing I've learned from my few years of teaching: Not every student is motivated by getting good grades. But it's important to me that he gets positive feedback. Eric shoots me a half smile, puts the phone in his pocket, and dashes into the hallway.

CHAPTER FIFTEEN

Katie juggles two guitar cases and a shoulder bag that keeps falling down her arm as she walks toward my front door. After parking, Zev runs behind and catches up to her. This will be our seventh time practicing together since we decided to throw in a couple of mid-week rehearsals.

We're still on the same page when it comes to the music we love and want to play. It's normal to be cautious, though. There's a lot that could go wrong with musicians. Someone's ego could get in the way. They could start showing up late to rehearsals or get sloppy when overindulging on alcohol to calm the nerves. It's hard to tell what the future holds, so I focus on the here and now, and the good energy we have when together.

After Katie puts a bag of cookies on the kitchen counter, we take our places downstairs: me behind the drum kit, Katie in front to the left, and Zev to the right. I check the lugs along the toms and tighten any loose ones that might make the drums sound out of tune.

"Do we want to go through the ones from last time?" Zev asks as he plugs his bass into the amp.

Katie sets her Les Paul, the one with a cherry sunburst finish, on the stand. "Not sure if we need to. Seems like we've got them down, especially the Green Day ones."

She fidgets with the mic stand, moving it up higher. I lean over and see she's wearing Doc Martens with chunkier heels that make her taller.

"Wouldn't hurt to run through them. It'll help us warm up," I say while doing stick exercises on the practice pad, allowing me to run through my single and double strokes without much noise.

"Emma's always right." Zev glances at me with a playful smile.

He pushes his hair to the side, and I'm reminded of the fleeting crush I had on him when we first met at Mo's. Since then, we've moved into the friend zone—actually, we never left it. Zev doesn't know about my crush, and we'll keep it that way. He talks about his boyfriend, Andrew, often and how they've been dating for almost two years. They seem happy, if only his mom would accept the relationship. That's what Zev dwells on and he's clearly hurt by her disapproval.

Once they're done tuning the guitars, I lean the practice pad against the wall behind me, and we get started. After running through a few easy songs, we move on to some others, the ones that keep giving me trouble and take up too much mental space when my head hits the pillow.

When I screw up, Katie and Zev would have every right to blame me, the drummer, the one who keeps the time and makes everything sound tight. But they don't. Both always encourage me, so we play the ones I find challenging until we nail them.

After taking a quick break, Zev comes back down from grabbing a drink and cookies from the kitchen. He overhears Katie telling me about one of her original songs. "Why didn't you mention something earlier?" he asks after setting his cup down on the side table.

She shrugs, her modesty poking through for a change. Most of the time, Katie's the queen of confidence, but in a self-assured, likeable way.

"Let's hear it…if you're ready." Zev sits with his back against the wall, legs stretched out in front of him.

I do the same on the wall by my kit. Katie plugs her guitar, the one she says broke the bank, into the amp. I've always loved the sound of an electric acoustic. Its crisper tone makes a meatier sound without being too heavy or distorted, the type of guitar that has always reminded me of Heart when Nancy Wilson would wail on hers. My mom used to watch their videos on MTV, and I'll never forget badass Nancy and her kicks, with her long blonde hair flying about.

Katie pulls out a chair, sits down in front of us, and starts to strum. She stops for a second and lifts her head. "It's called 'Scorched.' I wrote it last week between our rehearsals."

The song starts slowly and kicks in toward the middle, building up in all the right places. She repeats the chorus a few times.

The time to replace you
To no longer face you
My heart's on the run
With no place to call home
Scorched and left clinging
It's better off alone

Katie sings the chorus once more as her voice scatters through the air. We ask her to play "Scorched" again from the beginning. This time, it's even more powerful and the lyrics haunt me. Is this about her? Has she been hurt? How many times? She places her guitar back on the stand and stretches after playing.

"Loved it!" Zev says. "Not sure if that's for us, or just for your solo gigs, but would you want to play it together? Just need the chords. Emma, what about you?"

"Totally blown away. Would be cool if the fills came in right before the chorus."

"Right here?" Katie asks and, without picking up the guitar to accompany her, sings the part I'm referring to.

"Yes! What do you think?"

"Love that idea. Your drumming would do it justice."

Katie glances over at Zev, but he doesn't say anything. They lock eyes for a moment too long. Zev reaches for a pillow from the sofa, situating the cushion against the wall behind him. "You've been burned a few too many times, huh?" he asks.

"What do you mean?"

"Scorched and left clinging. So, what's better off alone? You? Your heart?"

Katie shakes her head. "Their hearts. I've broken too many. More than one at the same time."

"Ouch," Zev says but before he can continue, she cuts him off.

"I have a hard time committing. When they ask if we're exclusive, even if I really like them, it's like a signal gets sent to my brain that says, 'Watch out! Run the other way before it gets serious.' Figure it's better to bow out first or hook up with someone else. And I like the excitement of it, the newness that you don't have in a committed relationship." She puts committed in air quotes, making it sound even more serious.

"I get it," Zev answers. "That used to be me. Then I met Andrew."

"Are you saying I haven't met the right person yet?"

"Not at all. I'm saying that's how it was for me for many years."

Katie nods and looks my way. "What about you?"

"What about me?"

"You and relationships. Do you like casual or serious?"

"Oh, I don't care," I say, sounding like it's no big deal. "Depends on the person and my mood. Nobody special in my life right now."

"Sounds perfect to me. Well," Katie smiles and hesitates, "as long as you're cool with it."

"Yep, I'm cool with it," I reply, unsure and nonchalant, as if I'm trying to convince myself.

The truth is, I'd rather focus on my house and job. And lately, Josephine and that list of names are taking up space in my head. I'm not in the right mind to have a relationship. And I'm not sure I even want one.

"Not to change the subject…" Zev says. "I know we haven't played together that long, but I'm loving how we're sounding. Don't want to pressure but, I think we're ready to play some gigs."

Katie nods. "I'm not opposed to that. Small venues would allow us to get some experience and build up a following after a while."

My anxiety starts to build again. It's been so long since I've set foot on stage and in front of a crowd.

"Emma? What are you thinking?" Katie asks.

"That I haven't played in three years."

She continues in a soothing voice. "Yes, you have. You've played for us. And you're awesome."

"You know what I mean. I'd hate to let you down. What if I mess up big-time?"

"We'll all mess up. But guess what? Nobody's gonna notice because there will be like five people in the bar not paying attention. They'll be shitfaced or trying to hit on someone."

"Hitting on someone? Talking about yourself again?" Zev teases.

Katie throws a coaster his way. Zev tries to dodge the wooden object flying through the air but not before it hits him on the shoulder. He throws it back her way but misses. She dashes across the room and laughs until she's snorting.

Before we can start setting up gigs, we have to pick a band name. It's not that easy to get everyone to agree. Bands have broken up before they've even picked one. Bands have broken up over much less.

The three of us start calling out ideas, one after the other, and nothing sticks. We all have to agree, or we move on to the next one. We go around in circles, coming up with different names. Katie and I like several that Zev doesn't: Havoc Station. Pink Vespers. Downtown Banter. And others that don't make the shortlist.

"How about something short? Like Kez?" Zev shouts out.

"Hmm, sounds good, but what's the meaning?" Katie asks.

"Our initials, duh."

Katie snickers and then shakes her head. "Not feeling it."

We go through a few more and tease Katie about how we'll know when she's feeling it. Zev gets up to pretend he's plugged into the amp and twists and turns to show Katie's impending enthusiasm.

She rolls her eyes as we continue our brainstorming. "How about Unhappy Together?" she asks.

"That's cool, I like it. But…" Zev's words trail off.

Katie yawns and rubs the back of her neck while she waits for him to continue. I also wait, wondering if he's planning to say something profound.

"It's a better name for a song. And it makes me focus too much on the unhappy part."

"Well, we really aren't that happy, right? Because we're a bunch of losers," I joke.

"How about Even the Losers?" Zev asks.

"Nah, love that song but—"

"Let me guess?" Zev continues while looking at Katie. "You're not feeling it. Let's sleep on it and come up with a few more next time?"

Unhappy Together sticks with me. Katie doesn't like the name, but I'd love one that resonates with all of us that's in the same vein. My brain starts working. We're all imperfect or incomplete in our own way and that's okay—and it's what we know. Zev's bad relationship with his mom. Katie regretting her career choice. Me, with my grief, my parents' grief, and Cory.

"What about The Incompletes?" I blurt out.

"Interesting," Zev says while nodding several times. "It can have more than one meaning," he continues. "To be incomplete. Like 'to be continued' but more vulnerable, more for a person rather than an object. I like it."

Katie chimes in. "Me, too. And it sounds good to say. The Incompletes."

"So, we have a name?"

We all agree, and Zev says he'll work on our logo and website and then put together a list of places to contact. Katie grabs her electric guitar and plays the beginning of "Crazy Train."

"Wait." I jump up to sit on the throne. "Start over." When she begins again, I throw in the drum parts. "Crazy Train," a song I've played since high school, is hard to forget, even after all this time. It's practically muscle memory at this point as I fix the few mistakes with ease.

"Wait," Zev repeats after me. "Let's start over but give me a minute. We need to record a few songs so I can get us some gigs. We can't rely on your looks alone."

"Why not?" Katie teases and rips into the guitar part again, this time turning around to me with a camera-ready smile that accompanies her badass rock-n-roll vibe. She's putting on extra, but it works.

Zev sets his phone on the windowpane, turns all the lights up, and double-checks the mics and monitors. "Okay, I'm ready," he says and after hitting record, grabs his bass and leans into the backup vocals when it's his turn.

Chapter Sixteen

Josephine agrees to meet with me again, and this time I choose the location. Beforehand, I research a few more names on the list now that their identities have been revealed. There's one thing they all have in common: they've either disappeared, died in a crash, or had an accident, five years after their crime.

I lose sleep, thinking about them. They should have been put away. But we have to believe in the judicial system, right? To convict someone, we need to believe beyond reasonable doubt. Essentially, that's what Josephine has asked of me—to believe beyond reasonable doubt that someone evil deserves to die, at least before she'll tell me more about the final name.

A person in their right mind would forget about the list and go on with their lives like before. I've tried to forget. But then curiosity takes over. Who's the last person on the list? Are they still alive since the name isn't crossed through?

I walk toward the entrance of Maymont, a historic estate overlooking the James River. I pick a bench along the path and wait for Josephine, who approaches ten minutes later. She's dressed in all black again, except for an emerald-green beret and a gold brooch with pink petals on the collar of her jacket.

The beret complements her cherry-red lipstick to perfection and highlights her silver hair as the curls spill onto her shoulders. This time, she wears black combat-style boots with green laces and black cargo pants stuffed into them. It leans more trendy and less utilitarian, making me think she was a model in her younger days.

Josephine sits beside me and puts her purse on her lap. She pulls out a gray velvet bag cinched at the top with a delicate pink bow. "I bought you something."

"How nice, thank you. Should I open it now or wait?"

"Now's fine. Hope you like it."

I can feel her eyes on me as I reach inside and pull out a silver bracelet with two charms dangling from it. One has pink and yellow flowers with a dark etched border. The other's a musical note in white and black stripes.

"You were admiring my bracelet last time. I saw it at one of my regular haunts and thought of you. Hope you like flowers. I wanted to get you a drum charm. The musical note was the closest they had."

"I love it. It's perfect, thank you."

I put the bracelet around my wrist and as Josephine helps with the clasp, she tells me how she loves going to antique shops and estate sales. She gets animated when describing all the great finds like picture frames, gloves, silk scarves, and handbags.

It's an unusually warm day and we both take off our jackets as we find another spot in the shade a few feet down the path. Josephine brings up Dean and how his favorite season was summer, but it wasn't his style to be in shorts.

"Dean wore slim-fitted tees with his trousers," she says and smiles while strolling down memory lane. "He was as fit as a fiddle. Toned and lean."

As she talks about him, I imagine the two together, walking arm-in-arm down the street, a beautiful couple who most likely turned heads.

"Must have been from all that drumming."

"It certainly is great exercise. Whenever he played, he'd sweat up a storm."

We sit for a minute and watch moms with their toddlers run by. Josephine squints when a beam of sunshine beats down on her face. "Did you look in the bedroom closet?" she asks, shielding her eyes with her hand.

"I did. It was quite the find. Louie Bellson was an awesome drummer."

She smiles. "Good job figuring it out. He was Dean's favorite. They actually share something else in common, other than drumming."

"Oh yeah. What's that?"

She looks away when several kids giggle and speed past us on their bikes. "I'm surprised you haven't figured out the clue in the last name, considering your keen eye for detail."

I pull out the list and study it, feeling a tinge of annoyance from this cat-and-mouse game. "And you're not going to tell me unless you get the answer to your question? Or the answer you want?"

"Emma," she starts, sounding annoyed, as if she were my parents scolding me. "Isn't that why we're here? That you've thought about it and have your answer."

"I have thought about it. A lot."

She puts her arm on the back of the bench and turns toward me. Her dark eyes convey little emotion. Is she nervous? Excited? It's hard to tell when someone's this calm and collected.

Before answering, I think of Cory. How easy it was for my brother to get addicted. And how the doctor cut him off without a thought or care to help him cope after the fact, knowing she was the one who overprescribed in the first place. It was callous. Careless. As if she were playing God. "Yes, I believe evil people deserve to die," I say to Josephine. "But what do you want from me? I'm not the person who can make that happen."

"I never asked anything from you. All I said was if you answer my question, I'll tell you about the last person on the list." She looks at the sheet of paper resting on my lap before continuing. "Louie Bellson and Dean actually have a couple of things in common. They were born in the same year, 1924, and they both played Gretsch drums. Take a closer look at the list and the last name. See anything unusual?"

She gives me a few minutes, and I sigh, showing my frustration. Why is she making things so difficult? "Josephine, my brain hurts. None of this makes sense. All I know is this person has some connection to Sobibor."

"You know," she continues in a soft voice, "I knew very little about Louie Bellson's life but thought it was so interesting when I found out the name of his wife, considering he was a drummer. I knew about drumming from Dean, but not specific details."

Her clue puzzles me. I'm not finding this amusing at all, but her words motivate me, challenge me to dive deeper, similar to what my students go through when working on a tricky assignment. "Considering he was a drummer" could mean anything.

After staring at the list for a few minutes, I give up. "Josephine, I need a clue or two. And a bag of chips, that would help."

"I can't help with the snacks but let me see." She taps her fingers on the wooden bench. "The first name of his wife would be considered competition, not to Dean or Bellson—but to the type of drums they liked to play."

Her phrase repeats over and over in my head. Competition to the type of drums they liked to play. What does that mean? They both liked to play acoustic sets, so, having an electric drum set wouldn't really be competition. Besides, I can't remember when they began making electric ones.

Cymbals come to mind next; China cymbals in particular. China would be a cool name for a woman, and besides, I've always loved the harsher, more explosive sound they make. But that kind of cymbal doesn't quite fit the music they played, so when Josephine tells me China isn't the one, I'm not surprised.

Could it be competition in the sense of other drum equipment? I go through the alphabet in my head, starting with *A*, but nothing comes to me until I get to *E*.

"Evans?"

She shakes her head. "Keep going, my dear," she adds in a whimsical manner.

It's the first time I've heard a playfulness in her voice. She's getting a kick out of this and maybe enjoying the company.

Her comment confirms I'm on the right track, and I silently go through the alphabet and make it to the *L*s.

"Ludwig," I say with an air of confidence, and we both laugh as I move on without asking if it's correct.

"Majestic!"

Josephine shakes her head.

"What about Mapex?"

"No," she says, "but you're getting closer."

I skim through *N* and *O* and make my way to *P* and then stop. "Is it Pearl?"

Josephine throws her fist into the air and then claps at my success. "You've done it, my dear!"

She opens her purse and takes out a pencil. Before writing on the paper, she stops. "Are you sure you want to know?"

My heart races. At this point, there's no turning back. I nod, and Josephine circles the letters in the first and last name. "Once you remove the *P*, *E*, *A*, *R*, and *L* from here and here, you have the correct spelling of the person's name."

I take the note from her and, on a separate piece of paper, write out the name: Reinhardt Glichke. I say the name aloud, not knowing if it's the right pronunciation.

Josephine looks ahead in silence. A minute later, she stands in front of me. She reaches into her bag and hands me a thick envelope.

"That's everything you need to know. Oh," she adds as she puts on her jacket. "Not sure if you've learned more about the other people on the list."

"I have. People do some sick stuff, don't they?"

She nods and glances around before continuing. "How'd you get your information?"

"The internet. Why?"

"Well, if I were you, I'd delete my browser history."

As Josephine says goodbye and walks away with the same confidence as before, I hold the envelope and wonder what's inside.

Chapter Seventeen

The park gets busier, and people swarm around. Are some of them giving me the side-eye? My imagination goes into overdrive as I think about Josephine's comment: *If I were you, I'd delete your browser history.* What has she roped me into?

The envelope, in a brown distressed leather, has seen better days, but is intact. The top has a flap with a string-tie closure to keep the contents secure. I'm wondering whether to open the envelope here or wait until I get home. Mother Nature decides for me as gray clouds form, bringing rain a moment later.

I lift my shirt and put the folder underneath while making a mad dash to the car. My keys are nowhere to be found, and I take cover under a large pine tree and dig through my pockets. A young woman calls after me a moment later. She's holding a set of keys, asking if they're mine and, after sighing in relief, I thank her for the good deed.

After driving home in record time, I head straight to my bedroom, unravel the string, and pull everything out of the envelope. I set the stack on my bed before fanning out the contents over my comforter. There are copies of photos, one-page documents, and a newspaper article. The photos, some in color and some in black-and-white, include headshots of a man who appears, at quick glance, to be the same person at different ages.

I set them side-by-side for comparison. In each photo, the eyes, nose, and lips are a match. There's also a mole pattern on his upper right cheek that has been circled by a red pen in each copy.

After, I flip through several documents similar in appearance to a visa or identification card. Even though it's written in German—a language undecipherable to me—a quick scan of them makes my stomach drop. SS letters, in a slanted and jagged way, appear in all caps. There's only one thing SS could stand for—the insignia of the *Schutzstaffel*—the worst of the worst in Nazi Germany.

Another document looks like a passport with a Nazi stamp and the eagle emblem above a wreath with a swastika in the center. It has a picture of the same man in a military uniform. From teaching history, I've seen that Nazi emblem a hundred times, specifically on uniforms and caps. Again, it's hard to make out the German but there's one word that's easy to detect: Sobibor, which came up during my first search that made me want to know more.

I check the man's name, which is the same from the note: Reinhardt Glichke, born in 1923. He would have been young during World War II, eighteen or twenty at the most when Sobibor was constructed. I do an internet search and learn that SS recruits, at least pre-war, had to be between seventeen and twenty-three, and concentration camp guards between sixteen and twenty-three.

After that, I search for Sobibor again and click on the first entry in the results. Sobibor was a killing center where many Jews were murdered within hours of their arrival. The Nazis separated the Jewish men and women upon arrival. Then they'd go through a selection process: who would be kept alive for forced labor and who would be sent to their deaths.

After the selection process, the Nazis ordered the ones in the left line to remove their clothing and they were marched to the gas chambers. If any resisted, they were beaten. Around five hundred Jews were forced into the gas chambers at a time. Approximately two hundred thousand Jews were killed there from various countries including Czechoslovakia, Germany, Austria, and France, making it one of the deadliest Nazi camps besides Treblinka and Auschwitz.

About thirty SS officers worked at Sobibor. And there's no way they could have pretended they were just following orders or knew nothing about the operation. Considering the heinous crimes of those on the list found in the drums, Reinhardt Glichke has to be the worst. His crimes against humanity are immeasurable, a serial killer a thousand times over.

I put aside my laptop and fish through the pile. Under the photos and documents, there's an article dated September 1989, from a local paper. The headline reads: *Chicago Man Buys Spring Valley Manor.*

I pick up the article and learn how the manor, a venue that hosts weddings and other events, got a new lease on life. It was set to close down until a man named Rey Glover bought it at auction. He'd read about the rundown manor in the newspaper, and immediately fell in love with its history, so much so that he moved from Chicago to Virginia once the deal was made. After that,

Rey Glover spent two years renovating, bringing the space back to its former luster.

In August 1991, they had their grand opening. Glover, who was interviewed in the article, said, "I'd always wanted to own a venue where people could celebrate their happiest moments. And it was always my dream to be a business owner."

The article doesn't feature a photo of Glover, so I'm not able to confirm his identity by comparing the piece with photos from the folder. Since it's a different name, I can't be absolutely sure they're the same person. In learning about war criminals in hiding, it wasn't uncommon for them to change their names for fear of retribution. Maybe Glichke changed his name to Glover so he could fit a new narrative?

I open a new browser and type in the name of the manor. In the search results, the venue's website sits at the top of the page. I click over to the site. Beautiful photos sit on the home page, along with a few links of the space during renovations.

There's also a short video about bringing the manor back to life. It includes before and after shots of the gutting process as they repair the old wooden floorboards, patch the masonry work on the fireplaces, and strip and stain the window frames. Further down on the page, they feature photos of the finished manor with polished floors, new chandeliers, and stained-glass windows.

In the About Us section, they share the story of Rey and his dreams and passions, with a link to a few newspaper articles. Photos of his staff take up the bottom of the About Us page but don't include any photos of Rey. I go to a section called Work With Us. Vendors are displayed in alphabetical order and by category—caterers, florists, bands, DJs—along with their logos. At the bottom, there's information on how to become a premier vendor with a disclaimer that, due to the popularity of the venue, it could take up to six months to be added, if approved.

After looking at the photos in the article, the name Spring Valley Manor finally clicks. The 2007 article I'd read a few weeks ago about Dean and Josephine's anniversary mentioned the same venue—almost twenty years after Rey opened the manor. Was Dean planning to take care of Rey at their anniversary party? If so, why did he wait so long? Then I remember my real-estate agent telling me that my house was built in the early nineties and only had one owner. Did Dean and Josephine move down here for the sole purpose of murder? Was Dean almost caught in the act, so he had to bide his time and try again?

Now that I have more information about Glover—who's possibly Glichke—should I hand the details over to the authorities? He'd be in his mid-eighties by now and who knows his state of health. But should his age or condition even matter?

The photos and articles make my head spin. Should I put the list back in its hiding place and forget everything? Is there more to the story that Josephine isn't telling me? How would Zev feel, considering his grandmother was a Holocaust survivor, knowing there's an alleged SS officer walking free, practically in our backyard?

Part of me wants to ask Zev his opinion. But if I do, the secret's out and Josephine told me to keep it between us. At the same time, Josephine seems a little too carefree.

Is her nonchalant attitude a way to hide the pain and appear stoic? Does she want to say more but doesn't know whether she can trust me?

Josephine and her motives, whatever they might be, cloud my thoughts. The only thing that should matter is what to do with this information. And to confirm, with my own eyes, that Glover is, in fact, Glichke.

Chapter Eighteen

We've had a few more rehearsals since my meeting with Josephine, and tonight's our first gig at a dive bar known for rock, punk, and some reggae. It's a popular hangout with cheap beer and even cheaper décor, and I'm nervous as hell, wondering if I'll be able to get through a set, let alone on stage.

Broken Lane Café, a place where a few well-known artists got their start, books their bands months in advance. Turns out, Zev worked his magic and got us a spot when another act backed out at the last minute. The booking guy liked the tightness of our playing in the sample Zev sent over and said, "Cool you've got a drummer girl, let's see what she can do."

These unnecessary, tedious comments make me more self-conscious and under pressure to work even harder to prove myself. Yes, there are drummer girls out there. And, yes, we like to rock.

Tonight, we're the second band to go on, with little time to spare between lineups. Over the years, getting ready and setting up on stage became second nature. But tonight's different. Tonight feels like the first time all over again and who knows how long it will take to prepare.

I make my way to the venue with my snare, sticks, a drum key for tightening any loose heads, and my two favorite crash cymbals. The rest of the kit, which belongs to the bar and is shared by the other drummers, awaits me.

I don't tell my parents, or any friends, about this first gig. I need time to practice being on stage again, get back into the groove and out of the rustiness without anyone noticing.

As we wait our turn to play, Katie and Zev join me in the back room that's the size of a walk-in closet. Both sit squished on an oversized velvet chair, worn out and ripped along the cushion. I'm on a stool with my sticks and practice pad. It's about twenty minutes until showtime and a warm-up is vital for all of us, especially a drummer who plays for hours at fast tempos, keeping the beat without falling behind.

I've got the set list memorized but as a backup, it'll be taped to the floor next to my hi-hat during the set. Nerves get the better of me, thinking about what the booking manager said. *Cool you've got a drummer girl, let's see what she can do.*

Shit. In just a few minutes, I'll be on stage, playing in front of people. Strangers who might criticize and judge me, the drummer girl who's out of practice. I get up and pace while moving my arms and wrists around to warm up.

"You okay?" Zev asks while plucking his bass.

Katie opens her eyes. "Were you talking to me?"

Zev shakes his head, and Katie smiles my way. "You're gonna kill it."

She's trying to boost my confidence. She's done that since the day we met. Her volunteer work in music therapy comes in handy and helps me to refocus on what's important: having fun and living in this moment.

Zev gets up and stretches. "Anyone want a drink? I'm gonna grab a beer."

"I'm good, thanks," Katie says.

"Same here."

"Same here on what? The beer? The good? Or both?"

"Nothing for me, thanks," I say, knowing a drink would help before going on, but I prefer to stay sober and notice any mistakes with complete clarity.

After Zev leaves the room, Katie reaches into her bag and hands me a few fun-sized Hershey's. "Chocolate always does the trick when you're feeling a little edgy." She unwraps one for herself. "I always keep them around."

"You? Nervous? I would've never thought."

Katie taps on her iPad and starts to scroll. "I'm good at hiding it."

Her comment makes me think she needs a little encouragement, too, before going on stage. "I've said this before, but I love 'Scorched' and how your voice sounds."

"Thanks. Sometimes I get too into it."

"How could you not? You wrote an amazing song."

She turns and gives me a big smile. "Well, your drumming certainly helps. Brings it to another level."

At first, I don't want to interrupt as Katie mouths the lyrics to prep for our gig. But it's something that's been on my mind because writing music seems to come so easy to her. "Can I ask you something? How do you go about writing? Do you come up with the guitar and instrumental parts first? Or the lyrics? And is it always something about your life?"

Katie puts down the iPad and pulls out a memo pad from her bag, fanning through the pages. "I always do the lyrics first. I'm old school. I like to handwrite them and then use different color pens to denote different chords, whether they're major or minor and, for example, the verse or chorus. Although," she says, holding up the notepad toward me, "it's starting to look real messy." She snickers. "Kind of like my love life."

Katie puts the notebook away, but she's piqued my curiosity. I want to ask more about the sad songs she writes but I keep quiet, not wanting to pry, figuring she'd open up when ready. Maybe that's all there is to the story, though—just breaking others' hearts like she said when first playing "Scorched" for Zev and me.

"What about you? Have you written any songs?"

I shake my head and go back to practicing on the pad. "Wrote a couple in high school but not since then. They were pretty bad." I pause, reflecting on what it would be like to write a song now, ten years later.

"You should give it a try," she adds as Zev walks back into the room, juggling a beer and three water bottles. He sets his beer on the table and then throws Katie and me each a bottle. I drop one of the sticks and grab the water midair while keeping the other stick going in perfect single strokes. I'm quick on my feet, thanks to good technique and muscle memory.

"Damn, Em, that was awesome!" Zev says, and it stops me in my tracks.

I hold back the tears, remembering that's what Cory used to call me. Zev picks up on my emotions and worries that he's said something wrong. I lie and tell him I've got the jitters. I'd never want him to feel bad, especially before a show.

The manager from the bar peeks his head in and tells us we're up. We wait a few minutes and then grab our gear to head to the stage. The first band's drummer removes his snare and cymbals, and mine are put in the same spot until I rearrange a few things, including the throne. Zev tapes the set list on the floor beside my kit and another one gets taped to a monitor at the front.

My nerves get the better of me when someone calls out Zev's name from the audience. The bar is packed, not an empty seat in the house.

Pretend it's a rehearsal and nobody's here.

Pretend you're at home, in your basement, with just Katie and Zev.

I repeat this in my head several times until the anxiety wanes.

Katie walks toward the drum kit. "You've got this," she says, and it comes out as a whisper layered on top of a loud crowd. Zev waves to his friends at a table and turns around, giving us a cue that he's tuned up and ready to go.

Katie lets out a guitar riff that quiets them down. "Hey, everyone, thanks for coming out tonight. We're The Incompletes, and you didn't hear it from me, but this might be our first gig together. But rest assured, we'll be memorable. In one way or another."

The crowd whistles and claps. Some laugh and some hold their glasses up in a cheering motion.

"All right, all right, settle down," Zev says in a cute way, feeding off Katie.

He turns around to me again, and on cue, counting up to three, we start our first song. Adrenaline rushes through me a mile a minute. We get through it without missing a beat—and for me, not messing up the timing. I'm starting to relax as we go into the second one, and for the first time in years, I'm loving being on stage, wrapped up in the moment.

Before long, we pick up the tempo and a small crowd gathers in front of the stage. Once they take up space, it's hard to see behind them. This keeps my anxiety at bay, even when I miss the cymbal on one of the songs. Nobody seems to notice, not even Zev or Katie.

During our set, people walk up and put cash in our tip jar. We're not doing it for the money, but it never hurts to have some validation that we belong here on stage. When we get halfway through our set list, Katie switches guitars, straps on her electric acoustic and plugs it into the amp.

"Hope you don't mind." She puts her foot on the monitor. "I'm gonna channel my inner Nancy Wilson on the next couple of songs. Who here likes Heart?" Katie strums a bit and then swings her hair around and does a quick kick. The crowd gets louder. Some stand up from their bar seats and others snake their way to the front.

"Before Heart," she says, "we've got an original. It's called 'Scorched.' Hope you like it."

Katie looks at Zev and then at me. On her song, the tempo picks up in the middle, but the beginning is the hardest. All instruments come in at the same time from the first note. If it's not exact, we'll be completely off for the first chunk of the song. It took several tries during practice, making me hypercritical of my playing.

She counts to three and our extra practice has paid off. "Scorched" isn't a long song—only three minutes and twelve seconds—but it's intense and requires a lot of concentration, with fancier work on the ride cymbal and the bass drum. That's the main reason we put it in the middle of the set. It's like exercise. We warm up with easy songs, put the harder ones in the middle, and save a few easier ones for the end when exhaustion has taken over.

After "Scorched," we go right into Heart without a pause, and I choke the cymbal with my hand, reaching out to hold the side to stop the sound in its tracks. I remember hearing this term for the first time in my music class and how quickly I fell in love with the motion, hitting and then silencing the cymbal over and over again. We finish our set with a few more, ending with a slower Green Day song as part of the cooldown.

Zev throws a few picks, one by one, from the stage and, while the crowd's clapping, I get up and walk to the front. Every part of me is covered in sweat, and I wave and smile to the crowd. A teenager approaches and asks if she could have my sticks, and even though they're expensive, I oblige. She tells me her mom's letting her take drum lessons and that makes me happy because when there's one more drummer girl and a supportive parent, the world's a better place.

As Lenny Kravitz blasts through the speakers, we pack up our gear for the final band to take the stage. A few people gather around and compliment us on a great set. Zev introduces us to a few friends and his boyfriend Andrew. They make a super-cute couple, and, while chatting with them, I think about how Zev's mom doesn't accept their relationship. How could a parent be so judgmental and not accept a child for who they are?

After realizing one of my expensive cymbals is still set up, I jump on stage and unscrew the cymbal from the stand.

Katie follows me on stage. "Emma, you were nervous for nothing. You were so awesome!"

"Look who's talking? You're a natural."

She puts her arm around me. "Because of you and Zev. And the chocolate!"

"It was so much fun. Let's see if Zev can get us another gig."

"After that," Katie says, "I'm pretty sure we'll be booked by this time next week."

"It was a cool crowd," I add. "We might have to up the ante next time. Give them even more of your Nancy Wilson kicks."

She laughs as we walk to the back room to grab our bags and clean up anything left behind.

Zev rushes into the room and stops midway. "You're not gonna believe this. We're already booked for next month, same time, same lineup."

"That was fast!" Katie throws one of the guitars on her back.

"The manager loved us, what can I say? Sorry, I should have checked first. Got excited. I'll make sure next time. Hey," he adds, going a mile a minute, "let's celebrate with a drink at the bar?"

"I'd love to, but next time. Gotta get up pretty early."

"For what? A middle-school field trip?" he teases. "Need a chaperone?"

I shake my head. "Believe it or not, that might be more fun. Family obligations."

We wave goodbye after putting the gear in our cars. I wouldn't normally get up so early on a Saturday morning, but it's breakfast at my parents' house at nine. We've been celebrating Cory's birthday every year since his passing.

This year, it would've been his twenty-fourth, and Dad will be cooking up a storm as usual. We'll remember my sweet brother with his favorite meal: pancakes and eggs with a side of breakfast potatoes. It's a tradition of sorts, even without Cory here to celebrate with us.

Chapter Nineteen

I pull into my parents' driveway, deciding to surprise them by being twenty minutes early instead of ten minutes late. The local newspaper sits by the front step, and I grab it before opening the door. This time, I use my key, figuring Dad still wants me to feel at home, and most likely he'd already be busy whipping things up.

"Hey, you!" Dad calls out from the kitchen when he hears me. "Nice surprise! You're early."

"Thought you'd need an assistant. Considering how much you hate cooking."

His laughter echoes as I kick off my sneakers and glance at the front-page headline: *Deaths on the Rise from Opioid Epidemic.*

Sadness washes over me as I lean against the wall and skim through the pages. The article confirms my beliefs: doctors have prescribed way too much and too easily. Cory wasn't the only one. There have been many deaths, as well as those who still suffer.

The reporter states that with the recent crackdown, many who've become addicted take to the streets and buy illegal drugs to manage the pain. Several people are quoted, mostly family and friends who've suffered from the loss of a loved one. I hold back the tears and turn to the next page to read more.

"Did you get lost?" Dad calls out from the kitchen.

"Be there in a minute." I get to the end of the article where the author talks about physicians prescribing opioids without regard for their addictiveness or their patients' well-being. A retired doctor, who remains anonymous, states how some physicians were given gifts and incentives from manufacturers to prescribe their brands. "Many say we're not to blame for the epidemic and it's simply not true," the anonymous doctor adds. "It was a vicious cycle and a huge scheme to make money at the horrible expense of the patients."

At the end, there's a note from the newspaper: *We reached out to several medical practitioners for a response and received no further comments.*

For a moment, I imagine the newspaper contacting Cory's doctor and her dismissing them as she did my brother when he needed help.

I place the paper under my sneakers to hide the article from my parents. They don't need to read it, especially today.

Our cat Random meows and, after getting my attention, follows me into the kitchen and toward the counter. Dad plants a kiss on my cheek, and I wash my hands, ready to help out.

"Where's Mom?"

"Getting dressed. She'll be down in a few."

"What can I do?"

Dad pauses for a moment, eyeing the flour and sugar on the messy counter. "How about slicing the strawberries?"

He adds another pancake to the plate and pushes the spatula across the edge to keep them in line. "And maybe put the eggs away and set the table?"

"Hey, sweetie," Mom says from the kitchen entrance before walking toward me. Like always, she's naturally pretty with little to no effort, but today she's more put together, wearing a floral dress and gold-hooped earrings. Her hair's down; there's a splash of pink on her lips; her eyes pop with mascara and plum eye shadow. I haven't seen her wear a dress in months, let alone cosmetics.

She comes in for a hug, and I wrap my arms around her. We've always been huggers, but after Cory passed, we're holding each other a little tighter, a little longer than before.

Sometimes, I don't know what to say, whether to ask how she's doing or change the subject and try to make her laugh. I never want to upset her, but we're all reeling from the loss, especially today.

"Here, let me help." She takes the utensils from me, sets them and some napkins on the table, and grabs a few plates from the cupboard.

The shelf that once contained Cory's ashes now has a framed picture of the four of us during our vacation to the Grand Canyon. Our parents sold us on the trip as an opportunity to bond with each other and nature, so they decided we'd vacation without electronics. At first, Cory and I whined but the idea grew on us when Dad mentioned we'd be sitting around a campfire, telling stories.

When we got there, my parents took turns at night reading chapters from *The Three Musketeers*, and we'd listen intently, waiting to find out what would happen next to D'Artagnan. Cory would beg for another chapter and then another and another until he'd fall asleep in my mom's lap while listening. The next day, he'd ask them to reread the last chapter from the night before and my dad would always joke, saying, "You snooze, you lose."

It's a fond memory, one that hasn't crossed my mind in years. Today during breakfast, we share a few of those vacation stories, among others, and clink our glasses of mimosas together in remembrance.

When I think my mom's about to cry, because that's what happens each year, not one tear falls. She polishes off her mimosa in one swoop. "I'm tired of being sad all the time. I want to be happy again. But it makes me feel guilty to live my life and be joyful when Cory's not here doing the same."

Dad puts his glass down and reaches for her hand. "We want that, too, Deb, for you to be happy again. It's okay to enjoy life. You've been through way too much not to have that."

I'm about to add that Cory would want that for her, but it sounds so cliché to say. Besides, who the hell knows what he'd want. Or what happens once you die. "Dad's right, Mom. It wasn't long ago when you were always smiling, even when we were annoying you after school and during summer breaks. How'd you even put up with us!"

"I finally deleted Cory's number," she says out of the blue. "And I called my old boss. They have an opening, and they'd love to have me back."

I reach for her hand like Dad did a moment ago. "Mom, that's great. I'm really proud of you.

"Dad, how are you?" I always make sure to ask because he's suffered, too, and tries to play it cool.

"I'm fine, making the most of every day. Your mom told me all this yesterday, by the way—about Cory's number and her job. It makes me happy. All I want is for your mom to have peace."

Her progress and desire to move on takes me by surprise. I thought for sure we'd be crying, talking about missing Cory and hating on his doctor. Although, to be fair, my parents never hated her—it was all me. It's been hard to forget what she did, especially after reading today's article about the epidemic.

Mom and Dad don't know the half of it. I won't forget, even though that quack probably doesn't even remember his name. But I'll never forget hers—Dr. Dana Breznin. It was written clear as day on the empty prescription bottle in Cory's bathroom.

Our cat, Random, slides back and forth across my leg, begging for a petting. His timing is perfect and brings me back to the moment—a moment of calm we've been longing for these past few years. Seeing my mom finally living in the present and focusing on what the future holds makes me hopeful that I can also lay my demons to rest.

Since she's more upbeat than expected, I share my news. "Mom, not sure if Dad told you, but my house came with a drum set."

She smiles. "Yes, sweetie, your dad told me after you dropped us off from our road trip a few weeks ago. I think it's wonderful. And what a hoot that you asked for them to be included in the sale."

"It was meant to be, as they say," Dad adds.

"The bigger question is," she asks, "have you played?"

I nod. "Yep, and now I have a band, too. Remember Mo's, where you bought my first drum set? I met Zev in the parking lot there. He's our bass player. Met Katie, the other band member, in a parking lot, too, actually."

"So, naturally," my dad asks, "the band's name is The Parking Lots?"

Mom laughs and snaps her fingers. "Or The Parkers!"

"Nope! But close," I tease. "The Incompletes."

They nod and mouth the words, maybe trying to decide whether they like the name or not. They don't ask how we came up with it. Instead, Dad repeats The Incompletes aloud and says, almost singing, "Okay, okay, it's growing on me."

"Good, because, we'd have to change it if you hated it."

"Really?"

"Of course not!"

"If you need someone to play the cowbell, I'm your guy."

"Jim, hello?" Mom taps him on the arm. "I think she's covered in the rhythm department. Just face it," she says with a chuckle. "You just want to be a groupie again."

"Again? Are there stories you're not telling me?" I ask, loving the banter between them that has been missing for so long. It's so good to watch them laugh and tease each other again.

My mind wanders and I reflect on the band, drumming, and how it all started by finding the list of names. The thought of Dean getting rid of the others— and Josephine knowing and being so nonchalant about the outcome—makes me uneasy and mystified. Does she have a different moral compass and can justify the end result? Or is it me who has a problem with morality and knowing what's right or wrong?

There's no way I can share this news with anyone, especially my parents. They'd freak out and tell me to mind my own damn business. And then they'd start worrying, and I don't want to put that on them. But Josephine's words keep eating away at me.

Chapter Twenty

I feel bad asking Josephine to meet again and taking up her time. But I have no choice, considering the subject matter makes in-person conversations the only option. She doesn't seem to mind meeting, though, and reminds me that she's retired and spends most of her days reading, going to estate sales, and checking out the newest exhibits in Richmond's Museum District.

"You have a thing for ice cream, don't you?" I say when we meet at Triple the Scoop.

Josephine loads a portion of mint chocolate chip onto her spoon. "To be honest, it brings back memories. Dean and I used to come here the first Sunday of each month. I'd always get the same flavor." She digs her spoon into the cup for more. "He liked to vary his three scoops and would often end up eating half of mine. Now I get the kiddie size. Gives me just enough to satisfy my sweet tooth. Everything in moderation, as they say."

After our first meeting, we'd agreed that we'd never talk about anything over the phone or through email or text where our conversations could be traced. Fortunately, it's a quiet day here at the shop, with only a few seats taken and nobody within earshot. The bell on the door makes us stop mid-sentence and look toward the front. That's paranoia for you, when you're dealing with a murderous Nazi who potentially got away and lives nearby.

I fidget with a sugar package on the table, flipping it over and over.

"My dear, what's on your mind?" Josephine puts her spoon down on her napkin.

"It worries me."

"What does?"

"The person who's not crossed out and what he's allegedly done."

She gives a half smile and raises her eyebrows. "Allegedly? What about the documents I gave you?"

"They gave me chills. But how do you know for sure it's the same guy?"

"I don't know how Dean got the information or the names. He never shared that with me. You can dig all you want but let me make it crystal clear—Dean or I cannot be implicated in any of this. You do understand?"

She doesn't quite answer my question, but I nod right away because again, it sounds like a threat.

"There could be more," she says in a softer tone, "but Dean's no longer here to ask. I imagine it wasn't easy to get the information about this man or anyone else on the list. But I'm confident it's the same man who owns the manor."

I want to believe her; there's no reason not to. But this is a serious accusation. It's not like fibbing about eating the last cookie and putting the empty container back in the pantry. This is someone's life.

"Emma, did you notice the moles on his cheek?"

"It's not uncommon to have moles on your face," I say. "Millions of people have them."

"There are six moles, spaced out evenly, making a perfect triangular pattern. And, yes, I counted them but let's forget the moles for a moment. There's more to the story. Within the envelope is a document about an incident at the camp. Did you see it?"

I shrug and explain that my lack of German keeps me from understanding some of the contents.

"Not sure if you know," she continues, "there was an uprising by Jews at Sobibor and they got hold of a knife. During the upheaval, Rey got a part of his thumb cut off. That's something you can't hide…so, no, Emma, you won't find millions of people with the same mole pattern, a piece of their finger missing, who also happens to speak German."

She's right. If Rey fits the description, how could he *not* be the SS officer with a new identity? My head's spinning. What, if anything, should I do? Does she want me to take care of him? I'm a middle-school history teacher, for Christ's sake, not someone who'd stir shit up and live to regret it. There's still time to bury this news, go on with my life, and pretend nothing happened.

"While Dean and I were planning our anniversary party," she continues, "we took a tour of the manor to make sure it was to our liking. Rey, as he calls himself now, was too busy to meet with us until Dean made up an excuse to the manager that he knew him from Chicago. When Rey put out his hand to shake ours, that's when I noticed his disfigured thumb. I also noticed his thick, German accent. Naturally, Rey didn't recognize us, but Dean spun a story about how it had been many years back when Dean had more hair, which made them both chuckle. At the time, I didn't understand why Dean wanted to meet Rey so badly. I didn't put it all together until Dean told me about the list."

We sit in silence, our ice cream long finished, when a couple of families and their kids fill the place with noise as they fly through the door. A toddler runs to the counter, pointing out the flavors. He jumps up and down, asking for *bannilla wiff spwinkles*. It reminds me of my internship in college at a preschool when the kids were learning how to talk. So cute and innocent. Unlike the situation I'm in now.

"You know," I say, breaking the silence, "I did some searching and found out what happened to the other seven on the list. So, I'm curious: Why don't you finish where Dean left off? Why not do something about Rey like Dean did with the others?"

She wipes the corner of her mouth, taking a moment to fold the napkin over and over until it fits into her empty cup. "Because that was Dean's passion for justice. And I'm just an old lady, after all."

"So, you were a supportive wife."

"Emma, some people don't deserve to live after what they've done. How can you not see that?"

"But," I whisper, "Dean killed people, too. With all due respect, doesn't that mean he'd deserve to die, too?"

She snickers at my comment. "I'm surprised you'd say that, but I suppose it's up to interpretation. If you asked the thousands who died in Sobibor under Rey's command, I bet they'd think Dean's a hero, if he had a chance to take care of the situation."

"How can vengeance be sweet when it involves taking another life?"

Josephine pauses a moment. "There's quite a difference, my dear. Vengeance isn't sweet. But justice is."

Vengeance isn't sweet but justice is. I've never heard this before, and the phrase consumes me. There's no way

I can put myself into the shoes of Holocaust victims and survivors. But if I could, would it be easier to accept and believe in getting justice for those who couldn't?

"I'm not sure what else you want from me," Josephine says. "Just know that you'll never convince me that what my husband did was wrong. Even though it's a little too late for some, I'm proud that he brought comfort to those suffering from grief, loss, and trauma—and brought some justice to the world."

"Except he didn't get to finish the job. And I'm sure there are many more monsters out there who didn't make the list. Where do you draw the line?"

"From what Dean told me," Josephine continues, "he only added the next name when the previous person on the list was crossed off. That's why there's only one name that's not marked through. I'm not sure if he planned to add another once he took care of Glichke."

"The most difficult to-do list ever." I pause, still wondering about Dean. "I don't get why your husband would tell you all this. You'd think he'd want to protect you from knowing anything."

"He only told me a few weeks before he passed. It's as if he knew he didn't have much time left." She reaches across the table and touches my arm. "I know it's a lot to comprehend, Emma. And, yes, many might find it morally ambiguous. But there must be a reason why you can't let it go, and why you still want answers."

"True. In hindsight," I add with a wink, "maybe it was a mistake to ask for the drum set."

She grins. "But then we wouldn't have bonded over ice cream."

After our laughter subsides and we wave at the boisterous toddlers a few tables over, Josephine stands up abruptly like the first time we met. "Instead of asking me more questions," she says while picking up her keys and the empty ice cream cup, "perhaps you should pay Rey a visit and see for yourself."

Chapter Twenty-One

When we meet for rehearsal, Katie plays "Brevity." It's another one of her original songs, louder and longer than "Scorched." The lyrics are complex and when we ask about their meaning, she says they're up for interpretation, leaving us even more curious.

Zev asks her to run through the song again, and after she plays to the end, he asks if it's about the homeless crisis. I chime in, adding my thoughts that it's about the lack of a true connection with humanity. We're both off the mark when Katie opens up, telling us "Brevity" is about jealousy—how when you're jealous of someone, you disconnect from that person to alleviate the pain of not succeeding or following your dreams.

"You're making us look like slackers," Zev says. "I haven't written much. What about you, Em?"

"I dabbled with lyrics during high school. They were pretty lame. Haven't tried since."

"Guys, it's my outlet, what I do in my free time." She continues, "It has always been my dream to be a singer-songwriter, even during law school. Took three times to pass the bar. Guess they finally took pity on me. But it's my profession, not my passion."

"I get it," Zev adds. "It's hard to give up the job security. My mom would L-O-V-E love you. You'd be a shining example in her book, bragging 24/7 about you and your career to her friends."

"She still hasn't let up?" I ask.

He shakes his head. "It's wasted on me. But, she still tries. Now my visits are few and far between, sometimes for the occasional Jewish holiday when she guilt-trips me." He pauses while getting out the rest of his gear. "It's funny how she goes out of her way not to stop at the coffee shop where I work, even though it's the closest to their house. She probably doesn't want to run into Andrew since he hangs out there sometimes."

"I'm so sorry," Katie says.

There's not much we can say or do in this situation except wanting to slap some sense into his mom.

"Don't be. I'm dealing with it. So…our first couple of gigs went great," Zev adds, making me think he's trying to change the subject. "And we've got another one next month at the first place we played. Is there anything we should add or get rid of?"

He straps on his bass and tunes it. He turns on the amp and goes through the same motions to make sure the bass sounds good when plugged in. Katie does the same with her two guitars.

I sit behind my kit and warm up while giving Zev's question some thought. "I'd like to add one or two slower-tempo songs at the beginning. Warming up before isn't enough to get me through a ninety-minute set. My arms are usually on fire halfway through."

"That's cool with me. Any ideas?" Katie asks.

"Maybe another Fleetwood Mac one, or what about Muse?"

"Let's go with Fleetwood Mac," Katie says. "That way, Zev and I can sing together."

Zev stops messing with his bass. "Since when do you like my singing?"

"Since forever!"

"Bullshit."

She smiles and looks at me. Her cheeks turn red, and she winks as if she wants me to back her up.

"I realized," she turns back toward Zev, "how great your voice sounded when you were singing backup on 'Little Lies' at our gig. It was powerful, and you really hit the harder notes. Your voice didn't come across that way during rehearsal. You should sing more often."

"I don't mind. And, thanks for the vote of confidence," he says nonchalantly.

She blows him a kiss, and we get started. As always during rehearsals, we go through all the songs in our set list. At the end, we take a few minutes to decide which extra Fleetwood Mac song to add.

"What about 'Thrown Down'?"

"Never heard of it," Zev says.

"Yeah, same here."

"Really? It's a great song. Manageable tempo. Great harmonies." Katie pulls out her iPad and plays a few videos.

We decide the song's a perfect addition and call up the lyrics. These days, cover bands often bring tablets to gigs, so they have the lyrics in front of them. Katie puts her nose up to the idea, and says she'll have everything memorized by next week's rehearsal—and expects the same from Zev.

As they pack up, Zev asks if we're comfortable having gigs twice a month. Katie and I agree that it's manageable for now, and until it stops being fun, we'll continue to play, with Zev managing the bookings.

"So, guys," I say as they finish packing up their gear. "Playing at these dive bars is fun and all but they're not gonna pay much."

"For now," Zev answers.

"Sure. But, meanwhile, how do you feel about playing for special occasions, like weddings and bar mitzvahs?"

"Seriously?" they both say in unison.

I step toward them. "It'll give us some extra cash. We're getting better and have gigs to prove it, so why not get paid more?"

"Since when are we doing it for the money?" Zev says, beating Katie to the punch when she's about to respond. She doesn't say a word as Zev gives me a speech about how it's only about the fun and connection we have as a band, not about the money.

"Sure, but it wouldn't hurt. I mean, we don't have to do a lot. Maybe a few a year. All my savings went into the down payment for my house. I don't have an emergency fund right now, at all."

"What's that?" Zev replies with a smirk. "Yeah, the last thing I'd want is to reach out to my mom for money. She'd throw the barista job in my face and tell me 'I told you so' a thousand times."

"In all honesty," Katie says, "I really need to pay off these student loans."

Josephine's words about checking out Rey for myself have been on my mind. And this is the perfect opportunity. "There's a place called Spring Valley Manor. Have you been there?"

They shake their heads as I continue to fib. "We went as a family a couple of times for weddings. Why don't I check it out and report back?"

"So that means we'd have to play pop music?" adds Zev.

"We'd play whatever's on the bride's list. It could be anything," I reply.

"Well," Zev continues with his arms folded, "I'm not gonna agree to the weddings or whatever, unless there's some punk or rock added to the mix."

"I knew that was coming," Katie teases. "You and your punk obsession."

"At least they're short," Zev says.

"My arm's about to fall off, with their crazy tempo."

"Come on," I say, cutting them off. "We're not even there yet, so just chill."

"Just chill? No way." Zev straps his bass on and starts thumping. "For bar mitzvahs, I'll make 'Hava Nagila' so punked out their heads will spin!"

We laugh, trying to imagine turning every song into a punk version, and how it wouldn't sound that bad, at least to our ears.

After walking Katie and Zev out to their cars and waving goodbye, I go back inside and call up the manor's website on my laptop for their office hours. In my head, I concoct various stories for my visit and get ready to see Rey in person.

Chapter Twenty-Two

The ride to Spring Valley Manor takes longer than expected. There's a backup on the interstate and we come to a crawl, which isn't a surprise, as the traffic's always unpredictable, even outside of rush hour. I pass on Katie and Zev's offer to join me because the last thing I need is to get nervous or distracted while on a mission. Besides, they can't know my ulterior motives.

The thought of Rey being a former SS officer and living less than an hour away creeps me out, making me wonder whether anyone else knows his secret. Then again, I want to give this complete stranger the benefit of the doubt. That's why I need to see him face-to-face, to ensure Josephine's account isn't one of mistaken identity.

The parking lot sits close to empty, except for a few cars on the far side. I grab a spot and, before going inside, take in the grounds and the waterfront setting while watching a few people out on their kayaks. Pine trees and colorful floral gardens surround flagstone walkways, and the side of the building features a large patio with tables and chairs. Two large balconies jut out from the back of the property, offering guests breathtaking views of the James River.

I turn back around and take in the water view once more. The fresh air and light breeze invigorate me, and I close my eyes for a moment and listen to the birds singing until a voice startles me.

"Hi, can I help you?"

When I turn around, the sun blocks my view, making me reach above my head to pull down my sunglasses. A woman around my mom's age, with a dirty-blonde bob, walks down a slope and stops next to me. She's wearing a plaid blazer with a burgundy blouse and gray pants. "Sorry, I didn't mean to startle you. I saw you from the balcony, enjoying the view."

"I should be the one apologizing! Probably should have come through the front. I wanted to get a tour of your place, but the scenery lured me away."

"Upcoming nuptials? If so, congratulations!"

I giggle and zip up my jacket. "No, not yet. Still waiting to meet the right person."

She smiles. "Well, definitely keep us in mind. The more the merrier for us. So, what can we do for you? I'm Ingrid, the operations manager." She reaches out her hand. Her grip is firm and steady.

"I'm Emma, and my band would like to play some more weddings and events. I wanted to check out your venue—and see if you're looking for more live music."

"That's fantastic! Unfortunately, I'm not the one who manages the entertainment. And we already have an approved list of vendors. I suggest getting the word out to event planners and bridal parties. They usually share their thoughts with us and make recommendations."

"Oh, okay. It's just…" My words taper off as a concocted story is about to unfold, the one that came to me last week while checking out their website and doing a little research. "I have fond memories of coming here as a kid with my granddad. We'd often kayak on the river and pass the manor. He'd tell me stories—not sure if they were true, but they were all about how he worked on the garden back in the late eighties. He said the property was vacant for many years and the back was in disarray. He helped keep it from overgrowing."

"That was your grandfather? How wonderful! My father bought the place around that time. I came down to help with the business as he got older. He wondered how the inside could be in such disrepair when the grounds were maintained so beautifully. Then one day after he bought the property, your grandfather was out back, and they had a nice long chat. Now I can tell him the story. He'll love it."

Realizing that Ingrid is Rey's daughter, I continue, making my tale sappier by the minute. "I'd always imagined going inside with my grandfather to see if the interior did his gardening justice. I've heard about the amazing renovation." I pause to add more to the story. "I joined the band not too long ago. And I thought, wouldn't it be a nice way to pay homage to my pop-pop and play here."

"You know what…" She hesitates. "We don't normally give tours on Saturdays, but I can make an exception. And, besides, my father's usually here on weekends to check on things. Whatever I do, I can't get him to retire. It's his baby."

"Are you sure?"

"Of course. He'd love to meet you."

We walk up the hill toward the front of the property as Ingrid explains that, even though there's a back entrance, she wants me to get the full tour, starting from the front.

"There's nothing more inviting than our spacious lobby, along with the grand staircase that leads up to a beautiful landing," she says.

"Kind of like *Gone with the Wind*." I add, getting nervous with each step as we make our way inside.

"Exactly!" Ingrid opens the double door and holds it for me as I step into the stunning lobby with polished hardwood floors, large windows, and a ceiling that goes on forever.

She starts the tour and doesn't miss a beat. Her speech sounds right out of a marketing brochure as she takes me from room to room, describing each unique space. The parlor and its cozy setting. The Madison ballroom, the largest out of two, that holds five hundred reception-style or three hundred for a sit-down affair. Off to the side is the Crossway Gallery, perfect for greeting guests or a smaller reception. She takes me upstairs and points out a few holding rooms for the bride and groom to wait separately, and two small reception halls overlooking the river with their own balcony. They're all spectacular.

"When my father bought the property, it needed so much work. It took two years with full-on renovations to bring back the luster."

"I know. I read…" My words trail off when I almost slip up but then continue with a quick turn of phrase. "I read that more people want to have fancy weddings again, whereas before, people wanted to use the money for a down payment on a house or something more practical."

"Honestly," she whispers. "With the cost of weddings these days, I don't blame them." We walk back downstairs as she adds, "But there will always be brides who want to walk down the aisle and celebrate in the most glamorous way possible. And we're here for that or for smaller occasions, of course."

We continue toward the back of the building and walk down a corridor. The walls hold numerous photos of wedding parties and people smiling for the camera. Around us, attendants, wearing white button-down shirts and black pants, push carts with linens and silverware.

I inch back against the wall to get out of their way. After they've passed, I step forward and stop, realizing some of my hair has become stuck in a picture frame on the wall. Ingrid leans toward me and tries to pull the strands out. Nothing works, so she tells me to wait, and I joke that I'm not going anywhere. She comes back a moment later with a pair of scissors and, after I give her the go-ahead, she cuts the strands and sets me and my hair free.

"Well, that was awkward," she adds after apologizing.

"Sorry, my hair has a life of its own," I say and watch her cut off the tangled piece that's left on the frame. She holds the strands, unsure what to do, and then reaches down to place them in a trash basket.

I turn around to look at the photo and recognize Ingrid right away. She's standing between a man and a woman, with her arms around them.

"That's me and my brother with our mother. It's like you belong here."

"Or at least my hair thinks so."

We laugh at the ridiculousness of the moment and continue down the hall.

"I feel horrible—the thought of cutting your hair like that. I guess there's a first for everything."

"Oh, don't worry, it'll grow back. That's what my stylist always says."

When we get to the office at the end of the hall, she knocks, almost out of politeness, on an open door. Ingrid motions for me to follow her inside. Two leather chairs are perfectly aligned in front of a large mahogany desk, where an older man sits.

"Father, there's someone I want you to meet. Remember the resident gardener all those years ago who kept the yard in impeccable shape when you first bought the property? Well, this is Emma, and that was her grandfather, can you believe it?"

"Ahh, after all these years, I get to meet the next generation!" he says with a German accent, only recognizable from watching too many war movies with my father.

Rey puts down his pen, stands up, and tugs on his gray cable-knit sweater. He is average height, with some extra weight around the middle, and wears rectangular glasses with a thick tortoiseshell frame. He walks toward me, and I'm worried that I might stare too long searching for clues. I can't show my intentions or give way to the disgust building inside me while trying to confirm his identity.

My pulse quickens and as he extends his hand to shake mine, I see part of his thumb missing. He notices and without hesitation adds, "Kitchen accident from long ago. Let's just say I'm no longer in charge of cutting watermelon."

"He leaves that to us now," Ingrid adds. "I wasn't around when it happened, thank goodness."

"Ingie, you were too young to remember."

"Hope you've been able to manage okay." I feel sick to my stomach, standing this close to him.

"Managing just fine!" he adds while I focus on his upper right cheek. Rey looks the same as from the photos, except older, with less hair. A few moles on his cheek stand out but not enough to create the triangular pattern Josephine circled in the photos. The remaining moles could be hiding under the large rim of his glasses. I'm distracted by them, and at the same time, I need to act fast while trying to play it cool.

I quickly point toward his face. "I think you have something under your glasses, might be an eyelash. Getting one stuck in your eye is the worst!"

"Oh, I do? Ingie, could you take a look?"

He lifts his glasses and holds them up on his forehead while Ingrid searches for the eyelash and comes up empty-handed. Now, I can clearly see the mole pattern that was hidden away a few moments before: a perfect triangular match from the documents.

I'm shaken but I remind myself to continue with confidence. "Odd, it was there a minute ago. Either that or it's time to get my own glasses!"

"I've been blind without them, since my forties." Rey puts his glasses back on.

Ingrid shares a story about how, when she was little, they'd play hide-and-seek and tease their dad about not having to cover his eyes because once he removed his glasses he'd be as blind as a bat.

They laugh while reminiscing. "Haven't thought about that in ages. That's right. I'd try to scare you and Lukas as payback for teasing me."

"You sure did," Ingrid says and plays out a childhood memory, putting one hand on her hip. Once situated in a wider stance, she pretends to be her father. "I'll give you two minutes. And I'm starting to count now!" she says in a deep voice with a German accent. "And it wasn't just hide-and-seek," she continues. "It was whenever I'd leave a mess. He'd stand in front of my room, look at his watch and say the same thing. I'll tell ya, I've never cleaned up my room so fast!"

Rey rubs his chin and nods. "Scaring you little demons was part of the fun."

The reminiscing between them makes me uncomfortable, and as Ingrid changes the subject to discuss the afternoon's wedding with him, I glance around the office. Framed photos of various sizes cover the wall, featuring brides and grooms. Three large bookcases lining the opposite wall are filled with hardback books, wedding magazines, and a few decorative bowls.

I notice a black-and-white photo on his desk of several men sitting around a table. I can't get close enough to tell if Rey's one of them or what they're wearing. Certainly, Rey wouldn't display a picture of him in his SS uniform or time in Germany, especially if he's trying to hide his past. Rey sees me focus on the picture, and I look away, nervous as hell.

He moves toward the front of his desk and mentions my grandfather again, as I try to stay cool and keep my act going. The three of us chat for a moment longer and, before saying goodbye, Rey thanks me for sharing the story about the property's garden. As we walk out and toward the lobby, we pass more staff who make their way through the hall.

Ingrid glances at her watch. "Goodness, it's eleven? Time flies. We have a wedding at two. And it's a big one. Three hundred people."

"Wow, good for you!"

"Yes, we've been very lucky. The venue has a great reputation. In fact, there's a two-year waiting list for an event in our largest reception hall."

"The manor's definitely not the place if you want to get hitched quickly," I say to make small talk. "Anyway, I should get going—you must have a lot to do."

"We have a great staff, and all will be perfect. But, yes, I should make sure all's fine."

She wishes me well and as I get to the front door, Ingrid calls my name and walks toward me. "Do you have any videos with your band?"

I hesitate, not knowing what to say. But if I back out now, she might get suspicious. I pull out my phone and call up the website Zev put together. I'm picky with the videos I show her, focusing only on the more mainstream ones. After she watches a couple, I pull up the page with the songs we know.

"Emma," she says after skimming the playlist, "I never do this, but I feel like we've connected. Your band sounds great, so I'm going to add y'all to the approved vendor list on our website."

"Ingrid, thank you," I say, keeping up with my act.

"Not sure if you'll be thanking me. You might want to brace yourself for quite a few emails from some very demanding brides. But, it will keep you busy!"

"Oh boy," I say while worrying about ever coming back, knowing that her father, Rey, is Reinhardt Glichke, the SS officer from Sobibor.

Chapter Twenty-Three

Before my eighth-grade kids jump off the school bus, our driver, Mister Foley, gives the students a speech about sticking together and being respectful. Once he's finished, I do a quick head count and tell them to stand in a straight line outside and wait for me.

This is the first trip we've taken to the Virginia Holocaust Museum. It matches the curriculum, and the kids, aged thirteen, are old enough to process the material. Still, before the field trip, we send home permission slips in case any of the parents want their kids to stay back at school.

Out of the bunch, only two parents decline the trip. They send me similar emails stating that their kids are too young to visit the museum. I disagree, without sharing my opinion. Instead, I tell them that although I understand, the students will be given and graded on a comparable assignment. Call me a hard ass, but these are the same parents who probably have no problem letting their kids play violent video games or watch inappropriate stuff on the internet.

I do one more head count as they stand in line near the museum's three-story brick facade. A few of the girls hold hands and another one fixes the hat on the girl in front of her.

"The building looks like a prison," Casey states.

"Dude, how do you know what a prison looks like?"

"His mamma was there," Liam retorts, and the kids laugh.

It takes every bit of me not to yell at them. My phone pings and distracts me with a text from Zev.

Just parked. Be there in a minute.

I put the phone in my back pocket and raise my voice. "Listen up: Mister Foley hasn't left yet. We can go right back to school and forget all about the field trip. And that's exactly what's going to happen if I hear one more inappropriate outburst. Do we understand?"

They all nod in an orchestrated way.

"And like Mister Foley said, once we get inside, there will be no joking, laughing, or rude remarks. We will be respectfully quiet as we walk through the museum. I only want to hear your footsteps."

Zev walks up and joins me. He's wearing black jeans and an olive sweatshirt and matching beanie that complements his complexion and dusting of freckles.

"Students. This is Zev. He'll be our chaperone, so no monkey business because he's not very patient."

He leans in and whispers, "Making up stories again, huh? Bet I'm the most patient out of the bunch."

"Nah," I whisper back. "Imagine you're on stage giving one of your steely glares. That's the look you need to give them if they get out of line."

We walk a few feet ahead and motion for the students to follow us. As we enter the museum, we're greeted by a woman not much older than me.

"Emma Meade?"

I nod and shake her hand.

"I'm Haley. Unfortunately, Ms. Markowitz is under the weather. She sends her apologies, but don't worry, I've worked at the museum for several years and given numerous tours."

"I'm sure it will be great. Sorry to hear about Ms. Markowitz. Please send my good wishes." I turn toward the kids and put my finger to my lips, reminding them of my rules. "Kids, this is Haley. She'll be our tour guide. If you have questions, she'll be happy to answer them. No shouting them out, though. Put your hand up and she'll call on you, got it?"

Haley asks to speak to me separately and pulls me aside. "Before we get started, I'm not sure if you discussed this with Ms. Markowitz but there's an exhibit that may be challenging for the students. It's the remnants of a crematorium that was used to burn corpses at the concentration camps. Would you like me to skip that?"

I turn around and look at my students. Part of me wants to skip, then I quickly remember that humanity has all sides, even the most heinous that can't be forgotten. The kids need to understand what can happen when hatred spreads, and now's a good time to bear witness.

"Haley, I think they'll be okay seeing it," I wind up saying. "Thanks for asking, though."

She nods and gives her attention back to the class. "Okay, students, we're about to get started. Like Miss Meade said, if you have any questions, raise your hand and I'll be happy to answer. Before we move along, you probably noticed the boxcar at the entrance of the museum. It was made in 1928 and is identical to what the Nazis used to transport Jews during the Holocaust to concentration camps. Imagine. Each one, filled with eighty to a hundred people—no food, no water, no place to sit. Travel would take several days, so you can only imagine how hot it would get during the summer.

"Also, at the entrance," she continues, "you might have noticed train tracks. Those are real and were taken from Europe and placed here at the museum. Those exact tracks once led trains to Treblinka."

Haley pauses. She looks over at me, so I chime in.

"We talked a bit about Treblinka. Anyone remember where it is?"

Several hands go up, and I call on Jessica.

"Poland?" she says with hesitation.

"That's right. Do you remember anything else about the camp?"

She gathers her thoughts. "I think people from the Warsaw Ghetto were sent there?"

"Very good, Jessica," Haley says. "In 1942, they deported more than three hundred thousand Jews to Treblinka—many sent to their death or worked to death. A very sad part of history."

We follow Haley as she takes us into the main room and stops in front of a bench. She then explains how Jews were segregated from society and unable to use the sidewalks, sit on benches, use certain water fountains, or work in certain professions.

We continue our tour, from room to room, exhibit to exhibit. The kids are visibly moved, especially when Haley shares stories of those forcibly taken from their homes and separated from their families. She also mentions Holocaust survivors who came to Richmond. It makes me think of Zev and his grandmother, and if her name is in the archives.

When I look over, he's teary-eyed. I want to mouth, "Are you okay?" but he turns away, so instead, I sidle up next to him. "Is this too much?" I whisper.

He doesn't answer, walking ahead with some of the kids, taking his role as chaperone seriously. I'm worried about him, but I don't want to make it worse as we follow Haley to a display with a replica of where detainees would sleep.

She stops in front of it. "Students, remember how we talked about the boxcar at the beginning? Upon arrival, if still alive, the Jewish people would go through a selection process where soldiers and guards would decide their fate and whether they lived or not. Many who survived were young adults who could work. Many lied about their professions to have a chance to survive. For example, lawyers would say they were tailors or car mechanics, thinking that type of profession would be needed by the Nazis. Some who were much younger lied about their age, saying they were seventeen or eighteen, hoping they'd be kept alive to work."

Several students move in closer while Zev and I stand to the side.

"Here we have a depiction of life in the bunks," Haley continues. "Men and women were kept apart and given only scraps to eat. A little soup, an ounce of meat, but not every day." She puts her fingers in a circle to show how much an ounce would be. "Like a bite or two," she adds.

We make our way to a scene showing the International Military Tribunal in Nuremberg, similar to our discussion in class but with more detail and additional trials: how there were one hundred eighty-five defendants, twelve death sentences, eight life sentences, and seventy-seven imprisonments. I pull out my phone to do a quick calculation. That leaves eighty-eight who didn't get any punishment. Why wasn't Rey on trial with them? Did he vanish before that, never to be seen again? It's hard to believe he'd get away with his crimes, considering Nazi hunters' determination to capture war criminals and get justice for the victims.

Our museum tour ends at the Tower of Remembrance, a display created with barbed wire in the shape of a Star of David. There's a stained-glass window above with flames and the word *Zahor*.

One of the students raises her hand. "What's *Zahor*?"

"I knew someone would ask," Haley says with a smile. "It's a Hebrew word meaning 'Remember.'"

"Speaking of remembering," I add. "What lessons have we learned today by coming to the museum?"

The kids look at their feet, a telltale sign that they don't want to be called on. Lucky for them, Zev speaks out.

"We discovered what happens when hatred goes unchecked."

"Thanks, Zev. Class, what do you think that means? When hatred goes unchecked?"

My student Eric raises his hand. "That if one person hates another person and we let that hatred show, it could spread like a disease, making others feel the same way. And that's not good because it could lead to something like this, the killing of millions."

"Well said. And let's remember that it's not just about killing but the deliberate murdering of a particular set of people. The happy part of the story," adds Haley, "is that the people listed here survived and made productive lives for themselves."

"How was that possible?" Lindsey asks. "Oops, sorry, I'm supposed to raise my hand."

"That's okay," Haley says. "Because many non-Jewish people risked their lives to hide Jews, particularly children. By the end of the war, thousands of little ones were saved. But more than one million had been murdered, and we can't forget about that."

The students wear sad expressions as they listen, making me wonder what I would have done back then. Would I have kept silent or stood up? Would I have taken in a Jewish child or family, putting my life at risk?

Now, with Rey, there's a chance to get justice, and a choice lies in front of me. If he was responsible for thousands of deaths, it happened decades ago. Should someone in their eighties be punished for a horrible crime they committed in their youth? Rey was barely out of his teens when the Holocaust took place. Does age even matter when it comes to retribution? Josephine doesn't think so. And neither did Dean.

Maybe I should finally tell Zev and ask for his advice. The thought of him knowing, and how it might weigh on him, fills me with sadness. The idea that he'd be burdened with a dilemma, one so close to his heart, makes me tense. Does this make me a compassionate person, or am I simply a coward?

As we finish up the tour, Haley walks us to the exit and thanks the kids for behaving. One of my students is choked up, and two girls from the group give her a hug. It makes me reach into my pocket for a tissue. Zev notices and, this time, he asks if I'm okay.

I wrap my arm around his shoulder as the kids walk onto the bus and take their seats. "Just thinking about you and your family. I'm so grateful to the survivors who tell their stories, so we never forget. Must be so hard."

"That's why many don't talk," he replies. "One day, my grandmother opened up while we were sitting around the table. We were all weeping by the time dinner was over. I sometimes wonder," he adds, "if that's why my mom is so pissed I'm a barista. So many of our relatives perished. The ones who survived gave up their careers when they fled, ending up with minimum wage jobs just to get by. She sees me wasting my college years and not doing anything with my life when other family members didn't have a chance."

Zev has brought this up before. Maybe agreeing with him would make the pain go away, or at least hurt a little less. Before I can get anything out, he continues. "On the flip side, instead of giving me shit all the time, you'd think she'd be supportive of anything I'm doing— by the sheer fact that I'm alive and happy."

He pulls away, and we let silence take over while my thoughts about Zev, his unsupportive mom, and Rey consume me.

The students are getting rowdy on the bus, squealing, and trying to open the windows.

"Keep it down," Foley turns around and yells at them from the driver's seat, "or I'll confiscate your phones. And, if anyone tries to open a window again, I'm marking you all down for detention. Each and every one of you, no matter who's the culprit!"

I'm about to step onto the bus and do a quick head count to give Foley the go-ahead to return to school.

"Hmm, this is odd," Zev says while holding his cell. "Just got an email from a wedding planner named Colleen."

"What's it about?"

Zev reads the note aloud. "Hi there, I checked out your band's website and you sound awesome. I see that you're listed as an approved vendor at Spring Valley Manor. Are you available for a wedding there in three weeks? Sorry, it's such short notice. The band my bride-to-be hired double-booked. She just found out and is frantic! Have I mentioned frantic? I'm pretty sure I can get her to throw in extra funds for your flexibility. Please let me know as soon as you can."

"Wonder how she got our information."

"I checked out the manor…remember me mentioning them at rehearsal?" There's a nervous flutter in my chest, thinking about the Nazi's venue. "Anyway, I didn't expect to hear back so soon, or at all. Honestly, I'm not sure it's the right time."

"Wait a sec, didn't you need the money?"

"Yeah, well, I'm not sure if I'm ready."

"Really? You pretty much sold us on the idea. How many times has Katie already mentioned it'll help pay off her loans? Like a thousand?"

Zev's right. Katie sure as hell won't be ready to give up the money, now that we've got a possible gig lined up. If I tell her I'm not ready, the same excuse just fed to Zev, she's going to wave it off and try to build my confidence, like before. There's no getting out of this without causing suspicion.

"You know what? Forget everything I said. I'm in my head too much. Let's take the gig and get the song requests."

"Sounds good. I'll reach out to her. And don't forget we'll have to decide which punk song to throw in," Zev teases as he walks off and waves goodbye to the students.

Chapter Twenty-Four

Katie's running late for rehearsal for the first time, something about a fire she needed to put out at work. Zev's already in the basement and, instead of practicing songs on his bass, he's behind my drum kit.

"Hey, who said you could touch my Gretsch!"

Zev laughs and stands up from the throne. "Seriously? You're one of those, huh? Straight out of *Step Brothers*."

I laugh and think about the movie. "I've watched that scene so many times. Hopefully, we'll never get into it like that!"

"Any other house rules you haven't told me about?"

"I was kidding about the kit. But, yeah, there's one. Anytime you cuss, you have to put a buck in the jar."

"Really?" he exclaims.

"Fuck no. Don't you know me by now?"

Zev chuckles, sits back down, and plays an easy beat, keeping in time for a minute or two. It's obvious he's played before as he puts the sticks down. "One of my friends had a kit. I could never get past a simple beat. Once, he got sick right before a gig, so instead of cancelling, I sat in for his band. They kept it simple for me, you know, pretty much the same beat, over and over again with a few crashes here and there."

"See, you can do pop songs." I reach for my ear protection.

"Just because I can doesn't mean I want to," he adds before continuing to play. He throws in a slow, awkward roll before getting up to reach for his bass. "I'm mentally preparing myself for the wedding gig. A little pop and a little money in the pocket…suppose it never hurt anyone."

"Are those lyrics to the new pop song you've been working on?" I tease.

He rolls his eyes and plucks on his bass, switching from one Chili Peppers song to another. Before Katie gets here, I want to ask him about our field trip with the kids but don't want to upset him. If I don't say anything, will he think that I don't care?

"So," I say, easing into the topic, "was that the first time you'd been to the museum?"

He continues to play, his eyes following his fingers. "We went as a family once. My grandmother wouldn't join us, though. It was too hard. It was hard on everyone."

"I can imagine. Confession time: when you mentioned chaperoning, I almost said no. Thought it might be too much to handle."

"I appreciate that but wouldn't have offered in the first place. Although, seeing some of the kids upset got to me. Seems a little odd they'd teach it at such a young age."

"You have a point, but they're thirteen. We shouldn't shelter them from the harsh realities of history."

"That's the same age my grandmother was when they carted her off to the camp. It wasn't until I was seventeen that she shared her story with us. Once she did, it became a little easier for her to talk about. I always wanted her to speak about her experience at schools. She'd always nod in agreement, but it never came to fruition. And now it's too late."

"Were the two of you close?"

He nods. "She was like a mom, practically raised me and my brother because our parents worked long hours. She'd hang out with us, help build Lego cities, and put on puppet shows." Zev pauses and grins, recalling the memories. "She was an incredible baker, too. She'd make us so many treats, like *lekach* and *sufganiyot*."

"What's *lekach* and *sufganiyot*?" I ask.

"*Lekach* is a honey cake usually eaten at Rosh Hashanah to mark a sweet new year, but she made it year-round. And *sufganiyot* are those jelly-filled donuts we stuff ourselves with during Hanukkah."

"So that's what they're called! I always ate them at my friend Steph's house." Hearing about *sufganiyot* takes me back to when I'd spend Hanukkah with her. Steph invited me every year, and her family always made me feel like part of the festivities.

"To this day, it's hard for anyone's dessert to measure up. The other thing," he adds, "is that she was super chill with us. When my parents would yell to put our toys away, my grandmother would always snap back, saying, 'They're kids, leave them alone about the mess.' It wasn't until much later when I learned the real reason she was so easygoing."

"Why's that?"

"She never wanted us to fear punishment. When she was in the camps, the officers would yell at them to clean up their messes. They'd stand over the prisoners, glaring at them while holding their pocket watches and counting down. There was one woman who didn't clean up fast enough—the Nazi shot her, right on the spot, in front of my grandmother."

His words stop me in my tracks. "Really? Your grandmother told you that?" I ask, remembering Ingrid's story about her father's pocket watch and him counting down.

"Yeah, why, you don't believe me?"

"Of course! It just reminds me of a World War II movie, can't remember the name," I say quickly, thinking on my feet.

Ingrid's words—or rather Rey's—haunt me. The way she acted out her childhood memory and Rey's menacing laughter in response. *I'll give you two minutes. And I'm starting to count down now.* Did he say that as an SS officer to the camp prisoners? And if they didn't comply, did he also kill them on the spot?

"Have you ever thought of sharing her story, since she no longer can?" I ask. "You could come to my class anytime."

"Nope, no way." He shakes his head. "I'm not crying in front of a bunch of teenagers. But I'll tell you."

And while we wait for Katie to arrive, Zev shares how his grandmother survived, never to see her parents again. She was one of the lucky ones at Auschwitz, where, during the selection process, she was chosen to work instead of being sent to the gas chambers. She saw beatings every day. Inmates, as she called them, would be given shoes either too small or too big, and they never had enough warm clothes to wear during the winter.

It makes me think about all the victims and survivors. How scared they must have been. How many likely froze or were worked to death. How many blisters they had from shoes not fitting right. Or sores on their bodies from being malnourished.

I continue to listen, amazed at his grandmother's will to survive. I'm so tempted to tell him about the list. It sends chills through me, thinking about Rey and the other SS officers, imagining them having the same training, saying the same things, watching and goading with intimidation. I wonder about those who survived, like Zev's grandmother, and the thousands who were beaten and starved, and who watched their families be carted off.

Zev and I have only known each other a few months, but there's no clue how he'd take the news about Rey. Would he tell me to forget about him? Tell the authorities? Want to act on his own—to honor his grandmother and other victims? My thoughts sit with me until Zev mentions the doorbell, and I run up the steps to let Katie in.

"Sorry I'm late. Contract disaster. My paralegal forgot to check something. I took the blame because she's new and the partner can yell at me all he wants. After that," she says, carrying her guitars down to the basement while out of breath, "it's a good day to rock!"

She sets her electric guitar on the stand and the acoustic one by the bookshelf. "Which reminds me, I've checked the bride's playlist and there are only two rock songs. Actually, pop rock, so not sure if they count. And, if we keep playing these weddings," she adds, "we'll need to bring on a keyboardist instead of backing tracks."

"Well, we are The Incompletes. Anything could happen," I say.

Zev stands up from the sofa. "Oh, hell no! It has to be just us. Not that I'm antisocial but—"

"You're not?" Katie teases.

"It's just that we've got a good thing going," he says, "and I don't want to fuck it up."

Katie smiles. "If that's your way of giving a compliment, I'll take it."

I get what Zev means. It can be hard to find the right mix of musical interests, personalities, and professionalism. And we like one another! We don't always agree but our band is just about perfect, and a fourth person could upset the dynamic.

Zev picks up his phone and scrolls through the wedding party's song requests. He's mumbling while counting in his head. "Thirty songs here. I can play about twenty-five of them. The other five shouldn't be that hard to learn. Not a huge fan of their first song, to be honest. Then again, it's not my wedding, so…"

"Yeah, thank goodness," Katie chimes in. "The last thing I'd want is to get married."

"Now or ever?" I ask.

"Both. Enjoying what I've got. Or, actually, what I don't have."

Katie runs through the list aloud and adds a few more songs to learn that we don't know by Bruno Mars, Katy Perry, and One Republic. Then we talk about the schedule.

Even though it's broken up with a break, it's a long day—four hours plus transportation—and that's why we can charge our rate. To sweeten the deal, the wedding planner asked for an extra twenty percent to cover the last-minute request due to the other band's cancellation.

The thought that we can make fifteen hundred bucks each—and in one day—makes it all worthwhile.

At first, we weren't sure we'd get bookings since we don't have a horn section or a keyboardist, but the fancy lighting Zev came up with makes up for it. Plus, at no extra cost, we've thrown in Katie's playing during the ceremony, because it's at the same venue.

The three of us get the business talk out of the way and finally start jamming. Each practice sounds better than the last, and we're now nailing our cues. My timing is almost perfect, except for the transition into a song by the Killers. It's something most people at the wedding won't notice unless they're musicians.

"Do you still think we can play 'Hava Nagila' punk-style?" Zev asks. He brought it up last time, and we pretended not to hear him. "The song's on their list, and I think they'd love it—unless they're super traditional. But I don't get that impression from their requests."

"Let's try it. On three?" Katie says and counts in.

We dive in and the beat is faster, stronger, and spot-on. I'm laughing the whole way through, imagining everyone dancing in a chaotic circle. We follow up with the traditional version and realize we need more practice on the slower tempo.

"You know what would be fun?" I say. "We start with the punk version, stop after thirty seconds, and say, 'Just kidding!' and then go into the traditional version. They'll love it, and word will spread. So, we might get more gigs besides the manor. There are hundreds of wedding venues in the area."

"Hold on," Zev says. "I thought we were doing just a few of these a year. That's what you said. Katie's my witness."

Katie nods. "It's true. You did say that."

"Okay, hear me out." I put my sticks down on the snare. "Let's do this first gig and see how it goes. We might want to do more than three a year. Think about how much money we'd make."

Zev lets out a long sigh. "Was this your plan all along?"

"Not at all. Only to replenish my savings. That's it."

"Okay," he agrees. "Let's see. I might consider doing more on one condition."

"Uh-oh, what's that?"

"For every wedding, bar mitzvah, or whatever event we do, we have at least two or three dive gigs where we play whatever the hell we want."

"Fine by me. Katie, you okay with that?"

"Works for me. And if you're cool with it, that allows me to try out some new originals."

"Another already?" Zev asks. "When do you sleep?"

"Don't get too excited. You haven't heard it yet."

"Are you breaking more hearts?" I tease.

She shakes her head. "It's about my family moving when my dad lost his job. I was a senior in high school, and it totally messed me up. I mean, why couldn't my parents have waited a year or let me live with someone?"

"That's pretty harsh. I mean, your dad didn't plan on losing his job." It comes out in a rush, and they stare at me. I want to eat my words but do my best to explain. "I just wonder why we're still holding our parents accountable and letting the past define us—especially when we want acceptance from them in the present?"

"Who says I want their acceptance?" Katie stands up, folding her arms. "You have to work your way through shit to get to the other side. Why do you think I write songs? It's part therapy, part self-awareness. But don't worry. I've forgiven them."

"That's good of you." Again, the words fly out without much care. She has no idea what it's like to lose a sibling, becoming the forgotten child, while your parents—or at least your mom—drowns in grief for three straight years. It makes me want to scream *screw you, Katie, and your petty high school drama.*

"Good of me?" she says defensively. "You didn't have to give up your entire existence, your group of friends that took forever to find, after being bullied in middle school for being different!"

Zev looks at me with raised eyebrows. I've hit a nerve. And now it makes more sense to me: Katie's heartbreaks and how she ends relationships before they get too deep. Her song "Scorched" says it all.

I get up from behind my kit and walk toward her, putting my hand on her shoulder. "I'm sorry. You're right. I've never been through that. I was wrong to assume it wasn't a big deal."

She gets up and hugs me. "It has taken awhile to get over it. Guess I'm still not. I know my parents didn't mean any ill will."

"Sometimes parents are selfish. We all can be. Geez," Zev continues, "I don't think I ever want kids. I'd probably mess them up."

"You and me both," Katie says.

"Getting back to your song," I say. "I'd love to hear it."

"It's not complete yet, but I can share what I've got so far." She sits on the coffee table and starts to play.

While listening, my phone rings but I'm too engrossed to answer. It stops after a couple of rings and starts up again after a few seconds. Zev reaches over and hands it to me. Two missed calls from my mom. She never leaves messages, especially when she's upset. She confessed that to me and my dad a few months after Cory died. I want to call her back but want to wait for Katie to finish the song.

"That's it, that's all I've got."

"Love it," Zev says.

It's obvious, after hearing two of her songs, that sadness surrounds Katie, with her lyrics carrying the burden.

"That's beautiful," I say. "If you want to keep the song acoustic, I can accompany you with the Cajon instead of the full kit to match the feel. It would sound awesome, unless you had something different in mind."

"I like that idea. We could try both ways, rocked out and more melodic. Zev, with the acoustic version, maybe you can play along with me instead of bass?"

While they're discussing the guitar parts for the song, I text my mom.

> *Hi, everything okay? Katie and Zev are here for rehearsal right now.*

> *All is fine. I want to donate Cory's stuff. It's time. Would you help?*

She's continuing to make progress. Not long ago, she put on a dress and some makeup. She talked about working part-time. And now this. It's a huge step.

> *Sure, this weekend?*

She gives my text a thumbs-up and that brings me even more hope. Because it's no longer the crying emoji she has often used in the past.

CHAPTER TWENTY-FIVE

Mom comes to the door dressed in a baseball jersey and denim overalls. She pushes her long braid to the back and gives me a big hug. Like last time, she holds on extra-long before pulling away. I kick off my shoes and follow her into Cory's old bedroom. It's the same as before, with photos and baseball trophies on the bookshelves and posters of No Doubt and blink-182 on the walls.

Before his death, Cory had a tiny studio apartment in downtown, and Mom initially didn't want to get rid of anything. Dad thought the opposite, that getting rid of Cory's belongings would help with the healing process. Mom wouldn't budge. She thought it was insensitive, as if we'd be throwing away all our precious memories.

My dad, who only wanted to support her, packed up all his belongings and brought everything back to their house. Now, three years later, Mom seems ready, as piles of Cory's clothing and shoes sit on the bed, some stacked up and others in disarray.

"Are you good at making boxes?" Mom points to the flat packs of cardboard leaning against the dresser.

"The best!" I say and grab one. The directions confuse me as I fiddle with the corners until getting it right. She asks me to make five and, one by one, their corners get connected and taped up.

The dresser drawers are all open, with half of them empty. In the top drawer, Cory's wallet, keys, and cell phone sit in the far-left corner. It surprises me that my parents still have his phone, but then again, there's no rule book to follow when losing a loved one, let alone a child.

A few other drawers have sweaters, sweatpants, and T-shirts. One of the shirts catches my eye. It's from our high school, an oversized one in cream with red letters. I hold it up and ask Mom if she'd mind me keeping it. She nods and tells me to take anything I want.

I set aside the shirt, a VCU cap, and the wallet. His driver's license peeks through the see-through panel, and Cory's grin beams up at me.

"You okay?"

Mom startles me when she asks. I blink back the tears and pretend not to hear her because even though I'm not okay, she needs to think I am.

"Emma." She walks over to me. "You don't always have to be strong."

She touches my arm and that makes me want to cry even more but I try to keep the tears at bay. "I'm okay for a while and then something triggers me. Like when I see a photo of him, or I pass the Frosted Flakes in the cereal aisle."

"That's grief for you. Creeps up on you when you least expect it—at least that's what my therapist tells me. Sweetie," she says, "if this is too hard, your father can help me."

I shake my head and search for a tissue, choosing the sleeve of my hoodie instead. "No, you were right. It's time. It's been three years, for crying out loud."

"No pun intended," she says, and we both chuckle to ease the pain. "The amount of time doesn't matter. We'll be grieving for the rest of our lives. The other day, it dawned on me that I hadn't cried in a couple of weeks. At first, I felt guilty. Can you believe that? Feeling guilty for not crying?"

"Yeah, the guilt. I'm feeling it, too. Always will," I confess and continue to work through the drawers, pulling out a few more items.

"It's all about forgiveness." She walks back over to the bed to fold a few more shirts before placing them in the box. "Once we forgive ourselves, we'll be able to get over the guilt. It's not easy. I still feel guilty about him driving. And it's hard to escape because every time I get in the car, it's a reminder. Forgiveness is a slow process, but I'm working on it."

Mom would have never talked about forgiveness a few months ago. She'd always beat herself up when remembering Cory, and it makes me think that therapy's helping. We go through the rest of the drawers, make piles for donations, and another pile for stuff that's not in the best condition. We fill up three more boxes, tape the top, and write the contents on all sides in a blue marker.

Random jumps on the bed and rubs against the boxes before coming over to me for a good petting. He falls onto his back for a tummy rub while my mom opens up a box for one last look.

I grab a pink and blue striped blanket that's on top. "Hey, isn't this one of those blankets you swaddle a baby in?"

"Sure is. We took Cory home from the hospital in that."

"You don't want to keep it?"

She shrugs. "I went back and forth. Anytime I look at it, I get upset. And I'm trying my best to move forward." She reaches out to touch the blanket. "It's so hard…"

"Why don't I keep it at my place? That way we still have it but it's not within reach."

Before she answers, a pinging noise comes from the side door, the one that leads to the garage. "Hello, hello," my dad sings in an echoing manner, the same way he's called out for decades when he arrives home.

By the time we answer back, he's standing at the bedroom door. He walks toward us and plants a kiss on top of my head. "Looks like you've made a lot of progress. You must be hungry."

"You're always about the food."

"As it should be! Turkey with tomato, lettuce, and mayo? On wheat toasted, right?"

"Thanks, Dad."

"I'm on it!" He twirls his keys between his fingers, backs out of the door, and heads downstairs.

We tape up the open box, and I set the blanket on the dresser next to the few items I pulled out earlier. Then we stand the boxes by the wall. Random jumps off the bed and sniffs them, going down the line one by one.

"I'm gonna donate the furniture, too. Thinking about turning his room into an office since I'll be going back to work next month. They're letting me work from home twice a week."

Her words take me by surprise. Giving away the furniture is another step forward. To forgive herself and have a fresh start.

"That's great, Mom. This would make an awesome office. There's a ton of natural light."

As Dad sings out that lunch is ready, I notice his exceptionally good mood today. Mom's progress must be affecting him in a positive way. And that makes sense, knowing that someone you love feels better.

Random meows and runs toward the hallway. He either hears Dad opening a can of cat food or smells the turkey, hoping for some easy pickings that fall to the floor. We follow him downstairs and make our way to the kitchen, where Dad stands at the counter, tossing the salad.

I eye the sandwiches already on the table. "What can we do to help?"

"Not a thing. Go ahead and dig in. Actually, wait a minute for the salad. I've made a new dressing. See if you can figure out the secret ingredient."

"Normally I'd say I love a challenge," Mom adds, "but we went grocery shopping together, so there's no guessing from me."

I lean over and whisper, "You can tell me."

"I heard that, you know." Dad puts the bowl on the table with two wooden serving forks.

We sit down and they wait for me to take a bite.

"Is it Dijon mustard?"

"Nope. Two more tries."

"Ginger?"

They both shake their heads.

"Wait, I know! Salt!"

"Very funny. Give up?" Dad asks.

I pick up my napkin and wave it to surrender.

"Spicy honey," he says.

"Really? Never heard of such a thing. That's what gives it the kick, huh?"

"Yep! Getting creative in my old age."

"Oh yeah, totally. Fifty-nine is so ancient. Soon you'll be asking for all those special discounts."

"I can't wait," Mom says. "Movie theatres, restaurants, look out—here we come for our senior savings!"

Over lunch, I tell them more about our band, my job, and the recent trip to the Holocaust Museum. When we're done, Dad washes the plates and while I'm drying and putting them away, I notice an unopened envelope on the side counter with a return address from Kindred Lineage & Genetics. "What's this? Something about Cory?"

"Sweetie, I forgot to mention," Mom says after putting the leftover salad in a container. "I did one of those at-home genealogy tests. Just me. Your dad opted out."

"If you're not opposed to spitting in a tube," he says, "you'll get more accurate results, supposedly. But the privacy issue freaks me out, even though you can opt out of them keeping your DNA—or so they say. That's why I passed."

"Aren't you going to open it?" I'm taken aback that my mom didn't share this news with me. Didn't she think this was a big deal?

"Why don't you open it for me and read us the results?"

"Too much pressure. Dad, you do it."

He wipes his hand on a towel and walks toward me, picking up the envelope and ripping along the top. He pulls out the contents and sets one of the documents on the counter.

Dear Debra Meade:

Enclosed please find the analysis of your DNA test. Through the sample you provided, we have been able to identify your genetic ancestry. We have included the breakdown of your results in this correspondence. Please note that your information will be kept for twenty-five years. However, by written request, you can opt out of the data storage by sending your letter to the address below. You can also opt-in for your results to be shared by those searching for relatives. For now, your results remain private. If you have any questions, please reach us by email or at our toll-free number. Thank you for choosing Kindred Lineage & Genetics.

"Hey, drummer girl, can you give us a roll?" He flips the next sheet over.

"This is nerve-racking." I tap my fingers on the kitchen counter.

"How so? This is fun!" He winks at my mom as she leans against the table. "Are you both ready?"

"Wait a sec, Jim. Before you read it, let me guess what's there."

I beat her to the punch. "Ginger? No, wait. Spicy honey!"

Dad pretends to hit me over the head with the paperwork.

Mom does a quick guesstimate while looking up at the ceiling. "Fifty-two percent British; thirty-one percent Polish. And…" She waits to add the final one. "Seventeen percent French!"

"Ooh, so close, but yet so far: thirty-three percent British; twenty-one percent French; twenty-four percent Eastern European. And, this is interesting: twenty-two percent Ashkenazi Jew."

"No way, really?" She reaches over and takes the document from Dad. "So, I'm a Jew who went to Catholic school?"

Mom pauses, seeming to analyze the results. "This makes sense now. My grandmother always made pierogies and cabbage soup, but we always thought it was because she was part Polish. Maybe she was Jewish and didn't know."

"Or maybe she knew but didn't practice?" my dad says. "Surely, what makes someone a certain religion is if they practice."

"Not true. That's what's different with Judaism," I reply. "Someone who's born Jewish is always Jewish, whether they practice or not."

"Okay, but what if you've never set one foot inside a synagogue?" he asks.

"Think of all of the Holocaust survivors who couldn't practice or were hidden during the war and pretended to be Christians. Or those who converted throughout history. Besides, it's not for me to decide. Obviously, Kindred Lineage & Genetics did the homework for us. And, who knows, maybe Dad's Jewish, too."

"We'll never find out because I'm not taking the test. But I'm fine with that since I haven't stepped inside a church in ages."

"I'm not taking it, either. I'm going with Mom's results. So that means I'm at least eleven percent Jewish, right?"

"Not sure it works that way, sweetie, but sounds about right to me," she says.

"Can't believe we're part Jewish. Pretty cool, with all the stuff I've learned lately about the Holocaust for my job and…it makes me want to learn more about Judaism and the customs."

"If we're being honest, I'm all about the food." Dad snaps his fingers and goes to the pantry to pull out a cookbook. "I'd better learn how to make potato latkes. Always wanted to celebrate Hanukkah."

"Really? You've never mentioned it before."

"He just wants eight presents, that's all." Mom winks at me, then leans on the counter after putting away a few dishes. "Remember the goodie bags Steph used to give you at their Hanukkah parties?"

"You mean the ones she'd never share with us?" he teases. "Always keeping the good stuff for herself!"

I roll my eyes. "Dad, you're making stuff up now."

He lifts his head from the cookbook. "Remember that one time we fought about your outfit? Ahh, the teenage years, so much fun!"

"What did I miss?" Mom asks. "What outfit?"

"Can we change the subject? I don't want to talk about it."

"What's the big deal? It was so long ago."

"Then why'd you bring it up? I said I don't want to talk about it! And if you don't stop, I'm leaving."

Dad puts his hands up in a surrendering motion. "Okay, okay, didn't mean to upset you."

"I'm fine. Let's not rehash it."

Dad keeps his word. He doesn't bring up my outfit again and the tension begins to dull. Over the next hour, Mom talks about her newfound lineage and downloads books on Judaism while Dad focuses on a challenging crossword puzzle.

After saying goodbye, on the drive home, I can't get Mom's ancestry results out of my head. Zev's on my mind, and I imagine his expression when he hears the news. Josephine's on my mind, too, for different reasons. At a red light, I look into the rearview mirror at my reflection. My Jewish heritage wasn't known to me this morning, the day before, or when Reinhardt Glichke came into the picture. Now that it's part of me, should it even matter as I contemplate the Nazi's fate?

Chapter Twenty-Six

"You're a creature of habit," I say as Josephine approaches the table in our regular meeting place.

She sets her handbag and cup on the table, takes off a floral scarf, and adjusts her black beret. "Are you referring to the ice cream or my attire?"

"The ice cream, of course. Although I love the way you dress. Fashionable yet comfy."

"Comfort's my goal. And if I look put together in the process, even better."

"How have you been?" I reach for a napkin to wipe the table where ice cream has dripped from my cone.

"Doing well, except the community center at my condo is pushing all sorts of activities on me since I'm new there. They don't get it—I'm not lonely just because I'm alone."

"So, bingo's not your thing, huh?"

"Never has been. Ballroom dancing, on the other hand—"

"Josephine, is that you?" a voice calls out.

A woman with brown hair pulled back into a ponytail approaches our table. She's wearing a light-blue polo shirt and matching skirt, as if she came from a game of tennis. "It's so good to see you. Seems like forever! How have you been?"

Josephine introduces me as Claudia and says that I'm new to the area. They talk for a few minutes about the new exhibit at the fine arts museum in Richmond.

After the woman leaves, I stare at Josephine. "Claudia? What was that all about?"

She grins. "Being cautious, considering what we've been discussing. I've discovered the world's a small place, and you never know who knows who."

I nod and wonder if I'll remember the lie if the woman and I bump into each other at a later time. Richmond isn't that big of a city, and Triple the Scoop is one of the best ice cream shops in the suburbs from what all the online reviewers say. But I guess being overly cautious does make sense.

"So why are we here, my dear?"

"I took your advice and visited Rey. I met his daughter, too."

Josephine listens as the story unfolds about my visit to the venue and how I saw Rey's moles and disfigured thumb. "I tried scanning the room for other clues but felt his eyes on me."

"And?"

"And what?"

She puts her spoon down. "How do you feel, now that you've met him?"

"He didn't come across as a bad guy."

She snickers. "Aren't bad guys charming at first?"

"It felt so creepy being there, knowing what I know and confirming his identity. After going, while the visit was fresh in my mind, I looked at all the documents again. He hasn't changed much. It really brought home the horror of what he's done. Makes me sick."

A few rowdy teenagers rush through the door and catch my attention.

"In somewhat related news," I say, turning back toward Josephine. "My mom took one of those at-home DNA tests and found out she's part Jewish. Which means so am I."

"I've heard about those tests. Not sure if I'm supposed to say congratulations but the news is quite interesting. How does it make you feel?"

"It's a little bizarre, thinking I'm something one day and another the next. It's not like I'll start going to synagogue, but you never know."

"Does it change things as far as Rey's concerned?" She doesn't mince words, and her question makes me think she'd rather keep our conversation related to the matter at hand.

"A little. Makes me feel more of a connection to the atrocities committed."

"Should our heritage really matter?" she asks. "Shouldn't we want to take a stand or act because it's the right thing to do?"

I nod in agreement, but my words don't match. "Maybe," I add, "but it's human nature to care or pay more attention if it affects us personally."

She gives me a blank stare, making me defensive.

"Josephine, I've been to Holocaust museums, heard survivor testimonies, and taught the subject for a few years now. I don't need a reminder or convincing that Rey needs to be punished." I pause for a moment to soften my tone. "I just don't know what to do. I definitely don't want repercussions that could ruin my life."

"I completely understand. What Dean did with the other seven," she continues, "was definitely risky but must have brought peace to the victims and their loved ones. And probably prevented future crimes. In Rey's case, it's doubtful that an eighty-six-year-old man would do anything else."

"What are you getting at? That he should be left alone?"

"Not at all. Rey should pay for what he's done. Yes, he was a young man at the time, but he was old enough to know better. You didn't have to join the SS at the beginning. It was all voluntary up until a certain year. He knew exactly what he was doing, even if he were to deny it today."

I stare at the table, deep in thought, wishing it were easier to find the courage to do something. To take Rey's life and make it right for the murdered and traumatized survivors. To not worry about what's morally right or wrong, and not worry about getting caught. "I feel sick over what happened at Sobibor. I don't know…"

"Emma, you don't have to explain. All I ask is that you put the list back in the drum set and tape the second one back on the wall in the closet. Down the line, maybe you'll change your mind. Or you'll decide to sell the property one day, and someone else will do what Dean didn't have a chance to act on, if Rey's still alive then."

"Wouldn't it be better and just as satisfying to tell the authorities and have them do something about it?" Part of me hopes she agrees that we should go together to turn him in.

"I have no faith in that process. When Dean told me about the list, he said he'd never go after someone who'd already paid. They were only ones who got away with their crimes and were living a comfortable life. It doesn't make sense to go to the authorities. What's the point?"

When I ask her if she had to do her own digging about the other seven, she shakes her head. "Dean told me their names and what they'd done. He also made sure I knew everything about Rey, and I imagine that, like the folder you now have, there was an equally researched folder on all the others." She untangles the charm bracelet that catches on the sleeve of her cardigan.

I glance around anxiously. "Is it possible that someone else is trying to go after Rey? You said nobody else knows about the list, but you also told me Dean didn't share all the details."

She finishes off the last few bites of her ice cream, ignoring my question. "Today, I'm not going to be a creature of habit. I'm having another scoop. Would you like something?"

I pass on her offer, my stomach turning over with nerves. While she's in line choosing her next flavor, I wonder how she can be so nonchalant about what her husband did. Dean kept it a secret for most of their lives, only telling her weeks before he died. She overlooked his secret and admired him for the deeds, as if he'd given back to society.

While waiting for Josephine to return to the table, something she said last time consumes me: *Vengeance isn't sweet. But justice is.* She believes it with all her might, using her malleable moral compass to navigate life. Could I do the same? Get even without a second thought? And would taking one person's life make up for the millions lost?

"What did you get?" I ask when she walks back.

"Butter pecan with chocolate drizzle on top!"

"No whipped cream?"

"Not a big fan of the fluff."

I snicker, thinking about her answer. Is she talking about ice cream or life in general? *No added fluff. What you see is what you get.* The two of us haven't known each other for long but that would be a great description for Josephine. I'm tempted to ask about her life—to get to know her better—but decide to keep the focus on Rey. The thought of her changing the subject to avoid my questions makes me hesitant.

Could there be details she hasn't shared and is being aloof or cautious? Sometimes I don't know what to believe. But I remember what she said once before: that she has nothing to lose and could die tomorrow.

"To answer your question, if anyone else was going after Rey?" she says between bites. "Nobody was feeding Dean information. He worked alone."

She puts down her spoon and reaches for a napkin. "You mentioned you've listened to many survivors' stories. Have you listened to any from Sobibor, the one Rey commanded?"

I shake my head and wait for her to continue.

Josephine clears her throat and shares how, after Dean died, she'd often pull out the folder with Rey's information. "I studied him and the details so extensively, I could recite them word for word. When and where Rey was born. What year he joined the SS. How old he was when he arrived at Sobibor to start, or continue, his killing spree. The thousands of Jews he and other SS officers were responsible for murdering."

Josephine stands up, mid-story, and walks away to throw out her trash. I'm expecting her to wave goodbye and exit the shop as she's done before. Instead, she comes back to the table and sits down. "I'd studied Rey more than enough," she continues. "It was time to learn more about the survivors."

She catches her breath, and a sullen expression crosses her face, an expression that no amount of ice cream could make disappear. "I went to various websites to read their testimonies and one in particular, named Basia, changed me forever. Fourteen-year-old Basia watched her little sister get pulled out of line and sent to the left and never saw her again. Basia, who was old and strong enough to be kept alive, often suffered beatings by guards and witnessed horrors every day. She said music was piped so loudly through the speakers to drown out the weeping."

Josephine's voice cracks as she continues in a whisper. "What really got me about Basia's testimony was when she witnessed a soldier toss an infant and shoot the baby midair, just for fun."

She pauses, and I want to reach out, to take her hand, but she leans back in the chair, closed off, like my grief-stricken mom in the past.

After pulling a tissue from her pocket, Josephine continues. "While detained, Basia couldn't understand what she and her family had done wrong. She kept asking herself, 'What did we do to deserve this?' There were days she wanted to die but persevered. After the war, Basia discovered that out of the one thousand Jews from her village, only three had survived. Everyone in her family was murdered—her father, mother, two siblings, and countless friends and their families."

As Josephine continues the story, I wonder whether it's possible that some of my relatives also perished in a concentration camp. Perhaps my grandmother left behind cousins in Poland before the war even started? "The story's so heart-wrenching," I say, wondering why she's telling me all this.

Josephine sighs. It's a deep sigh, taking on a sadness that matches her mood. "At the end of the testimony, Basia says, and I repeat it word for word: 'When there's hope, you don't question it. You live and breathe it. And that's what kept me alive.' I'll never forget Basia's words, and it gives me hope that despite Rey enjoying a good life, his sins will catch up to him, somehow, somewhere. Whether you do something or not. That's my hope."

Her words haunt me. Offering hope for others might mean action from me. Do I have a moral responsibility to do something? Are my actions and choices free will?

Josephine pulls a pen and sticky note from her handbag, starts to write, and attaches the note to a piece of paper. Remaining silent, she puts the paper face down on the table and pushes it toward me. I wait to turn the paper over, scared to see what's written.

After getting up from the chair, Josephine tells me to splurge a little and try the peanut butter brittle ice cream. "You can't go wrong with that one," she says. "Unless you're allergic to peanut butter."

"No way, love the stuff. I practically keep them in business."

"Then you should definitely try it." While putting on her scarf, she adds, "Did you know that at least two percent of the US population has nut allergies? And other allergies, too, which completely astounds me." She walks off, waving goodbye with her head raised high, like each time before.

I wait for her to leave before turning over the paper. It's a copy of Rey's incident report, the same one that's in the envelope she gave me. She's placed the sticky note on the report with an arrow pointing at a line that says *Allergien,* which also has a few other German words next to it. On the sticky note, Josephine has written in red ink: fish—all types including crustaceans, mollusks, and finned.

Panic falls over me as I stuff the paper in my pocket. It's obvious what Josephine is spelling out to me.

Chapter Twenty-Seven

Our first gig at the manor starts this afternoon, and I slide my car into a parking spot two hours prior with Katie, coincidentally, showing up right behind me. Since it's our first gig performing here, we need extra time to get ready, warm up, and run through any last-minute changes.

Katie hauls out her equipment, and even with her three guitars, fancy pedals, and other gear, it's not even close to what I bring as the drummer. Katie's particular about her stuff, so even though the venue has mics and amps we could use, she brings some of her own. I don't blame her, considering the sound quality could make or break a band's set.

Zev pulls into the parking lot a few minutes later. He walks over and leans his guitars against the side of my bumper. An attendant calls out from the front door and points to a side entrance, where we can grab some luggage carts for our equipment. She tells us to use the same side door to access the reception hall.

Katie jogs to the entrance and pulls out two carts, pushing them toward us in a haphazard way as the wheels spin. We're about to rush toward her when she fixes the front and glides to us in record time.

I start to load my gear, first with the bass drum, and then place the toms, snare, and stands on the shelf. The cymbal and stick bags get placed on side hooks. The cowbell pokes out of the unzipped back, and I tap on it with my index finger.

Zev rolls his eyes. "I swore after high school, I'd never play another song with a cowbell, yet here we are."

"There's only one or two. You'll live," Katie teases.

"Maybe we need to add a disclaimer on our site saying we're not into cowbells," he says. "Or a playlist called No More Cowbell."

"That needs to be on a T-shirt somewhere, pronto," Katie says with a smirk, then leans her black guitar case on the other side of my bumper.

"Speaking of which," Zev continues, "I'm glad we're not wearing those matchy-matchy outfits like some band members. Imagine the three of us dressed alike!"

Katie nods in agreement. "No shit. Having a dress code was hard enough."

"Right? What's the big deal about wearing jeans and a T-shirt? I mean, we're all…"

"Guys! Really? What's with all the whining?" I realize my tone is harsh. I'm stressed as shit, and they have no clue that there's more to playing here than making a few extra bucks. I quickly change the subject, along with my tone.

"So, it turns out, I'm Jewish!" I follow my declaration with a few dance moves.

Zev stops in his tracks. "What do you mean, turns out? You adopted or something?"

"Wow," Katie jumps in. "Sounds like your parents dropped some family drama on you."

"Nope, none of the above. Well, not exactly. My mom did one of those DNA tests. Turns out, she's part Ashkenazi Jew."

While we walk to the side door pushing the carts, I finish the rest of the story and how my dad has no interest in his own test, only in making latkes.

"Well, I'd better get an invitation to dinner. And you know what that means? My mom would totally approve if we dated."

"But you're gay."

"Oh yeah, there's that."

"Yeah," Katie adds, "just a minor detail."

As we're about to get to the side entrance, Ingrid holds the door open for us. "Great seeing you again, Emma! If you follow this hall straight down, you'll get to a set of double doors on the left. Go to the one at the very end, for the closest to the dance floor. Behind that is a small platform. Not quite the elaborate stage a band hopes for but close enough."

We follow Ingrid's directions and start setting up our equipment. She peeks her head into the ballroom a few minutes later. "Hey, forgot to mention we're making y'all some sandwiches. We'll bring them by soon. Let me know if there's anything else you need."

We shout out our thanks in unison, and while Zev and Katie discuss the guitar intro on one of the songs, I think about Ingrid and if she knows about her father's past. How could she? He'd never tell them. He'd want to protect his family from harm. If I found out something this horrible about my dad, would I write him off? Or would I live in denial, pretending he's innocent, so I wouldn't have to lose him?

Zev straps on his bass and plugs the cable into the amp. The two of them set up their in-ear monitors as I fiddle with mine, adjusting the volume when they start playing their guitars. I situate the throne and tighten the screws on the cymbals before tuning the snare and toms.

When all the pieces sound perfect—or as perfect as they're going to get—we run through some of the set, starting with the couple's first dance. It's always a slow one and a perfect way to get warmed up behind the kit. We have fun with "Hava Nagila," then play two more songs, and consider rehearsal done. We hop off the stage with perfect timing when they set up a few lunch plates in the back of the ballroom.

I take a few bites, exit the back door, and ask an attendant for directions to the bathroom. More staff scurry past me, pushing a cart with a three-tier cake with intricate piping, silver beads, and a bride and groom nestled on top. The woman at the front hits a bump and the other attendant catches the tray before the cake goes flying. He cusses at her for being careless, berating her until he turns around and our eyes meet.

"Sorry, she's in training," he says.

"Sounds like you're the one who needs training, not her," I mumble under my breath as he disappears with the cart and his coworker around the corner.

A restroom sign hangs from the ceiling a few feet ahead of me. Ingrid mentioned her father comes here on weekends but didn't say what time of day. Could I get a closer look at his office for anything that jumps out at me?

I look at my watch. We have forty minutes before the wedding begins. I walk through the lobby and down the hall, stopping in front of Rey's office. When there's no answer after a few quiet knocks, I double-check nobody's around, open the door that's ajar, and step inside. Part of me says to go back to the ballroom, to not take this risk, but my need to know more takes over. I have to act fast. I close the door halfway and scan the room, making my way to his desk.

A few wedding magazines are piled neatly on the side. A wooden container, holding a letter opener and a few pens, sits next to a black phone. A large paper calendar has yellow sticky notes down the right edge, some with names and numbers, another with grocery items.

I step toward the bookshelf and eye the philosophy tomes and literary classics. Several photos act as bookends and as I pick up one of the picture frames for closer inspection, the books fall sideways. Before one tumbles to the floor, I grab hold and put the book back in its place, as my heart races.

On the shelf, there's a photo of Rey. He's with a woman and two kids, which must be Ingrid and her brother. They're in swimsuits at the beach, with glistening skin and wet hair, as if they've just gone for a dip in the ocean.

Another photo catches my eye on the same shelf, a young couple cutting a wedding cake and smiling for the camera. The groom has on a yarmulke, making me wonder why Rey, a despicable Nazi, would have a photo of a Jewish couple on display. I pick up the frame and notice a difference on the picture. The right edge is a few shades lighter than the left and sits crooked within the frame.

Could something be underneath? A secretive note or another photo? My mom used to put photos on top of others within picture frames, often saying she was too lazy to place them back into the albums.

Acting fast, I turn the frame upside down and shift the brackets sideways to remove the cardboard backing. Two other photos, both in black-and-white, sit underneath the one with the Jewish couple. In the first one, four men congregate around a table near a white one-story building. A soldier has an accordion strapped to his chest and the others are in civilian clothing, watching him play. In the other photo, Rey sits on a kayak near the water's edge. On the back, *Bug River* and *June 1943* are written in pencil. I take a picture of both sides and quickly put the frame together and back on the shelf.

Voices get louder in the hallway. I stand against the wall, praying the voices will disperse. A moment later, as they subside, I step out of the office and walk down the hall. I'm about to enter the lobby and run head-on into Zev. Right behind him is Ingrid. He has a puzzled look. Ingrid either hides her surprise at seeing me or it doesn't faze her.

Zev mouths, "What are you doing?"

I pretend not to notice. "Ingrid, by chance, did you find an earring near here?" I bend down to check the floor. "It could be anywhere. I noticed it missing after you gave me a tour."

"Oh no! Did you check by the wall where your hair got caught?"

I nod and continue down the hallway, scanning the floor. Ingrid does the same and, of course, we come up empty-handed.

"We do have a lost and found. I'll call up there and ask."

"That would be great, thank you." I describe the made-up earring as the three of us walk toward the central foyer. "How's your father doing, by the way?"

"He's well! You just missed him. He and my mother are attending a fundraising event at VCU."

"Did he go there?" I prod, hoping to find out what Ingrid knows about her father or the fabricated story she's been told.

"No, he didn't attend college. To this day, he says that's his biggest regret."

"It's never too late," Zev says.

"True. You should tell him. I always mention taking a class or two. Maybe he'll listen to you!"

Once we're near the ballroom door, Ingrid wishes us luck with our gig and talks into her walkie-talkie as she walks away. A moment later, she calls out. "Emma, I'll let you know what lost and found says."

I give her a thumbs-up as Zev pulls me by the arm.

"What was that all about?" Zev waits for my answer but instead, I focus on Katie.

With perfect timing, she grabs our attention by the ballroom door. "Emma, where have you been? Nerves get the better of you? Or did nature call?"

"Both. Just kidding. All good. Let's do one more quick set check?"

She nods and as we make our way through the ballroom, Zev gives me the side-eye, leans in, and whispers, "Seriously, your earring? What the hell's going on?"

CHAPTER TWENTY-EIGHT

The wedding gig's a hit and teenagers request Zev's punk-style "Hava Nagila" over and over again. We wind up playing an extra thirty minutes because there isn't another ceremony in the ballroom after ours. The groom's father loves the energy so much that he gives us an extra tip on top of our fee.

Katie wants to use the tip money to celebrate at a local pub, but I convince them to save the money and come back to my place instead. I'm exhausted after such a long set. My arms ache and more blisters have formed on my palms that need attention.

They follow me, and the motion light by my carport comes on as they walk up to meet me. I contemplate leaving the gear in my car until the morning. It's a safe neighborhood but the Gretsch set has become my pride and joy, and I'd kick myself if anything happened.

To make the unpacking go faster, they help me bring in the pieces and we set them out of the way, by the dining room wall. I grab a few beers from the fridge, and Katie and Zev pull the chips and salsa from the pantry and join me in the living room.

Sitting on the floor crossed-legged, opposite me, Zev pops off the top of the bottle and takes a swig.

"So, what did you think of the gig?" I ask while looking at Zev.

"Not as bad as I thought it was gonna be."

From the sofa, Katie leans in to grab some chips. "So, you liked it?"

"I like the money," Zev replies. "And I'm cool with doing them now and then, but not every month."

"A few a year is still okay, right?" I confirm.

"I'm keeping my word. As long as we can do other gigs in between. But not gonna lie, I'm pretty tired." He gets up and plops onto the sofa beside Katie.

"Yeah," she says. "It was pretty exhausting watching the teenagers ogling over you."

I laugh and put down my beer. "No shit. I'm surprised the mothers weren't trying to set you up. Or flirting themselves!"

Zev rolls his eyes and then stares at me. "So, did you ever find your earring?"

His question confuses me, and I almost ask what he's talking about until I remember my story from the manor. Zev with his bullshit detector isn't letting this go.

"Guys," I blurt out, about to change the subject, hoping he won't ask again or at least again tonight. "Have you ever played Morality Tales?"

Zev nods. "We used to play at home."

Katie shrugs. "Never heard of it. Cool name, though."

"It's a game," Zev continues, "where you ask another player stuff like, if someone drops a twenty-dollar bill in front of you, would you keep it or give it back to the person? I don't remember how you win."

"Nobody wins," I say. "It's just a way to have fun and explore deeper conversations."

Katie laughs. "More like a crafty way of revealing your character. We should play sometime."

"I'll ask my parents to borrow it," Zev says. "When I'm in the mood to go there and deal with the condescension." He finishes off his beer. "Any more booze?"

"Sure, there's more beer in the fridge." I'm about to get up but he tells me to stay put.

Katie leans forward and whispers, "I feel for Zev."

"Stop worrying about me," Zev calls from the kitchen. He turns off the light and walks back to the living room. "I've got killer hearing, by the way. I know it's hard to believe, considering I'm constantly plugged in."

"That's 'cause you're still young…or at least that's what the ENT told me about the ringing in my ears—after telling me to turn down the music," I say.

"Shit, I could've told you that without a medical degree!" Katie says. "So, back to Morality Tales. What made you think of it?"

"When my parents bought their house, it was the first game we played as a family. I've been thinking about having a housewarming party, but it wouldn't be the same without my brother."

I catch my breath for a moment and remember the last time we played. "Cory would sometimes pick the worst answer, as a joke. When we thought we knew what to expect, he'd throw us a curveball. It made me wonder if we really knew him or if he was just winding us up."

Katie puts her beer down and pulls down the fleece blanket from the back of the sofa. "How can we know other people when we barely know ourselves?" She sits quietly for a moment. "It's so easy for me to say, but you have to stop feeling guilty. I didn't know your brother and it's horrible what you've gone through—I imagine he'd hate knowing you continue to suffer. I'm not saying you shouldn't grieve. You'll never get rid of that. It's the guilt-ridden part that I'm sure he'd be upset about."

"Who knows." I reach for a few chips. "Who knows anything? He's dust now, and I don't believe in this afterlife bullshit or that they're still with you in spirit."

"You don't have to," Zev answers. "But I kind of feel it with my grandmother now that she's gone. It's gonna sound weird but on the way to get my first tattoo, my car wouldn't start. When I called to let them know I'd be late, they said I'd have to reschedule for another time because they were booked the entire day. An hour later, my car suddenly started, and I haven't had any issues since."

He hesitates, staring into space. "What if my grandmother was somehow telling me she didn't approve of a tattoo, after having numbers branded on her arm?"

Zev's comment about his grandmother moves me, even considering my beliefs, or rather lack thereof, in spirits of our dearly departed. A while ago, I'd come across a video of a Jewish person with tattoos who wasn't allowed to be buried at a local Jewish cemetery. I found the story fascinating and started to learn more about Jewish law, which then led to endless online searches of Judaic tattoos and their symbolism.

"A few of the Holocaust survivors who spoke to my class didn't have numbers. I wondered why but didn't want to ask."

"Maybe they weren't at Auschwitz? They only tattooed at that camp, a little fact my grandmother told me."

"To think," Katie interrupts, "we're supposed to be celebrating our first wedding gig. How'd this get so heavy so fast?" Katie stretches before making her way to the kitchen.

"I wound up writing a song after that whole car thing happened," Zev blurts out, "or at least lyrics."

"You're only telling us now!" Katie sinks back down onto the sofa, a beer bottle in hand. "Sorry. I mean, I'd love to hear it, if you want to share."

"Me, too," I add.

"What the hell, I'm half-drunk anyways."

"Isn't half-drunk the same as tipsy?" Katie asks.

"No, that's a quarter-drunk." He smiles and starts to scroll on his phone. "Are you sure? Honestly, the lyrics suck now that I'm looking at them again."

"We'll be the judge of that. What's the title?" Katie asks.

"It's called 'In Reverse.'" He sighs and reads the lyrics aloud.

The outlines on the dashboard
Seem too familiar
The link hasn't dried yet
Painful drops, in motion, etched
And near the surface

Shattered lives become one, undone
And beneath the skin
We take a final breath before escaping
There's no way out, no forgetting

Traditions hold onto us
How can we make new ones?
In reverse, I see you
In reverse, I remember you
In reverse, you cast your shadow upon me

Zev throws his phone on the sofa. "Oh my God, how embarrassing! What the hell was I thinking?"

Katie reaches for his phone, and he grabs it first and won't let go. "Come on," she whispers. "Please, let me see."

Zev reluctantly lets go while Katie reads the rest of the lyrics silently and then passes the phone to me. She rushes toward the foyer and flings the door open. A minute later, she comes back with her acoustic guitar and plops down on the floor in front of Zev. "The lyrics are great. And I'm not just saying that. I really mean it. Have you thought about the melody?"

Once Katie straps on a guitar, the creative juices flow, and there's no stopping her. She strums a few ideas as I sit back and watch them collaborate. They look over, as if they're worried I feel left out, but that's not at all the case. I'm basking in this moment, grateful we all met.

About twenty minutes in, they come up with a melody and Zev's song unfolds. Within another hour, they've got the entire piece done acoustically. Both take notes, and I record them to remember how they sound. I envision the song starting slowly and then ramping up like a Smashing Pumpkins one from the nineties once we add the drums and they plug into their amps.

They play the acoustic version a few more times while I grab three more beers. By the time we're done with the round, it's close to midnight and I tell them there's no way they're driving home half or even a quarter drunk. Katie wishes us sweet dreams as she heads to the spare bedroom, and Zev takes the living room sofa.

I clean up in the kitchen and then walk back to the foyer. As I put the chain across the front door, Zev calls out, half-asleep. At first, it sounds like he's talking to himself until he continues. "You didn't answer me," he says in a soft voice.

I step closer to him. "About what?"

Zev repositions the pillow and sits up. "Your earring at the manor."

"What about it?"

"Cut the bullshit. You didn't lose it. And you know how I know? Because you told me once the hole closed up and you haven't been able to wear anything. Didn't think I listen, huh?"

I sit on the edge of the sofa by his feet, my stomach in knots. "What do you want to know?"

"What were you really doing near Ingrid's office?"

"It's not her office. It's her father's."

"Father, shmather, whatever. You looked like you saw a ghost when we bumped into you."

We stare at each other for a moment. Can Zev be trusted? Even more, can he be trusted not to do anything if he finds out about Rey? Katie was right earlier. You don't really know yourself, so how can you know anyone else?

"Em, what's going on?"

"I need more time."

He sighs, pulling the blanket up to his chest. "Whatever it is, I won't judge you, promise. Hope you know that."

I nod. "If you knew, you wouldn't be able to sleep."

"I'm insomnia's nemesis. I can sleep through anything."

CHAPTER TWENTY-NINE

"Are you fucking kidding me?" Zev exclaims, then lowers his voice after remembering that Katie's asleep in the other room. He sits upright, and I share more about Rey being an SS officer when he was younger and how he now runs the manor, leaving out the part about my meet-ups with Josephine.

He can never find out about her. Those details need to stay under wraps so that Zev doesn't try to play detective on his own. If he contacted Josephine, she'd be livid with me for betraying the secret she asked me to keep.

"I told you wouldn't be able to sleep." I hesitate. "Are you mad at me for not telling you sooner?"

"Of course not. Why would I be?"

"Because of your grandmother, and you're Jewish."

"I get why you'd hesitate." He shakes his head in disbelief. "What else do you know? And how can you be sure it's the same guy?"

After I tell him about Rey's disfigured thumb and the moles, Zev asks to see proof. He won't let go and at this point, what's the harm in sharing a few more details? I go into my bedroom and pull out two documents from the folder, one to prove Rey was an SS officer and the incident report from Sobibor. I place them on the coffee table and hand Zev my phone to see the photos snapped from Rey's office.

"I looked up Bug River," I say as he looks at the photo with Rey sitting on the kayak. "Turns out it's like ten minutes from Sobibor. How convenient. He gets to enjoy free time between killing Jews."

As Zev studies the documents, my heart pounds. Suddenly, I regret telling him, wondering why I couldn't keep my mouth shut. How can I trust that he won't do or say anything?

After a few minutes, he pushes the documents toward me. "You need to tell the authorities so they can put his Nazi ass in prison. I can't believe, of all places, he's in Richmond."

"That's not how this works. You know how long legal issues can take, right? And this happened sixty-some years ago. Don't you think the authorities, or those Nazi hunters, would've done something by now? He's been in this country for decades. If it hasn't happened yet, it's not gonna happen now."

"You don't know that. It's worth a try." Zev snaps his fingers. "I bet with Katie being a lawyer, she can find out if he's in the system somewhere."

"Oh, hell no. There's no way I'm telling another soul," I whisper, without sharing that Dean only took care of those who didn't pay for their crimes. Zev can't know any more details that could lead him to Josephine. "Either I do something myself or forget about it. Those are the only options."

"What do you mean by do something yourself?"

I don't answer him, scared to reveal more, or involve someone else.

He glances down. "I get that you want to do something. But it's not worth the risk. Let the authorities deal with it."

"I already said no. It won't help."

"You know, it's a miracle my grandmother survived. Someone in the camp told her to make up a story about being a seamstress so that she had a usable skill. She survived by lying and taking on another identity."

"Rey shouldn't get that same chance," I reply. "He did horrific things and now has a good life. It's unjust. Look, I can't tell you more, other than this story is legit. And even if we told Katie," I whisper, "which we're not going to do, what would that gain us? If Rey's in the system, that means they didn't do a damn thing about him, and it would piss us off even more. And if he's not in the system, do you know how long it takes to get a case ready to prosecute someone? I'm not even a lawyer, and I know it can take years. The guy's in his eighties. It'll never happen."

Zev rolls his eyes, and it makes me nauseous thinking about how this news has made him an accessory—even without a crime. He gets up and heads to the kitchen, returning with a box of Honey Nut Cheerios.

"I have a bowl, you know. And milk."

"Nah, it's better dry and…"

"Stale?"

"Yeah, pretty much. And me being lazy." He tilts the box at an angle and pours cereal into his mouth. Between bites, he continues, his voice heavy with emotion. "You know all this stuff between me and my mom, right? Her not accepting me. Her wanting to live in denial or whatever the hell you want to call it. Well, before coming out to my parents, I came out to my grandmother…"

His voice cracks, and I put my hand on his arm. "From everything you've told me, your grandmother sounds like a wonderful person. If this is too hard, you don't need to rehash it."

He places the box of cereal on the coffee table. "Talking about it actually helps. My grandmother called me back later that evening to thank me for telling her, knowing it wasn't easy. But what I remember the most," he says, "was her telling me that she loved and accepted me. Something my mom has never done."

He looks away with bloodshot eyes. Zev's in pain, and I want to fix it, to make it better, to make his mom accept him no matter what. I lean in more and we hug until he pulls away. He takes a deep breath and, after composing himself, continues. "My grandmother also shared a bunch of stuff I never knew, like how the Nazis arrested thousands during the war. How gay men were sent to concentration camps and made to wear pink triangles. Many were forced to undergo medical experiments. It's sickening."

I nod, not knowing what else to say, but the stillness doesn't have a calming effect. Instead, it's deafening, making me question my silence and inaction, as I sit idle, wasting time by not doing a damn thing to make the world right.

"There's no way you can ignore the documents without feeling guilty for not doing something, I get it," he says. "On the flip side, the thought of you getting caught..." He stops talking, as if he wants me to make a choice.

I shrug in response and stare at the incident report on the coffee table. Josephine more than hinted at Rey's fish allergies. *Could I? Dare I sneak in and...*

"What are you thinking?" he asks after grabbing the cereal box.

"That you need milk with that."

"Really? Joking at a time like this?"

"You have no idea how stressful this is."

"I can't believe I'm going to say this, but…" He looks down at the table. "You need to get rid of these documents and forget about the guy."

His response and change of heart surprises me, and I sit up straighter and listen.

"First off," he continues, "this isn't about an eye for an eye. And second, how could you live with yourself knowing you've…I don't want to say it…but you don't seem like the type."

"Like what type?"

"The murderous type. What if you got caught and locked up for killing someone?"

A shiver goes down my spine.

"If you don't believe in our justice system," he says, "then leave it up to fate. That way, it's out of your control."

"What if fate led me to find out about him?" My voice cracks. "I wonder…what would your grandmother advise?"

"To leave things alone. That the past is the past."

"Wouldn't it feel good to get justice?" I ask.

"Of course! But seriously, what would you do? Strangle him in the middle of the night? Call him out and demand he turn himself in? Have you even thought it through?"

I shrug and play stupid, and, at that moment, Josephine's words stay front and center. *Vengeance isn't sweet. But justice is.* They keep gnawing at me.

"Zev, do you ever wish you could go back in time and stand up for yourself or someone else instead of being a fucking coward?"

"Are you thinking about your brother?"

I shake my head and open up to Zev about what happened years ago that still haunts me.

CHAPTER THIRTY

During high school, my friend Steph lived two neighborhoods over and, for many years, Dad would drive me to her Hanukkah parties. The year I turned fifteen, Dad agreed to let me take the bus, as long as Jenna came along. He had to warm up to the idea that his little girl wanted some independence, and finally gave in.

"Promise to call when you get there and when you're about to leave," he said from his comfy recliner that had seen better days.

"I promise."

"And if you change your mind and want me to pick you up, I'll be right here—me and the History Channel."

"Okay, Dad," I answered, and then ran up to my room to change for the party.

Reaching into my drawer, I pulled out several shirts, including a favorite tank top Steph gave me the summer before. She'd bought it during a trip to Israel, which she described as a way to connect with her Jewish roots for ten days.

The night after she got home from Israel, we sat on her bed as she shared stories about the ancient sites she explored and the salty sea she floated in. How she kissed a boy from Chicago named Jason and how he ignored her on the last day of the trip. Holding back tears after declaring her love for him, Steph pulled out a tank top from her luggage. On the front and in gold letters, *Chai on Life* sat centered above a Star of David in blue.

"I bought you a gift," Steph said as she held up the shirt. "Get it? Isn't it great?"

She laughed when I tried to pronounce *chai*, like those drinks you order at a coffee shop. "Not chai like the tea. Like high but with that extra sound, like you're trying to clear your throat. Chai on life."

"Now I get it!" I said, still wondering what *chai* meant but was too distracted to ask. After putting on the top, I admired the perfect fit and colorful graphic.

When Hanukkah rolled around later that year, it made perfect sense to wear the tank to Steph's party. So, on that December night, I threw on the *Chai on Life* top once again, pairing it with a cute denim miniskirt and a silver peace-sign necklace. As I fastened the chain, Cory called up to me from the bottom of the stairs.

"Jenna's on the phone. She wants to know if you're ready."

"Coming," I sang out, grabbed my lip-gloss, and ran downstairs to take the call from the kitchen. Jenna lived about a mile from us, and we agreed to meet at a stop in the middle, so we'd arrive within minutes—or even seconds—of each other.

"Heading out?" Dad bellowed. "Don't forget the chocolate and—" He stopped in his tracks after entering the kitchen, giving me a once-over. "No, Emma, not like that." He pointed at my outfit.

"Why not?"

"Because you're riding the bus."

"So? I've been on the bus before. Besides, Steph gave me this top, and it's perfect for the party!"

"It's too revealing, and," he added while following me toward the front door, "two young girls, alone at night? Absolutely not. There are a lot of creeps out there, and it's my job to protect you."

"You're not protecting me. You're smothering me!"

Cory slid into the hallway and watched us like he was front row at Wimbledon.

Dad stood up taller and folded his arms. "Either change or I'm taking you to the party. Simple as that."

"Mom!" I yelled and started walking toward the den.

"She's at book club."

"Did you make her change too?"

"Ouch!" Cory yelled out, not helping the situation.

"Dad, come on! Jenna's gonna be waiting at the stop all alone."

He stood in front of the door and didn't flinch or take his eyes off me. Instead of trying and failing to make my case, I ran upstairs, changed into jeans, and threw my Nike sweatshirt over the tank.

"Happy now?" I asked after coming back down.

He nodded as I grabbed my coat from the closet and put on my sneakers.

"Don't forget to—"

"Yes, I'll call if I want a ride home, okay?"

"Okay." He leaned in to ruffle my hair.

"Stop!"

"I love you too," he teased.

I smiled but didn't say it back when he opened the front door and let me pass.

"Have fun," he called out as I ran down the sidewalk to meet Jenna at the stop.

The moment we arrived at Steph's, I took off my sweatshirt and showed off my *Chai on Life* tank. Even though Steph still hadn't explained the whole meaning to me, I wore the top with pride. During the party, we lit the menorah and ate potato latkes and jelly-filled donuts. Steph's mom explained that the fried food commemorated a day's worth of oil lasting longer, eight days to be exact, a fact I'd learned at her first Hanukkah gathering.

About an hour in, Jenna disappeared. I went from room to room and found her talking to a cute guy at the kitchen table. She gave me a sly smile before giving him her attention again. Thinking three was a crowd, I left them alone and played dreidel with Steph and a few other friends. When I saw that it was getting close to my curfew, I headed back to the kitchen to find Jenna in the same spot. She introduced her new crush, Alex, this time around and after greeting him, I touched Jenna's elbow. "Hey, can we chat for a minute?"

She got up and joined me by the sink.

I leaned in and whispered, "We need to leave. My curfew, remember?"

"But he's super cute and new to Richmond. I'm just getting to know him."

"Yeah, but we said that whenever one of us was ready, we'd leave together."

"I know but can't you stay a little longer? For me?" Jenna looked over at Alex, who returned her glance. "Or would you mind if I stay?" she continued. "I'll get my mom to pick me up."

At first, I wanted to say no but after her begging, I nodded in agreement.

"You're the best, Emma." She leaned in for a hug. "Are you sure you don't want to stay? I don't want you taking the bus by yourself."

Part of me wanted Dad to pick me up but it was a matter of independence—to prove to myself that I wasn't a little girl, especially after our earlier disagreement. "No, it'll be fine," I wound up saying, checking my watch and planning to keep the bus ride to myself. Dad would kill me if he knew I was about to head home alone.

By the foyer, Steph leaned in for a quick hug and handed me a bag filled with Hanukkah goodies. While running to the stop to make the next bus, I threw on my coat, and as it flapped open in the wind, I screamed, "Wait," as the driver approached. A person at the stop turned around as the door of the bus flew open.

I stepped up and put money into the machine, and at that moment, it dawned on me: I'd forgotten my sweatshirt. And it was too late to turn back now. *How could I be so stupid?*

As I walked down the aisle, an older man with a camel wool coat took off his matching fisherman's cap. A woman with salt-and-pepper hair sat crossed-legged while reading a book. Another woman kept busy knitting what appeared to be a pink and burgundy scarf.

I settled in for the twenty-five-minute ride and caught my breath. At the next stop, the doors opened, and four guys ran up the steps and onto the bus. Loud and disorderly, the guys walked down the aisle and, as they spread out a few rows in front of me, their appearance caught my attention. Black bomber jackets unzipped. White tees and suspenders poking through. Jeans rolled up, revealing combat boots with red laces. They were all dressed the same.

One of them pulled out a beer from his jacket and passed the bottle around to his friends. I quickly looked away when he glanced over. While watching them through the window's reflection, I pretended not to notice when he got up and sat directly in front of me.

"Hey," he said nonchalantly.

I didn't answer.

"Hey! I'm talking to you."

His words shook me and, although dreading what might happen next, I reminded myself that we were among others. I turned to face him and returned the greeting, trying my best to hide my fear, hoping this would be the end of our conversation.

"What's your name?" He took off his black beanie, revealing a close-shaven scalp.

"Margaret," I lied and looked over at the woman knitting.

She glanced my way and then continued busying herself.

"Margaret," he repeated. "You don't look like a Margaret but whatever…I'm Milo. Margaret and Milo, has a nice ring to it, don't you think?"

He paused for a moment and turned in his seat. "Hey, Rudy, check this out."

"Check what out?"

"Get your lazy ass over here and I'll show you."

Milo stared at my shirt, making me wonder whether Dad was right all along about my outfit. It made me wish I hadn't been so defiant. It made me wish I'd remembered my sweatshirt or had a chance to zip up my coat.

I turned toward the window but could feel their eyes on me as Rudy walked over and took a seat next to his friend.

"Looks like we've got a little Jew slut on the bus," Milo said. "I call bullshit on her name. It's probably Rebecca, Sarah, or whatever those greedy, big-nosed degenerates name them."

He continued when I ignored them. "Hey, Jew girl, did you ask the bus driver for a discount? Or did you have a coupon?"

I started to panic on the inside. Why were they saying these horrible things? I'd heard of skinheads before but never imagined hatred so deep, or that it would seep out and be directed toward me.

Rudy laughed and leaned in. "What do we have here?" He reached over and grabbed my Hanukkah goodies.

He removed the blue and silver tissue paper as Milo pulled out a dreidel, chocolate coins, and a note. Fear grabbed hold of me as I tried to snatch the note. Milo pulled away and began reading, changing his voice to a higher pitch: *Emma, so glad we could celebrate Hanukkah together! It wouldn't be the same without you. Love, Steph.*

"Aww, isn't that cute?" Milo said. "And now we know your real name." He spun the dreidel in his palm and then gave it an angry toss up the aisle.

My hands shook as I took a deep breath and held back the tears. "I'm not Jewish," I whispered.

"Yeah, right," Rudy snickered. "Bunch of liars, all of you."

"Leave her alone!" the man with the fisherman's cap yelled out, his words as stern as his stare.

"Shut the fuck up, old man, or I'll shut you up!" Rudy yelled.

Why wasn't the bus driver doing something? Couldn't he hear all this? Just fifteen minutes until my stop. Fifteen minutes. If I started counting now, I'd be home soon. But would I have the courage to get off the bus, letting them know where my entire family lived?

When the bus came to a red light, I pushed my fear aside and got up, coming up to Rudy's chest. As he tried to block my way, I rushed past him and took a seat closer to the driver. The skinheads, including the two who minded their business until now, followed me and sat two rows away from the front. They kept harassing me, taking turns.

Don't touch her. You might turn into a filthy rat.

Hey, Jew whore, do you have any sisters?

Finally, my tears fell, and I wanted to scream, "Leave me alone," but instead sat in silence while they tormented me, repeating the same phrase.

Dirty Jew.

Dirty Jew.

Dirty Jew.

Rudy leaned toward me. I couldn't move fast enough before he grabbed my coat and tried to snatch it off.

Finally, the bus driver, who didn't seem to notice or care, slammed on his brakes and pulled to the side. He unbuckled his seat belt and turned around. "Get the hell off my bus. Now!" He stared at the skinheads.

They didn't budge. Instead, one of them tore pieces off the paper bag from their beer bottle. He balled them up and, one by one, pelted me until one hit me in the face, leaving a nasty sting.

"I said, get off my bus," the driver continued. "Don't try me. I'll make sure you never set foot on a city bus again." The driver stood up, holding a phone to his ear. "You have ten seconds. We're now down to five. Four. Three…"

The skinheads stood up, called me a dirty Jew a final time, and threw the remainder of the bag at me before they piled out. The driver closed the door behind them and continued his route. Nobody said a word. Other than my heartbeat, the only sound came from the empty beer bottle as it rolled across the floor. The silence was deafening but a welcomed relief.

I tried hard to hold back the tears, to be strong, to pretend like everything was okay. What would have happened if the bus driver hadn't intervened? How far would they have gone to torment or hurt me? How many others like them are out there?

Ten minutes later, I pulled the cord to request my stop and looked at the man who'd tried to come to my rescue. He nodded and closed his eyes. Maybe he'd seen this before. Maybe he wanted to do more but felt outnumbered. Maybe he was terrified, like me.

Before stepping off the bus, I made sure the skinheads weren't around, then raced to my house and unlocked the front door with trembling hands.

"How was the party?" Dad called from the den.

I triple-checked the lock and caught my reflection in the hall mirror, wiping away a tear from the edge of my nose.

"It was fun," I finally squeaked out. "Ate too many latkes."

"Did you bring leftovers? Asking for a friend, of course."

I tiptoed toward the den but didn't show my face. "Sorry, next time, for sure."

"Next time, right. Like how you forgot to call me when you left the party? Emma, you gotta work on that. Trust goes both ways."

"You're right, Dad, I'm sorry. It won't happen again." I still couldn't find the courage to look my dad in the eye, too afraid he would see that I'd been crying. "Dad," I leaned against the wall outside the den, "I'm gonna head to bed. All that food made me super sleepy."

"Okay, sweetie. Glad you and Jenna had fun. See you in the morning."

I ran up the stairs and closed the door behind me. After one more look in the mirror at my bloodshot eyes, I threw myself on the bed without getting undressed, pulled the covers over my head, and cried myself to sleep.

CHAPTER THIRTY-ONE

After listening, Zev comes in for a hug. He doesn't say a word until I break the silence.

"When it happened, I was so young and didn't know what to do. My God, what your grandmother and the millions went through."

"Em, don't diminish what happened to you. It was horrible. I'm just glad other people were around, and you weren't all alone."

"It's odd," I say. "For a long time, I thought I wasn't entitled to have these feelings because of not growing up Jewish. But experiencing anti-Semitism in my own way shook me."

"Did you ever tell your parents?"

"You're the only one who knows. I was too scared to tell them. Maybe one day. After that, my dad always took me to Steph's parties, and I made up some lame excuse that it was too cold to wait at the stop." My voice cracks. "I'm still scared to ride the damn bus, even during the day, can you believe it?"

"I don't blame you. What you went through was terrifying. But—"

"They called me a liar. A Jew whore, a slut, rat. And the only one who came to my rescue? A little old man who couldn't do anything after they threatened him. How can people have so much hate?"

"Em…" Zev says as he leans against the pillow and shakes his head. "Never mind."

"What? Just say it."

"Getting justice, or whatever you want to call it with Rey, isn't gonna get back at the skinheads who tormented you. And it's not gonna bring back those who were murdered at Sobibor. You know that, right?"

We stare at each other without a word.

"Right?" he asks again.

When I don't answer, Zev continues. "Look, the thought of getting rid of that Nazi piece of shit would be so satisfying but violence isn't the answer. You weren't put on this earth to go after criminals." He grins and knocks my elbow. "Be a lover, not a vigilante."

His comment makes me snicker. "Can't I be both?"

***

I wake up to the aroma of coffee and the sound of laughter seeping into my room. It's a little after eleven when I crawl out of bed, throw on sweats and a long-sleeve tee, and head to the bathroom to splash cold water on my face.

Zev kept me up way too late talking about Rey then switching to his life, his boyfriend Andrew, and how well it's going with them. He swore to me more than once that he would never tell a soul about our conversation. We also decided to continue, at least for now, playing at the manor if we get more gig inquiries, for the sake of our secret, as long as Katie doesn't get curious and start asking questions.

I head into the kitchen, where the two of them are sitting at the table, chomping on Honey Nut Cheerios—this time in a bowl with milk—like it's the first time they've eaten in weeks. They're cracking each other up with stories about college and their drunken escapades.

"Morning, drummer girl." Katie gets up, pulls a mug from the cabinet, and pours me some coffee. "Hope you don't mind." She says, handing me the mug. "We made ourselves at home."

"No worries. While you're here, can you do my laundry?"

She looks at her watch and makes a joke about needing to leave for an important appointment that doesn't involve chores. Zev's about to move down one seat, but I tell him to stay put. All I can focus on is my raging headache. Katie sees me eyeing the Advil on the counter and passes me the bottle in record speed. I down two pills, along with a tall glass of water.

"How much did you guys drink after I went to bed?" Katie reaches for her bowl. "I was out as soon as my head hit the pillow."

"Not an ounce. Just stayed up late talking."

"It's the wedding," Zev adds. "If it were a dive gig, we'd be at the bar throwing them back, eating cheese fries, and all would be great."

"For sure," Katie answers. "Nothing like an extra coating of grease to line the stomach. Honestly, I think that's what saved me in college. We always made sure to eat a shit ton before going out. Not once did I puke."

"Really?" I say, not believing her.

"Okay, maybe once, but that was because I had a salad."

"Serves you right! All that ruffage," Zev says, and they both laugh while I grab a bowl and join them for some cereal. Zev peers at me a little too long. "You okay?"

"Why wouldn't I be?" It comes out defensively. All I need is Zev spilling his guts. Even though we promised to take last night's talk to our graves, it puts me on edge.

"Okay, making sure. We've got another gig tonight, remember?"

"Shit, that's right. Are you sure you want to do it?"

He puts his spoon on the table and stares me down. "You promised. One wedding gig, two dive gigs. Don't go back on your word."

"Pretty bad timing, don't you think, to book two gigs back-to-back?" Katie asks.

"Not to throw shade," Zev says without missing a beat, "but that's because of the last-minute request from the wedding planner. We already had tonight's gig on the books. Next time, I'll make sure that doesn't happen. Actually," he continues, making us wait until he's taken a sip of his coffee, "this morning, we got a request from a different planner. She wants to book us at the manor. Guess word travels fast."

Chapter Thirty-Two

After breakfast, Zev and Katie head home, and in the afternoon, I take a nap to prep for tonight's gig. Belle Cantina, known for its Virginia beers and chicken and waffles, always has a mixed crowd, from college students to Richmond locals.

It's our third time here, and now, it feels like second nature. Katie's pep talks have helped me realize that, even though I hadn't sat behind a drum set in years, the skills had never left. But I still arrive earlier than needed to get into the right mindset and remember that if we screw up, most people won't notice.

I hang onto Katie's words to build my confidence and repeat them in my head while waiting for my club soda from the bartender. Zev and Katie turn up soon after and while the three of us watch the first band, there's a tap on my shoulder.

"You made it!" I say after turning around.

Dad, who's wearing a Steely Dan concert tee and VCU baseball cap, shouts over the music. "Heard The Incompletes were the best band in Richmond. Thought I'd check them out."

My parents never stayed for my shows during the

high school years but after I mentioned my new band, Dad's eyes lit up. Zev and Katie introduce themselves, and they immediately want the scoop on my childhood shenanigans. Dad disappoints them, only saying that I was a good girl and hardly got into trouble.

"That's because I was sneaky, and you never noticed."

"Now you tell me!"

"My parents grounded me more times than I can remember," Katie says. "Looking back, I don't blame them. My sister was the biggest troublemaker, but somehow I was the one who always got caught."

"What was the worst thing you did?" Zev asks.

"Hard to say. Probably that time I didn't put away my dolls. In the middle of the night, he tripped over them and broke his ankle. To this day, I'm pretty horrified thinking back at how he screamed out for help. He couldn't work out for two months, so that put him in a crappy mood."

"Yeah, I bet," Dad says. "All those stories about people tripping and falling, especially down the stairs. I bet the ER gets a lot of those."

"Great Sunday night conversation!" I say. "Next thing you know, we'll be talking about the bubonic plague."

Katie sips on her beer. "I had that once in college after a night of bingeing on burritos. Probably should've stopped at three."

My dad roars with laughter, a carefree moment that brings me hope for more moments like this. We turn to give the first band our attention and watch them finish their acoustic set, a cue to hit the stage in twenty minutes. Katie and Zev down their beers and say goodbye to my dad.

Before letting me go, he reaches for my arm. "You're gonna be great! I'd say break a leg but after hearing Katie's story, we should probably skip that."

"Good idea. Speaking of body parts, did you bring ear protection?"

He reaches into his pocket and holds up a neon-orange pair, twisting one between his fingers. I give him a thumbs-up, reach over the stool to leave a tip for the bartender, and follow Katie and Zev to the back room to warm up.

"I can't wait for the crowd to hear 'In Reverse.'" She leans her guitar by the door.

"Yeah, they might want to put their car in reverse to hightail it out of here."

"Stop." I pretend to throw a drumstick at him. "It's damn good, and you know it."

"After y'all put your spin on it."

"A song—or anything—is way better with collaboration. Like athletes and their coaches," she adds. "'In Reverse' is yours, and if it weren't for you, there wouldn't be a great song."

"I didn't think of it that way." Zev grabs his in-ear monitors and places the cable around his neck. "Why are you even a lawyer? Therapist sounds more up your alley."

"Not sure about the therapist thing. But you're right about the lawyer. Why am I doing it?" Oh yeah." She snaps her fingers. "Rent, groceries, and lots of guitars. Have I mentioned guitars?"

The venue's manager pokes his head in after a quick knock and tells us we're up in ten minutes. I place my accessories bag over my shoulder, pick up a cymbal bag and the snare, and follow Zev and Katie on stage. Like before, Zev tapes the playlist next to us and turns on his monitor while Katie attaches guitar picks to her mic stand.

Before sitting down, I stretch and look out into the crowd. For a Sunday night, it's packed: not a spare seat in the house or at the bar. This is the first gig I've told anyone about, and my friend Jenna sits near the front with her boyfriend and another couple. I wave at them, and they wave back, along with several others in the crowd who think my greeting is for them. Dad gives me a thumbs-up and lifts his beer in a cheering motion. He doesn't know this, but Cory used to do the same gesture, except with soda.

Dad's presence should make me nervous. But instead, it comforts me, with a "you've got this" voice whispering in my ear.

Zev, who's in front to my right, turns to Katie and then around to me like he always does before beginning our set as a confirmation that we're ready to go. Before we start, fear and excitement ripple through me, like every time. I glance at the playlist in hopes that muscle memory kicks in with each song.

"How's everyone doing tonight?" Katie asks as she gives her guitar a strum. The crowd whistles and hollers back. "Let's give it up for the first band, Eat Your Heart Out. How awesome were they?" Katie claps, and they cheer again. She's a natural on stage, always revving up the crowd. She talks to them as if they're in her living room, shooting the shit.

We begin our set and as the minutes pass, I become more relaxed and confident. As we pump up the tempo like a cardio workout, the crowd moves closer to the stage and dances in place. My dad, who's standing off to the side, sings along when we play the Rolling Stones.

After a few more numbers, Katie takes a break and grabs her water bottle. It gives me an opportunity to reach for mine. We've been playing for forty minutes, and we're soaked through. I take my T-shirt off, fan the bottom of my tank top to get some air, and remind myself to pack a fan next time. Zev grabs a towel to wipe his face, and Katie pulls her hair into a short ponytail as turquoise pieces fall onto the back of her neck.

She waits for the crowd to settle down before continuing. "I've got a great idea. For anyone working tomorrow, how about we call in sick?"

"You know," Zev says, gripping his bass. "Suddenly, I feel a cold coming on."

"Me too," Katie answers back. They smile at each other. If you didn't know any better, you'd think they were flirting.

Katie strums her guitar. "For all you night owls, we have a few more songs. And it's your lucky day because the next one is an original by our very own Zev Leiberman." Katie strums a quick lick and looks over at him. The crowd claps, and I do a quick drum roll.

"Zev, do you want to introduce your beautiful song?" she asks.

"Sure." He leans forward to adjust his mic. "The song is a nod to those who've passed on, but still have a hold on our hearts. I wrote the lyrics a few years ago. Katie, who's being way too modest, and Emma, our killer drummer, helped bring it all together. Anyway, it's called 'In Reverse.' Hope you like it."

Zev turns toward Katie and counts in. She begins the song, going into the intro with her acoustic guitar as Zev sings the first verse. The piece builds up when the bass and drums come together and later when the two of them begin the chorus. Their harmonies blend effortlessly as if they've sung "In Reverse" a thousand times before.

Zev's lyrics remind me not only of his grandmother but of Cory, and how it's up to us to decide when, and if, we want to let go. Zev knows I don't believe in spirits yet tonight, I feel Cory's presence for the first time. A distinct smell of his favorite aftershave wafts through the air, and moments later there's a slight prick on the back of my neck. Maybe I'm imagining all this because I want him here so badly. Or maybe it's a sign that I'm finally healing.

We finish "In Reverse" and go right into the next one by Siouxsie and the Banshees. It's a song that gave me some trouble during rehearsals. Tonight, we nail it, and the crowd goes wild. We play a couple of easier songs and end our set with the Foo Fighters as the crowd sings along.

I get up from the throne to join Katie and Zev at the front of the stage as the crowd cheers. Dad's going crazy with his applause and throws in a few whistles. Jenna and her friends stand up and clap some more. We wave to everyone and then step back to pack up our gear.

"I feel a sore throat coming on," Zev jokes. "Might have to call in sick, like you said."

"I think you should!" Katie adds with a chuckle.

"And give up making drinks with double this and extra shots of that, no way! Makes my day when customers call out their hundred-word orders. What about you, Em, calling in sick?"

I shake my head. "I've got bills to pay and kids to teach."

"Sounds like a country song," Katie teases, and before I can respond, she jumps off the stage and puts her arm around a woman in a black beret who calls out her name.

Chapter Thirty-Three

We've moved on to WWII liberation in my class, and anytime there's a new topic, we spend a couple of days in the library. The students love having a change of scenery and the opportunity to check out books. For this lesson plan, we're incorporating novels and working with our school's English teachers. My students can choose from five different books, and some go with *City of Thieves*, a coming-of-age novel about the siege of Leningrad.

While the kids make their choices and read quietly, I think about my next lesson plan, but it's hard to focus. Telling Zev about Rey has made me toss and turn at night, and I have a hard time concentrating at work.

Zev wants me to let it go. How can I, especially after listening to more testimonies about the concentration camps and what victims witnessed? No extra time should pass, and there's no more proof needed. Rey needs to pay, but should I be the one to make that happen?

Josephine's question stays with me, a steady wave of emotion: Do I believe someone evil deserves to die? If I could only separate myself from what Rey's done and not be fueled by emotion. If I could only stop reading the Holocaust testimonies. Not look at the images of bodies piled up. Not think about Zev and his grandmother or about the part of me that's Jewish, wondering if any long-lost relative, unknown to me, suffered persecution.

Zev says I shouldn't become a vigilante. Others might say that Rey's in his eighties now, so what's the point? But that's exactly the point. Rey has lived all these years without paying for his crimes. I rub my forehead, as the tension builds.

What if something happened to make it look like Rey committed suicide? What if a confession note was left behind, where he begs God or his family for forgiveness?

While in the library as the kids stay busy, I go through the non-fiction section, pulling out a book on vitamins and another with recipes. The librarian waves and, before she walks toward me, I grab a gardening book to place on top.

"Ooh," she whispers and glances at the cover, "that's a popular one. An exciting project in store?"

"Trying to spruce up my front yard, or at least make it halfway presentable."

"Let me know if you find some good tips. It's my dream to have a beautiful garden but, Lord knows, I can't keep anything alive." She spins around when two kids from another group argue as they play tug-of-war with the edge of a book. "Stop!" she yells before lowering her voice. "You'll break the spine, and I don't want to fine you."

As the librarian wanders off, I make sure my class is behaving before settling into a cozy chair in the corner. I skim through the book on vitamins, going to the index first. Under a category called supplements, there's a section on fish oil that takes me to page seventy-two.

Fish oil, the chapter reads, is an excellent source of essential Omega-3 fatty acids, which optimize overall health, immune system, and brain function, often lacking in many people's diets. However, the fishy flavor can be hard to manage.

I flip to the next page and read more. Fortunately, it's possible to disguise the taste through capsules while still reaping the benefits. Masking the taste is one thing. Getting Rey to consume the capsules, let alone any kind of fish, is another.

There's no mention of the daily dosage or how to disguise the fishy flavor until the next section: The best way to give the supplement to kids without them knowing is through peanut butter, as long as they don't have a nut allergy.

The author continues with useful tips and has me glued to every word. Puncture the capsule and add a few drops of oil into a small bowl of peanut butter. Blend well and spread the mixture onto a slice of whole wheat or sourdough bread. Add strawberry jam on top for some sweetness, slice up, and enjoy. The chapter ends with a word of advice: Be sure your child eats the whole sandwich to get the full dose.

There's no way I can bring a sandwich to Rey without the gesture seeming odd. *Think, Emma, think. How can I get Rey to ingest the fish oil?* After skimming through the cookbook, an idea comes to me. I jot down a recipe and make a list of items, before slipping the note into my pocket.

On the way home from work, I stop at the ATM and head to the grocery store across town. My shopping cart gets filled with cooking spray and vanilla icing, peanut butter, and chocolate chips. My last stop takes me to a different store, where I pick up a bottle of fish oil, a container to put cupcakes in, and one of those baby syringes, all paid for with cash.

I place the bags in my trunk and then settle into my car, in a daze. What has come over me? Taking matters into my own hands, acting like I have no conscience? Murdering someone, even to get justice, is still murder. My heart races when the person next to me slams her car door.

I make my way home and pull into the driveway, sitting for another moment too long, deciding my next move. Our upcoming gig at the manor is on a Sunday, three weeks away. The dessert could easily be stored in the freezer and taken out a day or two before. I could also change my mind at the last minute. I could also go to the authorities, against Josephine's wishes, like Zev suggested.

The groceries get put away, and I pull the note from my pocket, the one with the recipe for chocolate chip cupcakes. Prep time: fifteen minutes. Cooking time: twenty-five. A delicious and easy dessert, the cookbook had mentioned, but nothing about this seems easy. There's no telling whether this will work or what will happen if the reaction doesn't kick in and Rey or his daughter, Ingrid, figures out he's been poisoned.

What the hell am I thinking? I could lose everything. And for what? Because a lady tells me that evil people deserve to die as she walks away nonchalantly, hoping I'll do her—or her late husband's—dirty work.

***

For the next three weeks, the ingredients remain in the pantry untouched. The recipe, stuffed in a drawer but already memorized, has me changing my mind every other day on whether or not to take action. I can hardly sleep, waking up with a constant headache and dark circles that make me distracted at work.

My troubled mind continues to churn until Friday, two days before our gig at the manor. It's the afternoon and I'm in my classroom, reviewing the timeline projects from our final WWII unit. One student included survivors' tears on the poster's background, and another student used yellow stars. They all included at least one mention of a concentration camp in their timelines, and all the students who went on the field trip included a sidebar about the Virginia Holocaust Museum without me asking for its inclusion.

My students want to remember, and it takes me back to the class discussion a few weeks ago, where we talked about survivors deciding the punishment. What would the survivors say about Rey? What punishment would they choose for him? How would they feel about me choosing for them?

Zev's words ring true, from the night I told him about the skinheads on the bus and how they tormented me. Getting justice won't get back at them. And it won't bring back those murdered at Sobibor. In the end, should that even matter? Ridding the world of one more monster, like the other seven on the list, should be reason enough, in Josephine's eyes. And now in mine.

After getting home and changing into leggings and a tank top, I open the pantry and grab the chocolate chips, vanilla, flour, and sugar. The eggs, milk, and butter get pulled from the fridge. I throw on an apron, turn on the oven, and get to work. Fate is unfolding. Rey will eat a cupcake and never live to see another day—or, at least, one can hope.

While the cupcakes cool and the smell of chocolate fills the air, I pour several spoons of fish oil into a small bowl. I take the syringe and while steadying my hands, fill the nozzle with the concoction, injecting oil into the side of each cupcake. After that, the peanut butter, vanilla extract, milk, and a pinch of salt go into a separate bowl. The recipe calls for an electric mixer, but instead, I reach for the whisk and mix while pouring in the milk.

Once whipped close to perfection, I divide the peanut butter icing into two bowls, add fish oil to one of the batches, and do a taste test of the icing and cupcake. Luckily, there's no hint of fishy flavor. With a wide knife, I spread the peanut butter icing over the desserts and finish off by adding a few decorative chocolate sprinkles on top.

I'm tempted to take a picture to send to a few friends with a message that says: *Hey, look who can bake?!* But, that would be ridiculous and, of course, incriminating.

While looking out the window, I think of all the lost souls who didn't survive to tell their stories. I hope they're cheering me on, if only in spirit. If my plan works, justice will be served and how sweet it will be—from my countertop to Rey's despicable Nazi palate.

My kitchen's a mess, with flour and chocolate stains over the counter and sink. This day needs to get washed away quickly, like my questionable conscience. I clean up, pack the cupcakes into a decorative tin, and tie a thin blue ribbon around the container. The dessert gets set by the front door, ready and waiting for my visit to Spring Valley Manor.

CHAPTER THIRTY-FOUR

With my gear in the trunk and the cupcakes on the seat beside me, I sit at a red light, nervous as hell and second-guessing my decision. It brings me back to the day I bought the house. Why the hell did I ask for the drum set? Why couldn't I forget about the note? Why did I have to contact Josephine?

It's all too late now. I'm stuck in this mess. Damned if I do something and damned if I don't.

I pull into the parking lot and take a spot. A few more cars make their way through as I walk toward the side door like the last time. The cart in the hallway awaits me, and I push it back to my car and place my gear on top, carefully adding to the pile so nothing gets scratched.

Now that I'm playing again, Dad keeps asking if he can bring my old Tama set over, the one packed away at their house. But it still reminds me too much of Cory. One day, I'll be able to manage. Until then, I'll continue with the Gretsch that I've grown to love, even though the set comes with its own baggage.

"Hey, you," Zev says as he gets out of his car a few spaces down, startling me.

I throw a sweater over the cupcakes and decide to bring them in after setting up my gear. I've thought the plan through and through, but one detail is undecided: What if Rey isn't here? Do I leave the cupcakes on his desk? Would they accompany a note or be left anonymously?

"You okay?" Zev asks while setting his gear down.

"Yeah, why?"

He shrugs. "You seem quiet."

"Aren't I usually? Katie's the chatty one, remember? The one who actually likes people."

He laughs. "Yeah, except when they get too close. And then she writes songs about them." He hesitates. "Seriously, are you okay? I mean," he whispers, "after what we know about this piece of shit, I'm not sure I can play here again."

"Agreed," I whisper back, thinking about Rey's demise, especially if I change my mind at the last minute. "We'll have to make up an excuse to Katie since I've been pushing for extra gigs." Still shaking with nerves, I knock over a stand, and a cymbal crashes to the ground along with it.

"Shouldn't you wait for your drum solo?" Katie yells from a few rows down. Since our last time together, she's colored her hair platinum, effortlessly channeling a Debbie Harry rock-n-roll vibe.

Katie meets us in the middle of the lot as we make our way to the side entrance. She has a guitar on her back, another across her shoulder, a duffel bag and two amps on a small cart. She's in her usual gig attire: leggings under a black miniskirt, button-down shirt with a cropped blazer, complete with knee-high boots.

Zev and I are dressed in black trousers—his with stylish combat boots, mine with Converse hi-tops that will go unnoticed behind the drum set, allowing me to hide my dressed-down look and kick the bass pedal with ease. We're both in black cardigan sweaters, too, except mine's covering a sparkly silver tank top.

This time, we're playing at a bar mitzvah, and clearly, word got around about our punk version of the Jewish folk anthem. "Hava Nagila" was the first song requested on the form.

As we set up inside the ballroom, the door flies open and two kids crash through, running between the banquet staff setting up the tables. They sprint toward the stage and slide across the dance floor, stopping in front of us.

The taller of the two has a dark mop of curls, big brown eyes, and freckles across his nose and cheeks. The other kid comes up to his friend's shoulders and reminds me of a young Zev with his cinnamon locks.

"Hey," the boy with dark curls says. "Can I add a couple of songs to the list?"

"That depends," Katie smiles. What's your name?"

"Ezra."

"You must be the bar mitzvah boy," Zev says before the boy nods. "Congrats! What songs do you want to hear?"

"'Please Don't Leave Me' by P!NK."

"Done." Katie starts playing the guitar part.

"And 'DJ Got Us Fallin' in Love.'"

We look at each other, as I wonder who will have to let down the bar mitzvah boy.

"So, you're an Usher fan, huh?" Katie steps toward him. "Great song, but we haven't learned that one yet. What day were you born?"

"September 17."

"And the year?" She takes the phone from her pocket. "1998. Why?"

Katie types away and, after scrolling for a moment, holds up her phone while "Slide" by the Goo Goo Dolls plays. "Have you heard this one?"

"Yeah, my dad plays it all the time."

"Well," Katie pauses the song, "did you know it was released on the exact day you were born? Pretty cool, huh? How about we play this and the one by P!NK?"

He smiles and when he's about to respond, a woman from the front yells out, "Ezra! Stop bothering the band and get over here! The rabbi wants you to practice your *haftarah* portion again."

The bar mitzvah boy and his friend run off without a wave or goodbye.

"What's *haftarah*?" I ask.

"You expect me to know?" says Zev with a grin. "Just kidding. It's the Hebrew portion that we're tortured to learn. That was a stressful year, studying all that on top of regular school. My mom put so much pressure on me to be perfect. I feel for Ezra. I broke out in hives, hearing his mom scream at him."

"She wasn't screaming," Katie says. "She was calling from across the room."

He stares at her for longer than usual. "No, Katie, that was screaming. I know the difference."

Zev seems to feel the pressure still, taking him back to a time he'd like to forget. Maybe that's another reason why he didn't want to play these types of gigs.

We finish setting up, and make sure everything— and the three of us—sounds good. Zev digs into his bag, grabs a banana, and consumes half before looking up.

"Want one? I brought extra. Last time, I was so hungry through the entire set, distracting the hell out of me."

"Right?" Katie adds. "I was expecting them to feed us like the first time."

Zev reaches into his bag and pulls out another banana, extending his arm toward Katie.

She shakes her head. "I'm good, thanks. Learned my lesson and ate a big-ass sandwich."

I also decline his offer, after eating a salad and one of the extra cupcakes before leaving the house. We check our playlist once more, move a couple of songs around, and fit in the two requests from the bar mitzvah boy. Afterward, I pretend to need some air, and head out to my car, nervous as hell, to grab the cupcakes.

CHAPTER THIRTY-FIVE

Several guests brush by me within the parking lot. The bar mitzvah, which starts in thirty minutes, doesn't give me much time. I lean into my car, cover the cupcakes with the sweater, and make my way back to the entrance.

Part of me wants to ask Rey about his past. To show him the photos I'd found in his office and give him an opportunity to explain. To allow him to apologize for his crimes against humanity. But what good would it do? If he hasn't already confessed or felt remorse, why would he now?

As I open the front door, the lobby feels colder than moments before. My legs shake as if they're about to give way. There's time to change my mind. There's time to bring the cupcakes to Zev and Katie instead. But I stay focused, keeping true to my mission.

Somehow, the spirit of Dean urges me on. The anniversary photos of him and Josephine come to mind. I imagine how they met in France, young and in love. How they spent their beautiful lives together. I picture him behind his drums, smiling, and enjoying every minute playing one song to the next. I remember Josephine reminiscing about the love of her life while admiring his courage for eliminating monsters from society.

Will she be happy to hear the news? But what if my plan doesn't work? I haven't given as much thought to my fate as to Rey's demise. Now that I'm in the thick of it, I'm freaking the fuck out. I shake my head, try to snap out of it, and remind myself that anaphylactic shock often appears as cardiac arrest, a normal death for a man of his age.

Katie scoots across the lobby, and I duck behind a column and hold my breath. This is my last chance to forget the plan, to forget Rey ever existed. While waiting, the documents flash before me. His identification card. A picture of him in his SS uniform. The incident report, just one day after the Sobibor uprising. There's no doubt left in my mind. I peek out from behind the column, see that Katie's no longer in sight, and make my way down the empty corridor toward the Nazi's office.

The photos on the wall, the ones with Rey and his family, catch my attention. There's a strand of hair, possibly mine from that first visit, still stuck in the frame. Sadness sweeps over me, and I'm reminded of all the survivors. All the testimonies I've watched. All the stories I've read. One in particular still haunts me, the one where a woman talks about arriving at the concentration camp, and how they had their heads shaved right away, clipped so closely they were unrecognizable.

Was Rey there to see that? Did he have a part in the selection process—who would live or die? Did he hear mothers weeping, begging for the lives of their children? Did he watch with a smirk as people were tortured and sent to their deaths?

At this moment, any lingering remorse for what I'm about to do vanishes. Josephine's words make their way from my brain to my heart and remain there: *Vengeance isn't sweet. But justice is.*

Gripping the cupcakes even tighter, I move down the hall and stop in front of Rey's office. The door stands ajar, and I scan the room. The murderer is sitting at his desk, his fingers moving across an old-fashioned calculator, one that makes that satisfying sound as it crunches the numbers. My knuckles tap softly on the wooden door. He looks up and smiles before pushing his chair back.

"No, don't get up." I force a smile and walk closer. I need to get a good look at him, to hear his German accent, to see the missing piece of his finger. To have it etched in my memory forever and remind myself for the hundredth time that there's no mistaken identity.

"Nice to see you again," he says with his deep voice, making me look away.

Pull yourself together, Emma. Be strong. Focus.

I stand up straight and smile bigger. "Remember me?"

"Of course! The girl with the gardener granddad!"

"That's right."

"How have you been?" he asks while eyeing the container in my hands.

"Never better," I say while trying to remain calm. "I made you something. Hope you don't mind. My pop-pop and I used to bake these together, so I thought, why not make some for you!"

His eyes linger on the cupcakes after I remove the lid. "They look delicious. What kind?"

"The yummy kind! Double chocolate with peanut butter icing."

"What a lovely gesture! But," he continues, patting his belly, "sorry to say I'll have to pass. Unfortunately, I have diabetes and I'm on strict orders to stay away from sweets." He points to the Golden Delicious on his desk. "An apple a day…or so they say, especially paired with cheese."

My stomach sinks. A refusal never once occurred to me. Who passes on cupcakes? Especially homemade ones. After all my effort, I need to convince him. "Can't tempt you, huh? Just one? Nobody has to know…our little secret." I walk even closer, with the tin still open, hoping a whiff of chocolate will change his mind.

"Sadly, I cannot. Again, such a lovely gesture. I'd say leave it for the staff but since there's peanut butter in them, it might be best to keep them for yourself. With all the food allergies going around these days, you never know."

"Oh geez, you're right. Didn't think it through. I've been lucky when it comes to allergies." My face feels warm; my pulse quickens. "What about you, any allergies?"

"Yes." He rolls the pen back and forth on his desk. "Shellfish. All fish, actually. Honestly, I don't miss it. Never liked the taste all that much."

My stomach drops as our eyes meet. Is this the first time he has told the truth, at least to me? How can he even remember the truth, let alone keep things straight, since leaving Europe and hiding in plain sight?

Realizing I'm due on stage soon, I share my quick concern for his condition, extend another exaggerated smile, and say goodbye until next time. Out in the corridor, I sigh from all the built-up stress, and then quickly head back to the ballroom with cupcakes in hand.

"Where'd you get those?" Zev asks.

His question startles me. "Oh," I fib, "one of the moms from the bar mitzvah gave them to me."

"To you? Or to us?" Katie teases.

"I was planning to bring them to my class on Monday for the kids. Do you want them?"

"Nah, I was just joking, and honestly, I don't need to eat any more sugary shit this week."

I set the tin down behind my kit and begin the warm-up. With each stroke, the snare gets a beating, harder and harder until my hands ache. I'm livid. All that effort—the stress, the restless nights, believing this was the right thing to do—and of all things, he doesn't even cheat when the doctor's not looking. That takes some major discipline. Or, like every Nazi, he's good at following orders. And now, Rey gets to live out his life like before with zero consequences.

Starting the show is a welcome distraction, especially when Ezra goes crazy on the dance floor when we play his songs. He laughs as he's lifted into the chair, a tradition at every Jewish ceremony we've played.

Seeing them enjoy this moment feels bittersweet when, a moment later, another boy gets hoisted into the chair. He looks so much like Cory, with his dark-blond waves and broad nose. Normally seeing my brother's resemblance would open old wounds. But the agony of losing Cory eases a little, as if a piece of my heart is healing. Being a part of this band—and my friendship with Zev and Katie—has helped. Whatever shit we've been through, the three of us, The Incompletes, are complete with one another, something I don't ever want to mess up.

We finish the day with a second playing of P!NK, as a special nod to Ezra. After a thundering round of applause, Zev gives out our business cards. We start packing up and hear chatter among the staff cleaning up the dishes and tables. Some are visibly upset, and one sits down while being comforted by another.

Wondering what's going on, Katie jumps off the platform and approaches them. Zev and I stand still, watching and waiting.

Katie walks back toward us while shaking her head in disbelief. "It's really sad. Something happened to the owner."

"Of the manor?" I ask.

Katie nods and continues in a whisper. "He passed away."

CHAPTER THIRTY-SIX

It takes a minute to digest Katie's words. We stand in silence while my thoughts run wild. *This can't be real. He was alive just hours ago and seemed fine. Did my thoughts will this to happen?* Whatever the case, I keep my visit to Rey to myself.

"That's horrible," Zev says. "What happened?"

"They didn't say much, only that they found him in his office. I didn't want to be too nosy and ask for more details. The manager didn't want the news affecting the celebration, so they didn't make an announcement. The employees had to continue as if nothing happened. Damn, that's rough."

With a weird vibe hanging over us, we pack up a few things and walk to the lobby, where we spot the events manager. He steps toward us and explains, which isn't much more than what Katie shared. Rey collapsed in his office and by the time the ambulance arrived, it was too late.

We ask the manager to send our condolences to Ingrid and walk back to the ballroom to finish packing up, while saying how crazy life is: here one minute, gone the next. Katie asks me to send a condolence card to Ingrid from us, as a group. If she only knew how awkward this feels but, of course, I agree.

Zev drives off after helping me and Katie pack up our vehicles. I'm about to get into my car when I realize one of my cymbal bags is missing. I head back into the venue, relieved it's in the same spot by the stage.

During the drive home, my mind races, making me miss the turn into my neighborhood twice. I wonder what happened to Rey. Did he get dizzy, fall, and hit his head? Was it something related to his diabetes?

I send a condolence card to Ingrid and, for the next few days, search Rey's name on my laptop until a few entries pop up. First, there's a legacy page with information and then an article. After that, I check the manor's website.

Rey, a father of two and grandfather of five, died of a heart attack, aged eighty-six. Loved for breathing life back into the manor, he will be deeply missed by his family and the entire community.

I go back and reread the article, which goes into more detail about his life in Chicago before moving to the Richmond suburbs. The author shares stories from staff at the manor and how the venue offered many joyous moments to those who celebrated life events. At the end, I click on the article's comments and read through them.

Rey was such a great boss.

Rey was so nice and accommodating when my parents celebrated their 30th wedding anniversary.

Rey put a smile on everyone's face.

The Nazi created this new life for himself. One that will be remembered as helpful and loving. One that was a façade. Would the people who cherished him change their minds if they knew the real Rey?

I close my laptop and rehash the moments that led up to his death. Sure, I've saved myself by not becoming part of a crime, but I'm also angry at myself for taking so long to contemplate the decision. It allowed Rey to escape his past and, in a way, without the weight of punishment destroying him.

I lie awake, wondering how I lost an opportunity for revenge—to get justice for those who were murdered, and the survivors who had to live the rest of their lives with psychological and physical scars. The next morning, the thoughts continue to gnaw at me, and I call Josephine to see if she's free. I get dressed, slide on the charm bracelet she gave me, and make my way over.

This time, we meet near Presidents Circle inside Hollywood Cemetery, another place she's chosen. I park my car in Oregon Hill, a neighborhood close to downtown, and pass through the iron gates of the cemetery and down the rolling hill. A gray cat approaches and meows. He slumps to the ground and then rolls on his back in the sunshine, begging for attention. After a few pettings from me, he follows me toward a nearby bench. As I get closer, Josephine's already there—out of character by showing up first.

She moves her coffee and a paper bag to the other side, making room for me. After a minute of small talk about the weather, she hands me the paper bag and reaches down to pet the cat.

"Almost as good as ice cream," she says and describes her favorite bakery on Cary Street that makes the best oatmeal-raisin cookies.

"I already know about Rey," Josephine says, as I take a bite of the cookie.

"How's that?"

She reaches over and pulls a newspaper from her bag. "I read the obituaries every day. At my age, you never know; you might come across someone you know."

"Interesting."

"To me, it is. You get to learn more about people. Some people die so unexpectedly, and so young." She stretches her legs, and our new friend rubs up against her before getting comfortable next to Josephine's shoe. "Young or old…age shouldn't matter when it comes to dealing with death."

I want to thank her because, without knowing my past, people think I'm too young to understand the grieving process. I've never shared my story about losing Cory with her, but maybe it's time. Should I tell her how much my parents don't know due to my guilt and grief, and that sometimes, I'm the one who feels like the parent? But I hold back. Our meeting has never been about me and there's no need to make it about me right now.

"Are you upset with the way it happened?"

"What do you mean?" she asks.

"You know, heart attack. Natural causes or whatever you want to call it."

She picks up the cup and blows on her coffee. Josephine has never minced words, but is she buying time to answer my question?

"I wondered what you were going to tell me," she says between sips. "I'm glad you didn't fib because I would have thought less of you."

"Why would I fib?"

"In case you wanted me to feel like he got what he deserved, to be able to mark his name off the list with conviction. And to make me think that justice prevailed. All of those things."

Her words hit me hard. What she says is true. Justice hadn't prevailed. But what if it was divine intervention that took care of it instead of me, so I was absolved from being caught? It seems crazy, but now, instead of worrying, I have guilt for not getting to him sooner. As I keep these thoughts from Josephine, she tells me that, no matter what, Dean would've been proud of me, because I believed in his cause—that evil people don't deserve to live.

"Emma, what you've done won't be forgotten."

I nod and tell her nothing was done on my part, leaving out every detail about the cupcakes. She doesn't need to know I tried and failed.

"I know better than that," she says.

I'm not sure what she means, but then paranoia strikes. How could she know about my attempt? We sit in silence for a few minutes and watch people walk by. Hollywood Cemetery often draws many visitors as a historical landmark and for its beautiful setting on the James River. Our furry companion gets up and pounces toward a speed walker before settling back down next to the bench.

Josephine looks at me and picks up on my nervousness. "Wanting to do something is half the battle. You didn't turn a blind eye. You saw the list, tried to find out what it meant, searched for answers, and most of all, you believed me. You believed I wasn't making this up."

She reaches into her purse and pulls out her sunglasses as the sun beats down on her face. "Emma, there's something I haven't shared with you."

Chapter Thirty-Seven

Josephine begins her story about how she met Dean in France a year after the war ended. He was an American and the thought never occurred to her that they'd fall in love and move away. But her mother encouraged the couple, convincing Josephine that it was her destiny to marry him and live in the States, where, as her mom said, she could have a better life with more opportunities.

Her voice cracks as she continues. "When the war started, my family had Jewish neighbors who owned a convenience store a few blocks over. Their daughter Chava and I were best friends. We grew up together—same age, same interests, and we saw each other all the time. One day, I watched through the window as she and her family were taken away by soldiers."

Josephine reaches into her purse for a tissue, and I put my hand on her arm to comfort her. She takes a deep breath. "We didn't have time to help them. And if we did, our lives would have been at risk.

"After the war, I waited for Chava to come back, but she and her parents never returned. I worried day and night about what happened to them. If they managed to somehow survive or..." She hesitates and brushes off crumbs from her lap. "Then Dean and I got married and moved away."

"I'm sorry, Josephine. It must've been so difficult growing up during the war."

"Many decades later, after the Holocaust Museum opened in DC," she continues, "I took a trip there to search the database. Chava's name came up, even listed Monfort L'Amaury, the small town where we grew up, so I knew it had to be the same Chava. It showed her last destination as Sobibor. I mourned many years for the life she could have lived and wondered what I would have done if I'd been a little older. Would I have risked my own life and that of my parents? Would I have hidden her?"

Our new furry friend meows and stretches out his front legs. Josephine leans down to pet him again, and we giggle when he purrs and curls into a ball. It lightens the mood briefly.

"When our daughter was born, we named her Charlotte, a French name meaning free. It was our nod to Chava, a Hebrew name that means life. My family wasn't Jewish and because of that, we were allowed to live, to be free." Josephine looks up. "Chava reminds me of what we chatted about that day."

"What's that?" I ask, while wanting to know more about Charlotte, the daughter she has never mentioned.

"Remember when you told me you were part Jewish? I said that it shouldn't matter, that we should want to do what's right in the world no matter our backgrounds. After finding out Chava perished at Sobibor, I had many nightmares, feeling remorse and guilt for not being able to help. Dean told me I'd wake up in the middle of the night screaming. This went on for a long time. He comforted me as much as possible.

"When Dean confided in me about the list, he'd spent years trying to find out about the untried SS officers. Dean put all his efforts into finding Rey without me knowing. But, as you know, he never got the chance to do more."

"Sounds like he wanted justice for Chava and her family."

"Yes, and justice for me, too. I also wanted Rey to pay for what he'd done."

"Just curious…when Dean passed, didn't you want to do something yourself, considering what happened to Chava?"

"Ahh, the million-dollar question." Her smile disappears. "Emma, I've lived with the guilt every day since Dean's been gone and not doing anything. I may seem able, for my age, but it was too much for me. That's why he was still on the list, waiting for someone else to find, while taking my chances with my own mortality."

"That must be hard. I imagine Charlotte doesn't know about the note and what her dad did?"

"No, and I plan to keep it that way." She turns to face me. "Emma, you must promise me that you won't seek her out. I know how good your research skills are."

"Of course, I promise," I say and mean it, already so familiar with the desire to protect a parent even though I'm not one.

She reaches into her purse for another tissue. "Thank you. And for Rey, I'm glad he's no longer with us, whichever way he left this planet."

Josephine takes off her sunglasses and wipes away the tears. This is the first time, in all the times we've met, that she's cried. I thought she was tough as nails. Maybe she just didn't want to share her darkest moment with a stranger.

I connect with her on a different level now and feel her sorrow. Deep sorrow for the past and what could have been. I finally open up and share my story, the loss of my brother. In no time, we're crying together.

"Thank you for telling me about Cory. You know," Josephine blows her nose before continuing, "meeting for ice cream would have been so much better."

"You're right. It solves all of life's problems."

The cat, which I've nicknamed Hollywood, meows. We laugh at the same time, believing he agrees about our need for ice cream.

"Don't worry about what happened to Rey. Seems fate took control of the situation."

I nod and close my eyes, letting the sun beat down on my face. "So, what should we do about the list and documents?"

"You might want to destroy them. I'll be doing the same."

I turn toward her. "You have copies?"

"Of course. But they're no longer needed. What's the point in keeping them?"

I'm confused by her answer. "Don't you want people to know who he was—a Nazi and a murderer?"

She shakes her head. "No, my dear. Convincing people to believe something isn't my job. People believe what they want to believe. If he'd gone to trial, that would've been the jury's job. Not Dean's or mine. It was simply to get justice."

"Can I ask you something?"

When Josephine turns toward me, the paper bag falls to the ground. She reaches for it, along with the napkin that has fallen out.

"Why did you decide to trust me? There's no way you could have known whether I'd believe you or rat you out."

She gets up abruptly after putting the crumpled-up paper bag in her purse. Is she about to dash off with a smile and wave, like her normal self? Or have my words upset her? This time, it's hard to tell.

"Do you have a few more minutes? I'd like to show you something," she says.

"It's the weekend. I've got all day."

Josephine waits for me to get up, and we walk side by side up a hill and around a bend. As the James River and skyscrapers blend into a breathtaking view on the left, Hollywood, our furry friend, prances along next to us.

"Dean used to love coming to the cemetery for the uphill climbs and river views. He was always in good shape but would pat his belly and talk about walking off the calories from the ice cream. On Sundays, weather permitting, we'd come here after Triple the Scoop. It was a great way to take in the beauty and spend quality time together. We'd talk about all kinds of things," she adds. "Sometimes he'd give me advice on a project or how to handle a coworker who was being short with me."

This is the first time she's mentioned work. "How is it possible I've never asked about your profession! What did you do for a living?"

"I was an illustrator for an advertising agency. The local department stores would hire us to sketch models and piece the ads together for magazines and newspapers."

"That explains your great eye for fashion," I say, wondering if she'll ever answer my earlier question: Why did she choose to trust me?

"Here we are," Josephine says as we make our way up a grassy incline as Hollywood races off through the grass when another cat comes around the corner.

Most of the graves have tombstones that come up to my waist. Compared to the others, the one in front of us is modest and newer, with a sheen and cleaner edges to the words etched into the stone. She sweeps her foot across the base to brush away pieces of grass that have blown over the inscription. *Dean Mitchum Hensley* appears right above the dates of his birth and death. Under that, the words *Beloved Husband, Father, and Friend. Lover of Jazz and Drums.*

"Emma, I haven't forgotten your question—why I trusted you? Do you know what *bashert* means?"

When I shake my head, she continues. "*Bashert* is Yiddish. It means 'meant to be,' like destiny. Chava's parents used to say that about our friendship because we were inseparable. When you asked to meet with me, I wasn't sure if I should tell you more about Dean or Rey. But you wouldn't let go; you kept pressing me, even after putting you through those challenging exercises figuring out the names. You were determined, and I could tell it meant something to you, especially when you learned about the connection to Sobibor."

She looks in the distance when a couple of squirrels chase each other on a nearby pine tree. "But there's one thing I never told you. The first time we met, I knew who you were…well, sort of. About a year ago, you went to the Holocaust Museum. Do you remember that?"

This news startles me at first and then I'm taken back in time, to my museum visit. I'd gone alone, to make sure the exhibits were age-appropriate, because my school administrators had approved a field trip for the following quarter. "You were there?"

She nods. "It was one of my Saturdays to volunteer, so I was behind the desk. I remembered your name when you signed in and that interesting tattoo on your wrist. When reviewing the contract on the house, I thought your name sounded familiar, but didn't put two and two together until we met for the first time, and I saw your tattoo again. Then it all came to me."

"You have a really good memory."

"Not really. Your tattoo gave it away. When my agent reached out about you wanting to return something to me, honestly, I didn't realize it was going to be about the note."

"Wow, that's pretty crazy. It really is a small world."

"*Bashert*. It was destiny. Yes, I had hoped someone would find the list. Little did I know it would lead me to a courageous and caring drummer girl."

Her response makes me smile. *Bashert*. What a beautiful word. And yes, somehow, I did sense that inner calling, desperate to find the answers, and in the process, destiny brought us together.

"Now that Rey's gone, do you think you could ever forgive him?"

She bends down to wipe away a few pine needles from Dean's stone. "Someone isn't given a pass because they die," Josephine says as she steadies herself. "We should hold the same feelings toward them no matter what. Forgiveness, like respect, is earned. Glichke never wanted or cared about forgiveness. He was too filled with hate. Besides, forgiving him would only make it easier on me, and I don't want that. I don't ever want to forgive and forget. It would make me feel like I'm letting Chava down."

I lean over, wrap my arm around her shoulder, and look down at Dean's grave. *Beloved Husband, Father, and Friend. Lover of Jazz and Drums.* The words move me, making me wish the two of us had met.

"My dear," Josephine says after glancing at her watch. "I think we've come to the end of this particular journey. But we could still meet for ice cream?" She pulls a paisley scarf out of her purse and wraps it around her neck, tying a loose knot on the side. "The first Sunday of the month? Or, of course, whenever you're free."

"That's a great idea. Maybe," I tease, "you'll move up from kiddie size to triple the scoop?"

"Maybe. You know me…I can be easily swayed."

I giggle as she says goodbye and walks off, because I know that's far from the truth. There's no way Josephine, whom I lovingly consider stubborn and steadfast, would ever change her mind.

Chapter Thirty-Eight

The following month on a Thursday, I'm in a cab on my way to meet Katie and Zev. It's the six-month anniversary of us starting The Incompletes, and Katie suggests we meet to celebrate.

This time, I'm going to toast with something stronger than my usual club soda, not only because we're still together as a band but we've been booking more gigs. Zev is getting inundated with emails from event managers, and for the first time, we can be picky with which bars we want to play.

I've kept my promise to him since day one: two or three dive gigs for each wedding event. The variety works for now and keeps us all content. I've replenished some of my savings, Zev has started an emergency fund, and Katie has put a small dent into her student loans.

Upon my arrival, Katie and Zev wave to me from a cozy table. The bar is busy for a weekday as I squeeze past a few guys my age. One with dirty-blond hair, wearing a blue flannel button-down, catches my attention as he smiles my way. I look back over my shoulder and our eyes meet. It's been awhile since I've thought about dating, but my pulse quickens from the attention and fleeting connection.

"He's cute," Zev says with a wink.

"What?" I slide onto the chair beside him.

"You know what! I saw him checking you out."

"He'll have to wait in line. I'm here for the band. Wait a sec, I am the band!"

Katie cracks up and beer sprays onto the table as she laughs. Zev grimaces and gets up to grab some extra napkins from the bar. He's motioning to the cute guy from before, who looks over at me again. This time, I don't linger his way too long because tonight is about my friends. Tonight is about us, The Incompletes. The name always gives me a warm, fuzzy feeling because, for me, the band fills a void. The Incompletes. We're complete together. Something we said when choosing the name, and something I never thought I'd have again with a band.

The server takes my drink order and when he comes back with my cranberry and vodka, the three of us toast to friendship, the band, and our slowly growing savings.

After my second cocktail, an hour or so in, I'm tipsy and free, as if every inhibition and fear I'd ever had was melting away. I gaze at Zev and pull on his sleeve, while giggling. "By the way, I had a crush on you when we first met at Mo's."

"You did?" Zev raises his eyebrows. "Lucky me! Well, except that I'm taken—and you know, not into...." He snickers and rubs his chin. "But now that you're verifiably Jewish, I should bring you home to my mom. Fool her a bit so she gets off my back."

I giggle again, unsure what's even funny, and find myself nodding furiously. "Yes, yes, invite me over for dinner! I'll be very well-behaved." I giggle again until a snort comes out. "She'll love me! Moms always do."

"Instead, your mom should realize she has a great son." Katie takes a swig of her beer. "I mean, how hard is it to love you? You're awesome. You should just ignore her until she accepts you."

Zev shrugs. "You know, Katie, it's not that easy giving up your family."

I kick Katie under the table, harder than I realize now that alcohol's pumping through my veins. She stares at me and then takes another sip of beer. Maybe she'll get the message and back off, so Zev doesn't feel worse than he already does. But it's too late. Zev shoves his chair back and stomps off in the direction of the bathroom without saying a word.

"Oh shit," Katie says, her eyes glazing over. "I put my foot in my mouth, again."

"You've always been a straight shooter."

"And you're being nice. I need to ease up on the insensitive blabber."

I extend my arm across the table to touch her hand. We sit in silence and wait for Zev to make his way back to the table.

After a few minutes, he's still not back. I glance around the room and stand up, a little shaky. "I'm gonna check on him."

"In the men's bathroom?"

"Yes, in the men's bathroom. What's the big deal?"

"Nothing, you just need to give him…"

"Never mind," I say, as Zev walks toward us. "You okay?" I ask him, slumping back down on the seat.

"Yeah, why?"

Katie stares at him across the table, not believing him. "Are you sure?"

"Guys, I'm fine. Anyway, lately, I've been trying to focus more on the positive relationships, like the one with my grandma."

Katie taps on the table. "Do you have a pic of her?"

Zev places his beer down and pulls out his wallet. "Here's one with me and my brother when we were kids. I was about ten."

He hands the photo to Katie, who holds it close and smiles. "Cute! Wow, she's beautiful and so stylish with her bob. And her skin is flawless!"

"I know, right? Everyone called her Snow White. Even as she got older, she barely had a wrinkle. When people asked what her secret was, she'd always say she slept in cold cream."

Katie hands me the photo. They're sitting on the sofa with a beagle curled up in Zev's lap. "What a great memory. I can see why you loved her so much." I hand the photo back to him and before putting it into his pocket, he takes one more look.

"I really miss her. She read to us all the time. Her favorite was *Snow White*, like her nickname, go figure. Then, one day, my brother brought home *The Chronicles of Narnia* from the library and that was the end of *Snow White*."

"Don't blame her. That's why I don't eat fruit and veggies," Katie jokes. "Just look at what happened. That queen was brutal!"

Katie makes us laugh and then her words haunt me. Snow White. The deadly apple. Poison. I look at Zev, who's checking out the menu. He calls over the server and orders hummus and pita for us to share.

As the server walks off, I think of the cupcakes and how Rey died so soon after. What if Zev poisoned Rey by putting something in his apple? But how could he have known about his allergies? I fiddle with my hair. I'm being irrational, with my thoughts all over the place. *Snow White* is a fairy tale, a nickname, nothing more.

I peer at Zev, to see a glimmer of guilt in his eyes, but he doesn't notice, as he turns his head, fixated on the cute server.

Katie heads to the bar when she recognizes someone, and now it's me and Zev. I get up and sit across from him.

"What's wrong?" he asks.

"Nothing."

"Don't give me that," he says. "You always scrunch your eyebrows and get that crease in the middle when you worry about something. What gives?"

I lean in and whisper, "Don't you think it's odd that they found Rey dead in his office?"

"Why would I think it's odd? Honestly, I haven't given it a second thought."

"What I didn't tell you…" I pause as the server approaches to fill up our glasses with water and take away an empty beer bottle. "What I didn't tell you was after putting my gear in the car after our gig, I didn't take off right away. I'd forgotten one of my cymbals and had to go back inside. Something came over me to walk by Rey's office. An attendant was in there cleaning up, and when she saw me, she looked so upset. I'll never forget it."

I pause again to gather my thoughts. "She said, 'It's so sad about Rey. He was a good man.' And while she was talking to me, she picked up an apple from his desk."

"Em, this is getting cryptic as shit. Get to the point already."

"Right before she put the apple in the trash, I noticed only one bite was taken."

I wait for Zev to add something, anything. He stares at me, before gesturing with his hands for me to continue. I'm careful with my words because he can't know about my visit to Rey with the cupcakes.

"Who drops dead after taking a bite of an apple?" I ask.

"I thought he dropped dead from a heart attack. That's what you told me, remember?"

"That's what the obituary said. Look, I'm no detective but it takes a while for an apple to oxidize, so he didn't take the bite long before croaking."

"Not that it matters but your detective skills suck because oxidation doesn't actually take that long." He pauses for a sip of water. "Why do you even care? You're the one who wanted him dead anyways."

"Your story about *Snow White*. It's too coincidental. Did you…" I whisper. "Did you do something to his apple?"

He gives me a straight face and then laughs. "That's batshit-crazy. You should be a writer. Seriously, with that imagination?"

We stare at each other without a word until Katie returns to the table a minute later.

"Geez, y'all look grim." She picks up her beer and before taking a gulp, says, "We're supposed to be celebrating. To The Incompletes!"

We pick up our glasses and hold them high. "To The Incompletes," Zev echoes.

We clink our glasses. I set mine down to sober up, while Katie and Zev chug theirs down in one go.

A few minutes later, a woman with black hair strolls over. Katie smiles her way and then throws forty bucks on the table. "Guys, it's been fun," she grins and blows us kisses, "But I'm heading out. I love you, both."

She gets up, and the two of them walk away with their arms wrapped around each other. And now it's just Zev and me.

Chapter Thirty-Nine

Our server asks if we need anything else, and Zev pushes Katie's money to the side as the two of us decide to get some more nibbles instead of paying the bill. After a glance at the menu, Zev orders a pizza and watches the server walk away before giving me his full attention.

"Okay," I say, "this is the last time I'll bring it up, and after this, we won't talk about it again, cool?"

He nods and waits for me to continue.

"You really don't think it's odd Rey dropped dead like that?"

"Why? The dude was ancient!" He lowers his voice and leans in. "Rey's dead, end of story. Not sure why we're still discussing that Nazi piece of shit."

Maybe it's down to my overactive imagination, but Zev seems edgy, as if I've struck a nerve. During our rehearsals, he sometimes gets snippy when he's tired. Could that be it? He's had a long week at work, so I decide to drop it and heed his words: Rey's dead, the end, no need to mention it again.

We watch the crowd spill in and out of the bar and overhear a conversation about one of our favorite delis in Richmond. Zev says how much his grandmother loved their matzo ball soup. It's obvious he misses her.

He hands me his phone to show another photo of his family posing in front of the restaurant, the last photo they all took together. Zev's dad has his arms around his two sons. In front of them, Zev's mom stands next to his grandmother.

I study the image, focusing on his mom. She has brown, shoulder-length waves and wears glasses with burgundy frames. Right away, she's so familiar, as if we've met, with a kind smile, and not like a woman who would judge her son so harshly. But then again, appearances can be deceptive, as I've discovered.

"Your mom looks so familiar. What's her name?"

"Dana."

"Dana Leiberman," I say aloud while trying to place her.

"Breznin," he says. "She goes by her maiden name."

As soon as Zev says her full name, my heart races. He once mentioned his mom was a doctor, and I almost say that I know a Dana Breznin who practices off of Broad Street. But I can't. Instead, I rush to the bathroom, push open a stall, and lean over the toilet.

This can't be real. Of all people, Zev's mom is Cory's doctor. I'll never forget her lack of empathy. How she didn't return his calls when he needed help. How she dismissed me when I called, wanting my own answers.

After my brother's death, I did some digging and discovered a website where patients could leave reviews for doctors. Dana Breznin had a less than stellar rating and several negative comments posted underneath her photo and medical credentials. A few are etched in my memory:

Went in with a patch of poison ivy on my leg and came out with an addiction.

She gave me pain meds for a blister on my foot that she hardly looked at.

The doctor pushed an oxy rx on me, even after telling her I didn't want one.

That quack of a doctor ruined my wife's life. Yet, she gets to continue practicing.

I stagger out of the stall and lean over the sink. I can hardly breathe. The thought of looking Zev in the eye and telling him about his mom? There's no way. This has to be something else kept from him; otherwise, who knows what he'll do. Or what she'll say if she finds out we're friends and in the same band. Most likely she wouldn't remember me, but she might recognize my name. This band is my outlet, my heart and soul, and I can't lose it or Zev's friendship. Not now.

"Hey, are you okay?" a woman asks when she enters the bathroom.

I nod and stare at my blotchy complexion in the mirror.

"You sure?"

"Yep, just drank too much on an empty stomach."

I thank her and head back to the table.

Zev sets our glasses to the side and puts his hand out across the table to touch mine. "We gotta go out more often to build up your tolerance. Either that, or you need to eat beforehand."

"You're right. On both accounts." I can hardly look at him.

After finishing half the pizza, we pay the bill and head out. Zev calls us separate cabs, and within a few minutes, they arrive. He hugs me and it's a tight one. I don't want to let go of my friend, my bandmate, the one who has confided in me about his painful experiences. It's bad enough that Zev wishes for a more accepting mother. There's no way I can burden him with this truth.

"Text me when you get home," he says as we let go and walk to our separate cabs.

I give him a thumbs-up and after telling the driver my address, I call my parents to ease the knot in my stomach. My dad picks up on the second ring. We catch up, and he tells me that Mom is doing well. She's back at work part-time and getting into gardening again, something she has always enjoyed. He brings up the gig again that he came to a few weeks back and how much fun he had.

"You know…" He hesitates for a moment.

As I wait for him to continue, I'm fearful he's about to tell me some sad news.

"I'm proud of you, Emma. And Cory would be proud, too. Getting back into drumming and joining a band."

"Dad…"

"Sweetie," he continues, his voice breaking. "I miss him every single day."

I'm stunned. It's the first time he's shared his thoughts with me rather than focusing on Mom.

"I know how hard it is not to have your brother," he continues. "But he'd want you to be happy. He'd want all of us to be happy—and to carry on with what we love. You love drumming more than anything. You're beaming from ear to ear when you play. It's awesome."

I want to tell him about Cory's doctor but stop myself. "Thanks, Dad. It means a lot. Are you really doing okay?"

He's quiet for a moment, and I'm not sure whether he's gathering his thoughts or waiting for the choked-up feeling to subside. "Yes, sweetie, I'm doing just fine."

"I love you, Dad."

"I love you, too, Emma."

We hang up and ten minutes later, the cab pulls into my driveway. The motion light comes on with my approaching steps. I unlock the door, walk into my bedroom, and slump down on the bed. It's been an exhausting six months, with so many highs and lows. My first home, the band, learning about Rey, and now Zev's mom.

My mind stays unsettled with the latest news, making me uneasy. One thing's certain: nobody can know about this—not Zev, not even my parents. The only option, for now, is to keep the information buried.

A moment later, a noise from outside grabs my attention. I make my way to the living room, look out the window, and see a cab pulled into the driveway. Is it the one that dropped me off? Did I not pay the driver enough?

A second later, the car door opens. Zev steps out, walks up the path, and rings the bell.

CHAPTER FORTY

"Hey, you. Everything okay?"

Zev faces me with bloodshot eyes. He nods and opens his hand where he's written on his palm: *If you have your phone with you, turn it off.*

After giving him a puzzled look, I tell him my phone is in the bedroom. "Do you want to come in?"

Zev turns around to the cab and holds up a finger to show the driver he needs more time. He turns back toward me and leans close. "I didn't do anything he didn't deserve."

"What?" I snap before Zev tells me to keep my voice down. "Are you saying what I think you're saying?"

He nods and our eyes lock.

"You told me you weren't put on this earth to be a vigilante."

"That's not what I said," he whispers. "I said *you* weren't put on this earth to be a vigilante."

"I'm worried. What if the cops find out?"

"You weren't worried about yourself, so why worry about me? Besides, they'll never find out. He was eighty-six, with one foot in the grave. And everyone thought he was a great guy. Nobody's gonna do any digging."

"Are you sure you don't want to come in? We should talk about this. You can stay the night."

He shakes his head. "I have to work early. But I knew I couldn't sleep without telling you."

Even though I had my suspicions, I'm still shocked and in need of answers. "How'd you do it?"

"Hello? Have you forgotten I'm a barista?"

"I don't get it. What does being a barista have to—"

"*Ich spreche Deutsch.*"

"Huh?"

"My grandmother spoke German. I'm rusty now, but when you showed me that one document, I figured out pretty quickly he had allergies."

"Okay, so, I was right about the apple?"

He nods. "I snuck into Rey's office and switched it with one I'd injected with fish oil. Honestly, I'm surprised he croaked so fast. Not so much from the fish oil…I just didn't know when he'd eat the apple."

I take a deep breath and lean against the door, taking it all in.

Zev looks down at his feet. "You know, it's not that I didn't believe you, but I needed my own proof, especially if he was gonna go down."

"What kind of proof?"

"That, no matter what, he couldn't escape his past. So, this is gonna sound weird, but I watched Rey from the parking lot a few times, to see when he'd come and go. He was a creature of habit, always arriving at the same time. I hid while calling out names that started with *R*s, like Ramsey and Roger. And other random ones like Astrid."

"Astrid?"

"Yeah, I'll tell you about that in a minute. It's what gave me the idea. Anyways, he never turned around, not once. Then I tried Reinhardt. He stopped in his tracks, startled, as if a car had dashed in front of him. At first, he didn't move but then he started looking around the parking lot. When he got to the front door, he turned around for another look before going inside."

"Wow, when did you do this?"

"Right before the bar mitzvah gig."

I nod, wondering if that's the reason Rey hadn't accepted my cupcakes. Maybe he'd been spooked.

"So, back to Astrid. I had a classmate who hated her birth name. Hated it so much that she changed it to Ava—not officially, but if anyone called her Astrid, she'd ignore them completely, wouldn't even turn around, until they said Ava. One day, years later, I was walking through campus and there she was. My high school friend was with me and called out to her, using Astrid. She turned around right away—first happy to see us, then pissed that he didn't use Ava. I don't blame her. He's an ass, we don't even talk anymore."

I jump when the taxi driver taps on his horn. Zev calls out, asking the driver to keep the meter running.

"After you told me," he continues, "I couldn't sleep, tossed and turned, even called in sick one day—and I never do that. It's crazy. Once I decided to do something, I slept like a baby. There was plenty of time to change my mind and go through the whole 'don't live in the past, what's done is done' bullshit. Maybe I should have remorse, but I'm completely at peace. It's a nod to my grandmother and the millions who were murdered, and I can live with that."

"What do you think she'd say?"

He leans against the doorpost. "My brother asked her once if she ever wanted to get revenge. She said, 'Those Nazis are dead, so what's the point? And I can't hate the next generation for what their ancestors did.'" He gets choked up before continuing. "Which is true…you can't hold the next generation accountable. But since you gave me proof that there was at least one Nazi still around, I had to act and couldn't tell you."

I want to agree with him but agreeing would mean sharing my cupcake story. He's another person who doesn't need to know I tried and failed. "Saying thank you feels odd but thanks for having the courage to do something, knowing you could suffer the consequences."

"You were brave yourself."

As he hugs me and holds on tight, I wonder what he means but decide not to ask.

"Don't say a word to anyone, not a peep," he whispers in my ear. He pulls away and looks at me. "Promise?"

"Promise. I'll take it to my grave."

"And we'll never talk about this again. Ever. Okay?" he says.

"Never again."

I think about our connection and this secret we'll have forever. Zev's confession puzzles me. Why would he tell me in the first place? Then I realize how simple the answer is: Zev trusts me with all his heart. I reach for his hand and take in the tattoo on his wrist. It makes me want the same one to honor his grandmother.

After watching the cab drive off with Zev in the back, I wander into the living room, dazed and still taking in the news. Part of me wants to smile, knowing we got justice. Part of me wants to weep for all the suffering and death caused by this monster.

I make my way to the kitchen, turn on the light to the basement, and walk down the stairs. The set sits in the same place as the first day, always going back to its cozy spot after every gig. I sit on the throne and, with the drum key, remove the head of the snare and take off the note that's taped securely inside. Once open, the list of names looks the same, with the last one still unmarked. Now that Rey's dead, I can cross off his name to match the others.

I grab a pen from my music stand and draw a line through Reinhardt Glichke with satisfaction. I'm about to tape the note back into the set, but instead, I stare at the list of eight names. They might have committed different crimes, but they have one thing in common: they originally got away but eventually got what they deserved. What would Zev say if he knew about his mother, another person I consider a monster? But I can't tell him and never will. In this instance, I need to trust my gut. Zev has been hurt too much by her already. He deserves to be happy, not burdened even more.

With the marked-through list in my hand, this moment should feel absolute. It seems that way to Josephine, but not to me. I pick up the pen and add one more name—Dana Breznin—in caps like the others. I walk upstairs to the bedroom and do the same on the note stashed within the closet's wall.

Maybe one day, Dana Breznin will no longer practice medicine so callously. Maybe one day, she'll feel remorse for the lives she's ruined. And maybe one day, she'll accept Zev for who he is. Until then, the list will remain incomplete.

Thank you for reading

Dear reader, I'm so grateful you chose my story when there are so many books out there! You probably already know this but, just in case, word of mouth is an author's best friend. If you liked *The Incompletes*, please spread the word. Tell your family, friends, anyone you think would enjoy this story. And if you have a moment, I'd be grateful if you left a review. It really helps readers decide what to read next.

LYRICS

"In Reverse"

The outlines on the dashboard
Seem too familiar
The ink hasn't dried yet
Painful drops, in motion, etched
And near the surface

Shattered lives become one, undone
And beneath the skin
We take a final breath before escaping
There's no way out, no forgetting

Traditions hold onto us
How can we make new ones?
In reverse, I see you
In reverse, I remember you
In reverse, you cast your shadow upon me

Should it feel this real?
You were young once—laughing, seeing, being
Interpreting life in quiet motion
With this pause on memory lane
How can we avoid the pain?

One day, I'm afraid I'll forget you
Your love made me stronger
Your acceptance makes it harder
Will you still be proud of me
Of what I haven't become?

Traditions hold onto me
Should we make new ones?
In reverse, I see you
In reverse, I remember you
In reverse, you cast your shadow upon me

Traditions hold onto me
Upon me
On the dashboard in front of me

Lyrics by Zev Leiberman of The Incompletes

"Scorched"

We were tattered like pages
In a story worth forgetting
Skipping, repeating
Wading through lies

You didn't believe me
I tried to tell you
A bastion surrounded us
Filling you with envy

The time to replace you
To no longer face you
My heart's on the run
With no place to call home
Scorched and left clinging
We're better off alone

Don't stay too long
Don't pray for true love
Why keep the door open
As I pretend to be tough

The time to replace you
To no longer face you
My heart's on the run
With no place to call home
Scorched and left clinging
We're better off alone

Lyrics by Katie Perone of The Incompletes

An Author's Note

As an author, I'm fortunate to be able to share my words with the world. Novels offer an escape, entertain us, let us walk in someone else's shoes, and sometimes break our hearts. I've often said that the characters in my stories are braver than me. They're willing to take more risks. Willing to break the rules. Willing to be vulnerable.

I bring up vulnerability because, as the daughter of a Holocaust survivor, there wasn't much of that growing up. My dad would often say: Be strong. Don't cry. Don't sweat the small stuff.

It never felt right to have a bad day. It never felt right to think my problems were actually problems. How could I when my father's life began—and my grandparents' lives ended—so tragically?

When I was a child, my father would sometimes scream in the middle of the night and brush it off as a bad dream. It wasn't until my teenage years when he told me he was a Holocaust survivor and that my grandparents were murdered at Auschwitz. After telling me, my dad often spoke about it, sharing stories about his parents, how he was orphaned at seven, and how he hid during the war.

Later in life, he couldn't get through a conversation about it without choking up. I'm glad he finally opened up, for all of us, but mostly for him.

I share this brief family history because of the themes in my novel, *The Incompletes*. There were a few times, while working on the story, when I thought, "What would Dad have done if he'd come across someone like Rey?"

My father passed away several years ago, and I often hear his voice in my head. But it's not the answer to this question. Or a reminder to be strong. I hear him calling out my name (not Linda, but Lindy, his nickname for me), wondering how my six-hour drive was, and like many Jewish parents, asking if I'm hungry and when I want to eat.

ACKNOWLEDGMENTS

About one month after getting my edits back in late summer 2023, my editor, Sherron Mayes, passed away. It's still hard to believe. Yes, she made *The Incompletes* so much better by being brutally honest and providing great edits. But my relationship with Sherron wasn't just a professional one; I considered her a friend and miss her. I'll never forget our talks about writing, life, relationships—and how she came to visit me in 2019 from England. Sherron's legacy lives on in every word of this story, and I'm so thankful we met.

Working on *The Incompletes* involved a lot of research. To the many historians, authors, journalists, documentarians, and various organizations and museums including the United States Holocaust Memorial Museum, Veterans History Project at the Library of Congress, Virginia Holocaust Museum, and National Institutes of Health to name a few: Thank you for collecting data and testimonies, and for bringing to light the tragedies surrounding the Holocaust and the U.S. drug epidemic.

My advanced readers, Jeffrey Malone, Jill Sabban, Libby Cox, and Marla Handelman-Greif, there wouldn't be a book without you:

Jeffrey, in 2021, I promised a certain cymbal would make it into a future book. It took a few years but here we are! Thank you for reading my story and lending your expertise as a drummer and songwriter. But what I'm most thankful for, other than our connection: You encouraged me to write lyrics! I'm super excited to see how you'll bring the song to life now that it's in your talented and creative hands.

Jill, thank you for reading (yet another!) story of mine in advance. Your insight and feedback helped so much, and I'll never forget your emails and texts. Your words were filled with so much love and encouragement.

Libby, I'll never forget the message you left me when you finished the book and read the ending. That's because I listened to it on repeat! And without spoiling anything for the reader, your keen eye for detail and making sure I had my facts straight in certain scenes helped so much. I'm grateful for your friendship and advice. And, of course, hearing your voice on the regular warms my little heart.

And, Marla, I thank my lucky stars the day we met in the journalism hall all those years ago. We're still standing and so is the building! Since then, we've spent hours talking about life and this novel. Thank you for brainstorming ideas, reading the book more than once, and encouraging me to add that extra (and necessary) chapter the story needed.

Christine Chirichella, Elyse Cooper, Beth Falk, Rosalie A. Lacorazza, Natasha Moussavi Lewis, and Uniqueka Walcott, for supporting me and always sharing my book news.

Family and colleagues, for cheering me on, encouraging my literary endeavors, and always asking about my next book. Guess what? It's finally here!

My proofreader and copyeditor, Faith Williams, who also worked on two of my other books. Thanks for making sure everything made sense, flowed, and matched up.

Authors Edwin Fontánez, Rochelle Weinstein, and Allison Winn Scotch, for offering advice since day one. You, more than anyone, understand the rocky road of the publishing business. Thanks for lending your ear.

Christina Huber, one of my biggest cheerleaders since my debut novel came out in 2017, and countless book lovers, BookTokers, and Bookstagrammers who've read and mentioned my books and supported the writing community near and far.

Sasha, your creativity amazes me. Thanks for the awesome book cover (and other beautiful covers), social media posts, and story advice. For many reasons, I'm so proud of you. I hope, throughout your life, you always do what you love and never stop being curious.

My parents, almost the last ones on the list but the first I think about. They've been gone a long time, but I always remember my mom's beautiful smile and my dad's silly jokes.

And, finally, my grandparents, I remember you often even though we've never met. If you hadn't given your seven-year-old-son to a stranger in hopes he'd survive, I wouldn't be here today and writing this story.

A Conversation with the Author

**How long did it take you to write
The Incompletes?**

Before writing, I always outline a novel, and that took about two months this time around. Then, the first draft took about six months, with many disciplined days because I work full-time and write around my job. The novel went through several additional drafts before I sent it to my advance readers and then to my editor. After that, I had more revisions! The entire process took about two years.

What inspired you to write *The Incompletes*?

I often think about book ideas, whether it's when I'm walking, in the shower, or staring out into space. One day, I got to thinking: Should someone who is considered evil deserve to die? And who's to decide? From there, the story took off. I wanted the book to have a morally gray aspect to it, where someone would have a difficult choice to make, as well as a story that included a variety of people from different generations. I love reading and writing books that are considered "genre mash-ups." I've been told *The Incompletes* is a good mix of contemporary, historical, and suspense.

Do you have any favorite writing spots or rituals?

I don't have a designated spot, but my writing is mostly done at home. I almost always need to be looking out a window, though. Somehow that inspires me. Sometimes, I go to a coffee shop or plop myself on a park bench. For some reason, people-watching helps with ideas and keeps me motivated.

Did you always know how the book would end?

Yes! This is the first book I've written where I knew right away. For my other novels, the endings either changed from what I'd originally planned or weren't thought up from the beginning. If my advance readers weren't thrilled with an ending, I contemplated changing it and did for two other books. For *The Incompletes*, all my advance readers (and editor) loved the ending, so that was a relief.

Did you consider any other titles for the book?

For my others novels, the titles weren't what I first came up with, but with *The Incompletes*, it was the first and only—and it stuck with me. It was fun writing the scene where Emma, Zev, and Katie brainstorm to come up with the name of their band. I thought it would be cool to have the band's name the same as the book.

Which is your favorite character from the book?

If I had to choose one, it would be Josephine. I loved coming up with her character. I could totally picture her in my head, as she walked in and out of the ice cream shop and as she fed Emma the clues.

Which parts were hardest to write? Which came easiest?

There are some heavy topics and moments in this story. I had to do a lot of research about WWII and the Holocaust. That was hard emotionally. I learned more about Sobibor, listened to many survivors' testimonies, and wanted to get facts and dates straight even though it's fiction.

Writing the parts where Emma and her parents remember Cory was also hard. I needed to learn more about this type of tragedy, watch documentaries, and read stories about an epidemic that has ruined so many lives. The loss of a loved one is so painful. With a loss, everyone grieves differently, and I wanted to show that.

The easiest parts? Writing about drumming because I'm a drummer! And the scenes where Emma meets up with Josephine and her bandmates were easier to write because they were fun to imagine and put on the page.

So, what's next?

I have a few other book ideas—it's just whether I can turn one of them into an interesting story that's hundreds of pages! Sometimes I think it would be cool to incorporate a character from a previous novel into a new one, but I haven't figured out a way.

Book Club Questions

If you're reading or considering *The Incompletes* for your book club, thank you! Here are a few questions to help jumpstart the conversation:

Did you have a favorite character from the book? If so, what was it about the character that you liked or found interesting?

Josephine made Emma answer the question, "Does an evil person deserve to die?" How do you think you'd answer this question?

How did you feel about the way Emma handled her dilemma regarding Rey?

Did the ending surprise you, particularly what Emma decided to do with the note?

There are historical elements sprinkled throughout the book. Was there anything new that you learned?

If *The Incompletes* was made into a movie, who would you choose to play the cast of characters and why?

About the Author

Linda Smolkin always wanted to be a writer—ever since she saw her first TV commercial and wondered how to pen those clever ads. After graduating with a journalism degree, Linda landed a job at an ad agency, where she worked for several years before joining the nonprofit world. She's also the author of a few novels and a short story. When not in front of the computer, she's behind the drums escaping into her rock-star world. For more information, visit lindasmolkin.com and follow Linda on Instagram @lindasmolkin.

Also by Linda Smolkin

Among the Branded

The Secret We Lost

Love the Way They Lie

The Obituary Tales